On Gravedigger Road

◄●►

Rod Little

This book is a work of fiction. All names, characters, places and incidents are either the product of the author's imagination or are used fictionally. Any resemblance to actual persons, living or dead, or to actual events or locations is entirely coincidental.

On Gravedigger Road
ASIN: B08MCJYHBS
ISBN: 9798557363082
v1b

Copyright © 2020 Rod Little.
All rights reserved. Including the right to reproduce this book or portions thereof, in any form. No part of this text may be reproduced in any form without the express written permission of the author.

Special thanks to my editor, Laura Hall.

For other books by Rod Little, visit:
www.rodlittleauthor.com

What's buried at the end of the road?

Four college students are spending their summer break trawling the back roads of the South for photos of old relics. But when they witness a man bury a boy alive by the side of the road, they are thrust into an all-night chase through a foggy swamp of fresh graves, deadly creatures and dead bodies.

With no phones and no hope of rescue on this remote dead-end road, they must pull together to survive the night, rescue the boy, and uncover the road's secret … before it kills them.
And those who tend its graves have secrets of their own

Who will live to see the sun come up

ON GRAVEDIGGER ROAD

PART I

*Three men can keep a secret,
if two of them are dead.*

CHAPTER 0

"On Gravedigger Road is where it all started. I suspect that's where it will end. I spent a year there one night. That's the way I see it, anyway. The worst night of my life. We saw something we shouldn't have seen. But no one believes me, do they?

Not even you. That hurts most.

Sure, I'm feeling sorry for myself. I do that a lot these days. I'll get over it.

I doubt I'll see you again, and sorry for that, but I have to do this.. So please pass this story on. Maybe someday someone will care. Maybe it will have meaning. Don't come looking for me. I won't be found. I can't be found. You see, I'm going back. Back to where it all started. I fear I left something there on that road, and I'm going back to find it."

— <u>Love</u>, K.D.

ROD LITTLE

Note found in a manila envelope with a four-hundred page handwritten manuscript, collected from the Fifth Avenue drop box, postmarked October 1.

CHAPTER 1

The body of the man who had tried to save him lay six feet away, as it had for more than a day, filling the cellar with the stench of decay. The eyes stared through him. The eleven-year-old boy who shared the cellar tried not to look back.

The boy flinched at the sound of boots on the ceiling. It was the other man, the big man, moving around upstairs. Every stomp of his boots sent a thin mist of dust sprinkling into the cellar. Andy closed his eyes and mouth and struggled not to cough for fear it would alert his captors. They thought he was sleeping, but he had spit the pills into the floor drain. Now he fumbled in the dark for a tool.

A small window well near the ceiling admitted a sliver of moonlight that led him to a metal shelf unit. His small hands felt the smooth glass of jars. He touched nails, screws, and finally what he needed: a Philips-head screwdriver. He also discovered a roll of tape and shoved it into his pocket.

The cellar door opened, and light flooded in. Andy scooted to the corner and pretended to be asleep. The big man clomped down the rickety steps and picked up the dead body as if it were nothing. Such was his strength that he tossed it over his shoulder and made his way back upstairs without losing a breath. For him, carrying the body was as effortless as the murder itself.

When the door closed, the boy pushed two wooden crates together and stacked two more on top, creating a precarious pyramid ladder. Now was the perfect time to escape, when they were getting rid of the body. The dead man wasn't part of this; he had merely been in the way. The boy had heard the two kidnappers discussing how they would place the body in the swamp and not bury it in the small graveyard where Andy's mother was buried yesterday. Andy was destined for one of those graves. Tomorrow morning.

The boy didn't intend to be here for that.

He climbed the boxes and reached the window well. Concentrating so hard that he bit his tongue, his small fingers worked the screw out and placed it on the ledge. The second and third screws were almost as easy.

A new rain of dust fell on his head. He stifled a cough and swallowed hard.

The final hinge screw was corroded. It resisted his efforts, and the screwdriver slipped and scraped his hand. He ignored the blood until it made his grip too slippery to hold the tool. Quickly, he wrapped the cut in the tape he'd stolen. It was surgical tape and disappeared against the skin—what luck! He bent back to the task, and this time the screw turned. But when he got it loose, it fell to the floor. It bounced and struck a dozen pings before rolling down the drain.

He paused to listen. Upstairs, the man stomped across the floor.

He heard that. He'll come down.

But he didn't. It was only a tiny sound in a house full of noises, most of them born of rage.

With the hinged holders gone, the window fell open. His body fit through with inches to spare. He twisted and worked his bony torso into the well, but when his buttocks rested on the glass, it cracked. He wriggled further up into the well.

Fearing all the noise he was making would attract unwanted attention, he stopped for a second. Was the dog near? The night was calm but full of life. Sounds emanated from the swamp—loons and toads and crickets—but that was two hundred yards away, maybe more. He tried to remember how far. He could barely see anything beyond the outline of the willow tree across the road.

Andy squirmed out of the window and crawled onto the dead ground. No grass grew here, not on this side of the road. He rose and dashed for the tree on the other side. He did not look at the graves to the left. His mother had been buried in one of them earlier today. Or was it yesterday? He couldn't remember. Another hole was dug shallow and waiting for him.

Tomorrow. They said they'd bury me tomorrow. After the new moon ritual.

The words he'd heard them say were indelibly etched in his brain. Right now, he didn't want to think about that, or about her.

The boy hit the tree and pressed his body against it, making himself one with the trunk. The house he had escaped was the sole house on this dead-end road. No one was around for miles to help. If he screamed, it would only bring the man down on him. A single lamp gleamed through the front window of the living room, and Andy saw the man's silhouette inside. He didn't think the other one was there. He waited and listened.

Where is that dog? If it's loose, I'm dead.

But the dog wasn't around. He wondered if she had taken it, that woman. Had they left him alone with the man?

Andy tied his right sneaker and checked the other in preparation to run. He crept first on all fours, then stood and sped up the road, his shoes pounding dirt and gravel. He veered into the shallow grass to soften the sound of his footfalls but avoided the taller grass. There were things in the tall grass, poisonous and deadly, that he didn't want to meet.

He advanced past a line of skulls poised on metal spikes. Last night they had been set on fire, tinting the road with their glow. Tonight, they were lifeless and dark. For that he was grateful. The darkness helped spirit him up the road.

Three-quarters of the way, he changed course and headed into the fringe of the swamp. The roads wouldn't be his ally. He knew his captors had friends in the area, bad people privy to the kidnapping. Instead, he planned to stay in the swamp, but only at the edge. Even there, the danger was real.

Gators and snakes and shit. Screw them!

He prayed he'd see none of that tonight. If he crossed at the right spot, a mile up, he could skirt the next road and duck if cars came. Best to avoid being found until he reached the highway. Only the highway was safe. So damn far—at least twenty miles off, by his guess. His chances of finding it were slim, but he refused to be buried next to his mother. Not without a fight.

The swamp suddenly lit up, suffused with hues of orange. He turned and saw the skulls down the road had been set aflame. That didn't mean the people knew he had escaped; he believed they lit the skulls every night. But it meant one of them was on the road. Andy squatted and rested to catch his breath.

After ten minutes, he crawled forward.

A shadow passed over him, and he sprang to his feet. He sprinted away from the road, his arms swinging and his lungs gulping air. His small sneakers tore through the grass.

For the second time this week, he ran for his life.

CHAPTER 2

Zach put his head in the alligator's mouth for kicks. Half sure the jaws would snap his head off, he did it anyway to get a good photo. Bragging rights were king on social media. The creature was dead and stuffed, but Zach felt a tingle of doubt. Was anyone sure it was dead, or was it *playing dead*? As soon as his friends clicked their photos, he yanked his head free. His grin was as wide and toothy as the gator's, but Zach's was whiter. This place reminded him of the crocodile farm he'd seen in Thailand two years earlier, his first trip to visit grandma.

"Are you happy now?" Jessie asked, straining not to roll her eyes. She tried to be tolerant but found the entire alligator farm to be ridiculous.

Jessica Hampton was the main reason for this trip and the one who had planned it. In the middle of her graduate degree in history and archival studies at the University of Pittsburgh, she wanted to spend five weeks of summer break sifting through the remote back roads of the Deep South to document little-known monuments and relics of the past. Not everyday relics, she wanted something unique, something with dazzle.

Milton Peltner, known as Pelt to his friends, was the second reason. A photographer in need of a new portfolio, he wanted to photograph the unknown, the rarely visited culverts of the country. He had dreams of finding that rare totem only he would photograph and make viral on the net.

Zach Saetang came along for the experience. He was a criminology major and held a place on the Pitt track team. He ran every morning before each outing. Though he wanted to put his criminology skills to the test, he came along mainly for the fun. To him, alligators, spiders and snakes were fun.

Cole Diaz Ramirez only came because his girlfriend, Jessie, had asked. And because Zach and Cole were best friends. He and Zach were rarely apart. Their college baseball team had a month off until pre-season warm-ups—he was their best hitter, but only a fair center fielder—so he had the time. And the car. As the strongest athlete in this group of four, he considered himself the "muscle" of the group. In reality, Jessie was more likely to defend them from any tempestuous strangers. She usually packed both Binaca and mace and was more likely to get into a fight.

Friends since childhood, they stuck together even when Zach's parents moved to Chicago. He returned to Pittsburgh to study at U Pitt with his friends, in both their undergrad and graduate years. They were inseparable, even on their summer breaks. Even when one of them suggested a harebrained trip to nowhere.

The four students were on day six of their planned thirty-five-day trek across the South, a long way from home. Not a promising start, though. They hadn't yet found anything of value to buy, document or photograph. That's why they had agreed to stop at Bud's Gator Museum on their second day in Louisiana. Zach and Cole were delighted by the attraction; Jessie and Pelt, not so much.

Jessie watched Cole and Zach fondle two small alligator skulls that had been stripped, boiled and cleaned, and were now for sale. Cole touched his ever-present baseball cap, which meant he was thinking. Whenever he adjusted his cap, he had something to ponder. She hoped it wasn't the purchase of a reptile skull.

Pelt leaned into her. "You've been grumpy all week. What's up?"

"I'm not grumpy. I just think this is a stupid waste of time."

"I take that back. You've been grumpy all year. What's up with you, Jess?"

"Things." She shifted away from him. "Are you two about done playing around?"

Zach held up a set of alligator jaws and maneuvered them like a puppet.

Cole laughed. "Sure, babe. Almost done."

Bud, the owner, frowned and slipped his thumbs into his overalls. "You break it, you buy it."

Jessie grabbed Zach and Cole by their shirts and

moved them along to the next room. Pictures of giant alligators lined the walls. Pelt was sure at least one was a photoshopped fake. But there was nothing fake about the stuffed eighteen-footer displayed on a platform in the center of the room. It dominated the exhibit and got more than one *wow* from the group.

"Things this big are out there?" Pelt asked. "Are you serious? That side camping trip you planned for tomorrow… it's off, man. I'm not camping outside with these monsters out there." He made a mental note to get backup from Jessie on this.

The end of the room housed a live twenty-foot yellow Burmese python. It coiled around a tree trunk inside a glass enclosure big enough for five people. It rested its head lazily on a heated rock, unimpressed by the tourists.

Zach said, "Awesome," twice, but Cole gave it a wide berth, eyeing it suspiciously as he left the room. Pelt and Jessie had to push Zach onward to the souvenir shop, which led them outside. Late morning had arrived, and the heat already smothered them. They fanned themselves with their t-shirts to cool off.

"Lovely," said Jessie. "Snakes inside, and gnats and bugs outside." But the trip had been her idea, and she only complained because she wanted to get back on the road to find something of value. She believed that strange pieces of history were buried all over the region, but none would be here at Bud's Gator Museum.

For the grand finale of the tour, Bud took them out behind the building to a kid's swimming pool filled with baby alligators. They climbed over one another and formed a pile in one corner to get some sun. A sign said they were for sale as pets, only $10 each.

"I'm no expert," said Zach, "but that sounds like a bargain to me. We need to get one. No! Two. A pair, so they have each other to grow up with."

"No way in hell," said Jessica.

"Yes! This is happening."

"Let me sort this out," Pelt said. "You want to… what, put them in a plastic bowl and carry them around for four more weeks in the car? Sloshing around the back as we drive from town to town? And then when you get home, put them in your kitchen sink until they're big enough for the bathtub. Then… after about a year or two, they're too big to keep, but no one will take them. And you can't afford to feed them anymore, even after you've stolen the neighbors' dogs and cats. In the end, they eat you." He removed his glasses and cleaned them on his t-shirt. "Yeah. That works for me."

Zach thought for a moment. "But they're so damn cute. Right?"

Jessica shook her head. "Not even a little."

"They're adorable." Zach stuck a hand into the pool and tapped one on the head.

Bud looked concerned. "Uh, a few of them are gettin' big enough to bite. Don't lose a finger there, son. We ain't liable." He pointed to the faded wooden sign above the pool: Not responsible for injuries.

"When we get back home, we'll buy you a baby

chick, all yellow and furry," Jessie promised. "Chicks are cute. Or ducks. But this…" she waved a finger at the pool, "is not happening."

Pelt captured a photo of the baby alligators and slapped his friend on the back. "Come on, Big Z. I'll buy you one of the little skulls. You can put it on your desk when we get home."

That appeased Zach for the moment, and he beamed a smile. Bud's wife appeared again. They had met her at the souvenir shop and heard all about her gout flare-up in excruciating detail. She wore a simple flowered dress and had three butterfly pins in her gray hair.

"The tour includes lunch," she reminded them.

"But we got no tacos," Bud said to Cole, then shifted his eyes to Zach. "Or sushi." He shuffled into the gift shop to let his wife handle the food.

Zach scrunched his nose. "That's fine. I don't like sushi. Why would you—"

"I think he's being racist," Cole explained. "I must be a Mexican and you must be Japanese, ya know."

"I was born in Pittsburgh," Zach said, feigning confusion. He enjoyed that. "And I'm not Japanese. My mom is Thai."

"He meant no harm," Jessie said softly, always the peacemaker. "It's just the way they are down here. He's old. Old people are… you know."

"So, what am I?" Pelt asked.

Cole winked. "A.W. B."

"Average White Band?"

"No, Pelt. Average White Be'atch."

"You know," said Pelt, "that was a real band in the 70s. Average White Band, not the other."

"I don't think so." Cole didn't believe anything he hadn't seen with his own eyes. "No one would name their band that."

"In the 70s they would!"

Bud's wife returned with a plate of meat on a stick. "I've got grilled gator kebabs. If you grill it right with plenty of sauce and a thin slice of cheese... well, it's to die for. You won't regret it. It'll be the highlight of your trip."

They looked at her.

"Are you serious?" Cole asked.

"About what, dear?" She didn't understand the question.

Zach whispered to Pelt, "Dude, isn't that like eating horse at a horse race?"

Pelt pursed his lips. "Hmm. I think it's more like eating chocolate at Hershey Park."

"Ah."

"We don't really have time for that, ma'am," Cole said. He wrinkled his nose at the meat. It smelled like hamburger, but the idea of gator grub turned him off. "We need to move on."

"Oh, that's a pity. You're missin' out. You kids need to stop an' eat an' enjoy life, or you'll miss it all. And you're skinny as straws, every last one of ya." She giggled. There was something sweet about her. She was everyone's grandma. "Well, the meat doesn't travel well in the heat. I tell ya what, I'll make you some peanut butter an' jelly for the road."

"Drinks cost extra," Bud shouted from the gift shop, lest anyone think their one-dollar soda or iced tea was on the house.

"We need to get back on the road," Jessie said. "We're in a hurry." They weren't, but she wanted to get out of there.

"I'll pack you a bag," Bud's wife said. It wasn't an offer or a request, it was a statement. She was already off to complete the task.

They piled back into Cole's Accord with their souvenirs and drinks. Pelt held the bag of sandwiches from Bud's wife; he cradled them on his lap like a delicate baby. Gravel spun under the tires. Zach waved to Bud and his wife while Pelt snapped two more photos of the couple in front of their gator museum slash farm. Cole focused on the road while Jessie glared at the morning with second thoughts about the entire trip.

The car turned up dust and rolled out.

"Someone get the map. Where to next?"

CHAPTER 3

Cole slammed on the brakes, jerking them forward in their seats. A standard rectangular street sign said *Dead-End Road*. It was the sign they had been searching for, but its simple presentation was a bit of a letdown. It looked deserted.

The lane clearly stretched much deeper than the fifty yards indicated on the map. From the looks of it, the dirt road spanned for miles into the weeds and brush. A tall willow tree guarded the entrance, a wooden sign nailed to it with the words *Dead End* painted in red, the letters misshapen and uneven as if from a child's hand.

"I guess this is it," Pelt said. He rolled down the window and snapped a few photos of both signs. "C'mon. We need a selfie at the end of it."

"It looks empty," Jessie said. "Tell me again why we need this?"

"A selfie at the end of Dead-End Road? It's classic. It'll be internet gold."

"It's stupid," Cole said. "But it might be cool."

Zach folded the map on his lap and re-examined it, running his finger along a line. "It shouldn't go that far.

It only shows an inch here on the map. I mean, like a hundred feet maybe."

"Well, we gotta go to the end," Pelt said. "That's the whole point. Right?"

"It's narrow," Cole complained. "If another car comes the other way, where are we supposed to go? Into that mess of weeds? They'll scratch my car."

"What car would be coming the other way? Seriously, there's no one out here. And it's a dead end! No one else is on this road, dude. And weeds won't hurt your junkyard car, anyway."

"He has a point," said Jessie. "I love you, babe, but your car's a piece of crap."

"Easy," Cole said. He rubbed the dashboard. "She doesn't mean that, sweetie." Cole thought every car was a special lady.

Zach reminded them they were fifty miles from the highway. "Let's not waste too much time, guys. I want a real bed in a real motel tonight. Last night sucked."

Pelt slapped his palm. "True that, my friend. We'll be fast. This is something no one else can say they saw. It'll be what stands out in my portfolio."

"Doubting that. And doubting anyone will care. But I'm okay. Let's check it out."

Jessica shrugged. "Alright. Let's do this. But if we see any more snakes in the brush, you two back there will have to carry Cole out on a stretcher."

Cole hated snakes, and the group had already seen three in their first six days on the road—not counting

Bud's python. Snakes, bugs and lizards, but very few antiques or unique items to photograph. It was going to be a long summer if they didn't find something good soon, anything to make this trip worthwhile.

Cole turned the car onto the dirt road and sped past the painted sign. The Accord jostled over rocks and twigs, while Cole complained incessantly that his car wasn't built for this. According to the map, they should have already reached the end of the road. Instead it bent slightly to the right and continued on.

"You see that?" Jessica asked.

A tree branch extended several feet over the road, a cardboard sign hanging from its knotted arm. It twisted in the breeze, but during moments of lull they caught its message. Written in thick black marker were the words:

Gravedigger Road.

No Trespast.

Misspelled, and the first S was written backwards.

Zach got out and tried to touch the sign. Even jumping, it evaded his reach by a foot. "Not a good omen, gentlemen."

"Get back in," Cole yelled out the window. "We'll go to the end and turn around."

After another mile, he insisted they give up and turn back, except there was no good place to do that. He wondered how stable the grass was on the right or if it was a marsh that would swallow his car. Trees crowded the left side, leaving few safe places to make a U-turn on the narrow path generously called a road.

Then they saw something that made them sit up and take interest. The left side opened into a wide clearing of grass and bushes with a church at its center. Old and weathered, angled to one side as if it might one day fall over, the pains of old age spilled off it, and that's what the group had been hunting for.

"Oh snap! What is that?" Jessica shouted. She leaned forward into the windshield, her interest spiking.

"Holy crap," Pelt said. "No pun intended."

He began snapping photos before the car even slowed. They pulled off the road onto a gravel lot in front of the church.

"Hot as hell, man," Zach said. "Park in the shade. Over there on the side."

Cole eased the car onto the grass alongside the church and parked underneath the wide boughs of two willow trees, safely sheltered from the sun. Everyone except Zach opened their doors.

"You're too close to the tree, man."

"Climb out the other side. Don't be a wuss."

The church side held little more room. Zach had to squeeze through without scraping the door against the rotting wood of the church, forced to trample a row of violets to get out and away from the car.

"Sorry little flower dudes," he apologized.

The front of the church was covered in unpainted wood with no finish, decorations or signs. A simple cross towered on its steeple, nothing more. The only color was from a few patches of wildflowers growing around the building's base. Modest and rustic, it was as plain as buildings get.

Zach opened the church door to a shrill creak, and poked his head in. Splinters of light seeped through crevices in the wood, and a murky glow shone through ten dirty windows on each side. The ceilings stood remarkably high.

"This looks horrid," he said. He motioned inside with a flourish. "Ladies first." That was directed at Cole.

They stepped inside.

A musty odor hit them hard. The church hadn't been aired out in years; the smell was a testament to its age and abandonment. They wondered when the windows had last been opened, or even the front door. They might be the first visitors in a decade, but if that were true, it was in surprisingly good shape. Twelve rows of oak pews lined each side of the sanctuary. A lonely pulpit made of darker wood sat on a riser at the front.

Jessie ran her hand along one of the pews and checked her fingers. "There's almost no dust. Someone has been here to clean it. This place… it's been cleaned. Recently. Don't you think?"

"They should have aired it out some more," Cole said. He stretched his t-shirt over his mouth and nose. "It's gross."

Pelt snapped photos at every angle. The design and structure fascinated him. He squatted and took photos of the light rays as they hit the pews. There was no stained glass, only plain windows high up in the walls. They badly needed a cleaning, but the high arched roof gave the church an air of nobility. Built like a large shack, it somehow still retained the characteristics of a church, no less impressive than the great cathedrals in the cities. Pious and elevated. But it stank.

On the floor before the pulpit lay three crosses fashioned from tree branches and cut with a saw, the cross pieces nailed together and reinforced by twine. The supplies to make them—the nails, twine, hammer and saw—had been cast across the floor in a haphazard manner. Zach sniffed the ends of the branches and felt the bark with two fingers. They were cut recently. Someone had made these crosses in the past few days.

"Why?" Jessica asked. "Why now? I wonder what they are for."

"I hope whoever made them comes back," said Pelt, always snapping photos. He captured the pulpit and the crosses. "I'd bet dollars to donuts they have a ton of cool stories to tell."

"That would make for a great paper," Jessica agreed. She was always thinking of her next thesis, grappling for something that would make her work stand out. It drove her. Sometimes it drove her crazy. "But we can't hang out here forever and wait for them to come back. It might be weeks."

They inspected the dark wood that held the church together, the moldy trim and the rotting floor boards. This church was in great shape for its age, despite its slant and strange build. They pegged it at two hundred years old, at least. The stories within its walls spoke to the group's sense of wonder in different ways. Cole was the only one immune to its charms.

An organ sat in the corner, lonely and forgotten. Jessie tapped a key, but no sound came out.

Behind the organ, a doorway led to a back room, then a staircase to a baptismal chamber. An opening allowed the congregation to view the baptism from their pews. Now the baptismal basin was empty, but a ring around the rim told of water it once held. Pelt took photos and speculated how many people were baptized here over the years. A hundred? A thousand? How many decades had this church served its parishioners before being abandoned?

"It's a bit odd, the location, don't you think?" Zach asked. "There are no houses on this road. Not even broken down homes or any remains. There were never any other buildings on this dead end. It's not been deserted, it's more like it was never inhabited."

"Your point?" Cole asked, his voice muffled by his shirt tent.

"People usually live near churches. Why not here? Why didn't anyone live near this church?"

"It was different back then," Jessica said. "In the 1700s people lived on farms, far from each other. It was normal to get on a horse and ride a long way to town to buy supplies. Or, I guess, even to church."

"I still think it's not normal," Zach insisted. "Weird as hell."

Pelt agreed but was more concerned with getting every piece photographed. "I'm going outside to get some shots of the exterior."

"Me too. I'll go with," Cole mumbled into his shirt. He was eager to escape the smell.

"You're such a lightweight, man." They passed through the doorway and let a wave of fresh air in.

Zach examined the crosses again; he traced his fingers along the grooves in the wood. "What are these for? I mean, there aren't any other crosses in here. And only one on the roof, but it's not like these." The roof cross was carved, finished and painted, but these were make-shift; branches put together the way a child might do for a pet's grave.

"There's nothing in here; no icons at all," Jessie said. She knelt next to him and touched a cross. "Not even a picture of Mary or Jesus. This church is abandoned. Are you sure these crosses are new?"

Zach sniffed the wood once more. "Yep. Fresh cut this week. And the end has been sharpened to a point. These were made to stick in the ground. Either that, or as a weapon."

"Why? Why now, after all these years?"

"I don't think it's part of a remodel. These were meant for outside. A garden, maybe. Out front?"

She took a moment to study the sanctuary again and gazed up at the windows. Dust danced in the sunlight that fought its way through the grimy glass. Dust. Had they stirred that up when they entered? Or did it always swirl like this?

And the church was cold. Hot as it was outside, the air was twenty degrees cooler in the sanctuary. She felt a cold draft. Zach felt it, too; she saw a shiver run through him. What ghosts still rode these pews?

"I want to leave," she whispered.

"Go ahead. I'll be out in a minute."

CHAPTER 4

They spent half an hour in and around the church before Pelt pleaded for them to continue to their objective, the end of Dead-End Road. He used his zoom lens to spot the weeping willow tree that marked the terminus. Only half a mile, so they agreed to walk. They brought the sandwiches and the drinks they'd bought at the alligator farm and planned a quick picnic and a victory lap before heading on.

They noticed a remarkable decrease in green on the left as they approached the end of the road. The trees became thin and bare until covered only in dead branches, spindly and twisted. The grass yellowed and then disappeared entirely. Aside from patches of brown weeds, the earth was barren.

Further along, they spotted thirteen crosses similar to those inside the church, but these had been planted in the ground to form a small graveyard at the end of the road. A display so heartbreaking, even the birds avoided it. This sad little graveyard was the purpose of the crosses someone had assembled in the sanctuary.

Only a rat found the courage to wander the graves.

When it heard the four intruders, it scurried across the road and into the swamp grass. Cole threw a dirt clod at it but missed.

At the gravesite, they counted two rows of six crosses. A third row held only one cross and one covered grave, but it also contained a second hole that had been dug and left open. Fourteen graves, but the last plot had not yet been filled.

"Cree-ee-py," Cole said. "Who would bury someone way back here?"

"It's not people, I'm sure," said Jessie. "It's probably pets. A pet cemetery or something like that."

Zach counted the steps from head to toe of each grave, then from cross to cross lengthwise. "These are seven feet apart. That's big enough for people."

"So?"

"So, how many cats do you know that are seven feet long? How many dogs?"

"Might be gators," Cole offered. "I mean, it is the bayou, sort of."

"Yes, and twelve people had pet alligators they were so fond of that they made a little gator cemetery for them. Don't be stupid, man. This is for people. People are buried here."

"You can't bury people anywhere you want," Jessica laughed. "There are zoning laws. You can't bury your aunt in the front yard."

"Out here? What zoning laws do you think apply here? We're in the middle of nowhere. Anyone wants to bury their grandpa out back, he can. Who's gonna stop them? Who would even find out? This isn't only the middle of nowhere, it's miles from the middle of nowhere. We're in *Nahnia*, man."

Jessie frowned. "That's not how it's pronounced."

But Pelt agreed. "That's how people used to do it. My grandma told me that when she was little, her mom had a stillborn baby and her dad just buried it on the farm. Nothing more was said or done about it. Back then when people were poor, that's how it was done."

Jessie didn't buy it. "This isn't 1920. You can't do that anymore. I'm sure of it."

Zach knelt and ran his hand through the dirt of the unfilled grave. He smelled it and felt its texture. "This was dug recently. It's fresh. The dirt is new."

"How can you tell?"

"The way it feels and smells. It's moist. This was dug today, this morning maybe. Or last night."

Zach stood and clapped his hands free of the dirt, then wiped them on his jeans. "Check out the house."

They had been so mesmerized by the unexpected gravesite, only now did they notice a small house built fifty yards back from the road. A rundown shack that had never been painted, only bare boards nailed together formed a structure that looked as sound as a popsicle fort. A small porch sagged badly at its front. All the windows were covered, two boarded up, one with a black curtain drawn. No lawn, no green, only dirt and patches of dead weeds cast a rug of despair to the front porch, and more dead trees peppered the landscape around the house. The scene was dreary, a portrait of death.

"Who the hell would live in that?" Jessie asked. "You think anyone's home?"

"I doubt it." Cole touched his cap. "Looks abandoned. Besides, would *you* live here behind a bunch of graves?"

"I wouldn't live anywhere on this road or in this town. Not even if you paid me. So, no, not me. But someone did, at one time."

"No one lives there," Zach said with conviction. "But I bet they store tools and shit for the graves."

"But they made the crosses in the church back there. Remember? Why not make them here, in the house?"

"Yeah. You're right. Maybe they make them in the church to bless them. A ceremony. There were three back there. I guess they expect to bury more bodies. More cats, dogs or gators."

"Or Aunt Margaret," Cole said.

"There's room for eighteen. Three rows of six. This row can fit a few more. Only thirteen things are buried here, thirteen people or pets. So, they plan to eventually need three, four, five more. This is a work in progress, guys. Not some ancient burial ground. It's ongoing."

"That's very unsettling," Pelt said. "We should get out of here. Let's take our big photo and go."

"I think we should check out the house," Zach said.

"No way in hell. No way," Jessie insisted, and Cole echoed her sentiment. Whoever lived in that hellish-looking shack, they didn't want company.

Zach held up his hands and backed off. "Fine. I thought this was our big Pee-wee adventure. Could be something old and historical in there."

"We'll pass," Cole said.

"Could be gold!"

"Or a box of chicken heads and voodoo dolls. We'll pass, thanks."

Pelt clicked a set of pictures of each side of the road and the house. "Guys, you notice how dead this end is? Lots of green trees and grass up there, but down here only dead twigs and dirt—no grass at all."

"It's only this side of the road, though," Zach said. "The other side is covered with... swamp, or whatever the hell is over there. But it's green. It's alive."

"Yeah." Cole saw it now, too. "Only the graveyard and the house are on dead land. It's almost like it's contaminated."

"Pesticide dump, maybe."

"This whole trip is one big pesticide dump," Jessica complained. "One long string of freaks and weirdos. That bizarre garage of jars two days ago. Yesterday's freak-show antique auction, today's gator farm, and now this. None of this trip is turning out the way I had planned."

"What did you expect? You'd discover Sherman's sword and his last will and testament?"

"I expected more."

Cole had had enough. "I'm hungry. Let's get that

selfie and then lunch. And then back on the damn road to the highway."

After the obligatory stream of pics taken with Pelt's camera and each of their phones as they stood at the end of the dead-end, and one in front of the little graveyard, they crossed the road and sat under the shade of a giant willow tree that resembled an umbrella. It was one of the few trees on the swamp side of the road—the green side—opposite the graves. Behind them lay miles of tall grass and likely some marsh ground in the middle. The blades stood four to five feet high, reaching six feet in some places. Snakes would be a certainty, but no one mentioned that. Cole didn't need to be reminded. If it hadn't occurred to him yet, it was best not to bring it up.

They relaxed and ate the peanut butter and jelly sandwiches Bud's wife had made for them. The jelly was strawberry and definitely homemade, as was the bread. No one complained. They were delicious.

"That ground is badly contaminated," Zach said. "That's why nothing grows there."

"You mean cursed?" Jessica asked.

"No, I said contaminated. Like I said before: pesticide dump. Gas or chemicals or something like that seeped into the earth. I wonder if anyone realizes it. They shouldn't be burying anything here. The whole area should be checked out by the EPA."

"Like the EPA would ever make it back here. It's miles from any homes. No one cares if the ground is leeched or poisoned or whatever."

Zach shrugged. "I care."

Though a closet environmentalist, he rarely let it show. Part of his Thai-American heritage, he supposed, even though he spoke no Thai and had only visited his grandparents once. His parents were avid environmentalists. More than that, they were focused on getting him into law school, environmental law. They hated his love for criminology but got by with false promises that law school was next. It wasn't. To them, his overachieving came first, family second, then the Earth. To him, running came first, then everything else in shifting order, depending on his mood.

After lunch, they relaxed and drank their sodas and tea. It was becoming a lazy afternoon.

Until the gravedigger arrived.

The sound of a truck's poorly tuned engine disturbed more than the road; it woke the whole swamp. Louder as it barreled toward them, the tree hid it from view until it was nearly upon them. A badly rusted relic —a pick-up truck that might have dated back to the fifties—stirred up dust from the road, then turned left and parked next to the graveyard. It spat black exhaust fumes as the engine sputtered a few seconds after shutting down.

A man dressed in a brown robe jumped out of the driver's side, grabbed a shovel from the truck bed and went to work on the open grave. They couldn't see his face. The man kept his head down with the robe's hood pulled up, but they could see he was a big man. His robe swelled and ballooned in the wind while he worked to deepen the grave.

"What is he, like a monk?" Pelt whispered. "Damn hot to wear all that."

Hypnotized by the scene, no one replied. They watched him tidy the grave and wondered what they were witnessing. If this was a sacred ceremony, they should announce their presence. It wasn't polite to trespass on a funeral, especially in t-shirts and jeans. Even a pet funeral deserved better.

But this wasn't a funeral; it was only the gravedigger. And yet, before he broke earth, he bowed his head and prayed for a few seconds, or seemed to do so.

In the shadow of the tree, they sat still, observing the man at work. They didn't think their presence was a problem, and they'd certainly leave before the funeral started. But no one wanted to break the silence.

Then the unexpected happened. The man opened the back gate of the truck bed to reveal the body of a pre-teen boy, ten or twelve years old. He wasn't in a casket. His body was out in the open. While that in itself seemed odd, the boy's hands and feet were tied, and duct tape stretched across his mouth.

"I told you it was people," Zach murmured. "People are buried here."

But why tie up a dead body? Makes no sense. What kind of ritual is this?

And where's the coffin?

They all wondered the same thing but didn't say anything. They were frozen, captivated by the scene unfolding across the road. And glad to be hidden under the tree. It was clear the man hadn't seen them. They weren't sure how he'd react to their intrusion. Most of all, they wanted to see more. Sometimes you can't look away.

Ceremoniously, the man spread a wide burlap blanket on the ground and bowed his head again, pausing several seconds. A second silent prayer, perhaps. Then he threw the boy's body on the ground. A *humpf* sound came from the body. It was almost as if it felt the pain of being thrown down. The man whistled an old gospel tune, Amazing Grace, as he wrapped the body in the burlap covering and lifted it in his arms. It was then they realized how large the man truly was; it took no effort for him to lift the body that had to weigh at least ninety pounds. He tossed the corpse into the open grave as if it were a pound bag of sugar, with no more effort than stocking a pantry.

And he continued to whistle.

Amazing grace, how sweet the sound…

The man lifted a handful of dirt and let it fall through his fingers onto the boy.

… that saved a wretch like me…

The ritual shot goosebumps over the four spectators. It wasn't right. Spiritual but not holy; it felt somehow less divine and more depraved. This was no church funeral; it was… something else. Why were no other people here?

Jessica took Cole's hand, and he touched the rim of his cap with the other. The group stayed silent, afraid of what the man would do if he saw them. Their eyes followed the robed figure as he reached into the passenger side of the truck and took out a jar of tiny pebbles. They looked like white crystals. He spread three handfuls onto the body and over the dirt in and around the grave, then closed the jar and laid it carefully on the ground. He handled the jar gently as if it contained valuable gems or hallowed tokens.

Again he seized the shovel and drove it into the earth. As he filled the grave, he resumed whistling. When the first clods of dirt hit the body, it made another *humpf* sound. The man ignored the noise and shoveled more dirt into the hole.

Then the absurd happened.

The body moved. The kid started thrashing about under the burlap, and the dirt roiled.

He's alive. That boy is alive.

"Fuck! That kid's not dead," Zach whispered. He fought to keep his voice down. "Why doesn't he stop? Doesn't he realize it?"

"He realizes it," Pelt whispered.

He knows.

The four began to understand the gravity of their situation. This was no funeral.

"Shit. What do we do? What do we do?"

"I don't know," Pelt hissed. "What the fuck."

"Try your phone," Jessica said, but she was the one opening her phone. Even before the screen lit, she knew there was no reception. There hadn't been any, not even one bar, for miles.

The robed man raised his shovel and struck the boy through the burlap sack. The sack moved no more, and the man continued filling the grave.

"What the holy hell," Cole said through clenched teeth. He wanted to rush the man, but had a good inclination that would be suicide. People who bury kids… those people don't go down easy.

"Shit! I should be photographing this." Pelt yanked his camera to his eye and focused the lens. He started snapping shots in rapid succession.

That's when they saw his face.

With the first click of the camera, the robed man's head shot up. He spun around and looked straight at them. The man's face was covered in costume makeup, entirely white with black on his nose and around his eyes. Stitch marks striped his lips. His face looked like a skull, a well-made Halloween costume meticulously applied. If scaring strangers was his goal, mission accomplished.

The man threw his hood back to expose a bald skull with white coloring over his entire head. He stared at the four students for a full minute, surprised by the intruders. The five locked eyes, transfixed, waiting for one of them to act. While gauging his next move, the man freed himself of his robe with one sharp pull of the drawstring. Underneath, he wore work boots and overalls from which huge sinewy arms emerged like pythons.

No Trespast.

The sign had warned them.

They had infringed on his land, interrupted his work, and earned his wrath.

Suddenly, the man sprang into action. He grasped the shovel in both hands and marched toward the road. He didn't run, he walked, but there was strong purpose in each stride. He stomped straight for the four of them. The drive in his eyes cut into their hearts; he was on a mission and it likely included four more graves.

They shrank into the tree and scrambled to their feet, backing away from their attacker. Cole was first to bolt. He grabbed Jessica's hand and raced into the tall grass. She held tight and followed. Zach pushed Pelt into motion and the two of them also flew into the thick grass. The weeds parted to let them through.

The man pounded across the dirt road.

Cole bent his head down, trying to shrink from view; he pushed Jessie's head down, too. The grass was four feet here but taller deeper in. If they moved fast and stayed low, they could vanish in its green labyrinth. The man was taller; harder for him to hide. They might see him coming or hear him; he moved like a bull. They weaved away as fast as they could, bent over and fighting against the weeds. Cole initiated a zig-zag pattern and Jessie held on.

After ten minutes, he felt they had gone far enough

to take a minute to rest. They looked up at the sky but dared not peek above the grass. The wind rustled the weeds, but no other sounds came. They listened, trying to still their breaths. Somewhere in the distance, two large birds flew off from the marsh. Their winged outburst was followed by a fresh silence.

"What the hell," Jessica whispered. "We have to do something."

"Stay low. Just wait. He'll go away eventually."

"We have to help that kid."

Cole looked at her; he had no answers. "How?"

"I don't know. We need to… do something."

"One of us could get hurt. Or killed."

"That kid is gonna get killed if we let that freak bury him. We have to help him," she pleaded. "He'll die, Cole. Right in front of our eyes."

Better him than us.

Cole thought it but didn't say it. Selfish, maybe, but he was just thinking of her. He grappled for a plan, but his only ideas were bad ones. "We need to get back to the car. You'll go for help. The guys and I will… I don't know what we'll do. We'll try to rescue the kid."

"I'm not gonna leave you here, Cole. We'll all drive away and get help."

Cole shook his head. "I don't know where Zach and Pelt are. If they're not at the car when we get there, you have to drive for help. I'll try to find them."

She didn't agree, but nodded. For now. But they weren't at the car yet, and it was a long way up the road.

Traveling through the grass was taxing and painful. They both had tiny cuts on their arms from batting the blades of grass aside.

Cole pointed.

"C'mon. That way. We'll make our way up and over, back to the road across from the church."

Jessie held his hand tighter. Her other hand guarded her face from the weeds. Slowly, they melted into the sea of green.

CHAPTER 5

They carved into the thick grass, Zach always nudging Pelt forward, making sure he didn't slow down. Though Zach was a runner in good shape, he worried Pelt would stop to catch his breath too soon. Stop too soon, and it could end badly for both of them.

They hacked the tall grass aside with their arms, often rewarded with a stalk to the face, as they forced their way through. Zach changed their direction twice, always veering away from the road, and only halted when his sneakers hit soggy ground. He grabbed Pelt by the arm and yanked him down. There they squatted, waited and drank in the surrounding sounds. The noise of their own breathing rose above all else, the wind shifting the weeds, the drone of insects.

"The ground is getting too wet," Zach whispered in Pelt's ear. "Marsh must be up ahead. We gotta be careful. It could become water and we'd fall in. No telling how deep."

Pelt nodded, panting.

"And there's gonna be nasty shit in the water. Leeches, snakes, who knows what else. We need to stay on dry land."

No argument from Pelt, scared and out of breath. He checked his camera and confirmed it was still hanging from his neck and in one piece. The lens cap had flown off, but that was easy to replace.

Two minutes went by. Zach was considering standing up to risk a look around when something disturbed the grass fifteen feet away. Now ten feet, nine, eight. Closer. It fought its way fast through the thick brush and didn't care what noise it made. That had to be the strange man with the shovel. Zach motioned for Pelt to crawl back farther. Quietly, they inched their way deeper into the marsh on their hands and knees. They hit mud but dared not turn around; they allowed themselves to sink into the muck and forged on.

The sound came straight for them. The man knew where they were. And then a growl, low and guttural. It shocked them both. That's exactly how they imagined the costumed man might sound, speaking in demonic animal-like sounds, utterances from hell.

Their pursuer thrashed forward and burst through the reeds. They flew back on their hands and scrambled away from him, but it wasn't the man. It was a juvenile alligator, no more than three feet head to tail, winding its way back to the water.

Zach stifled a nervous laugh. "Oh man, I've never been so happy to see one of those bastards in my whole damn life."

No doubt the young alligator could still have bitten

off a chunk of Zach's leg, if it wanted to, but it wasn't a demon man with a shovel. Zach pushed Pelt behind him and kicked mud at the creature. Equally startled by the humans, it wasn't eager for a fight today. Instead, it shifted direction and thrashed onward through the reeds, skirting the men, on its way to the water. That provided them with useful information: it confirmed their suspicions that a body of water was nearby.

Zach breathed again and smiled. "Oh shit. That was scary." He put a hand on his friend's chest. "You okay, man?"

Pelt looked pale. "No. Fuck no! I think I peed myself a little."

"Get it together, man. I have an idea."

CHAPTER 6

Jessie and Cole crept to the edge of the road and parted its curtain of grass. They could see the church still guarding their car across the street. Nothing stirred there, but noises echoed from the gravesite. They heard the clang of a shovel being thrown into the truck bed, then the driver's door slamming shut.

"He's down there," Jessica said. "We could run now, run to the car."

"No way. He'd see us for sure."

"But couldn't we start the car and get away before he catches us? I mean, your car isn't great, but it's better than that freak's piece-of-crap truck. Right? We can outrun him, can't we? If we get to the highway before him, we can get help."

"Sure, unless he runs us off the road. You think a guy like that plays by the rules? How do we know he doesn't have a gun? He could shoot our tires out."

"But—"

"And what about Zach and Pelt? You want to leave them behind?"

"Crap, I didn't think about them. You're right. Where the hell are they?"

"In the grass, same as us. But I didn't see which way. Did you?"

"No. It was so confusing. I followed you."

The truck started up with a bang—a rude, disagreeable sound. Cole lay flat on his chest and peered through the grass. He could see it now; its rusted frame shook as it reversed out of the driveway, belched a cloud of black smoke, then sped forward. Cole inched back into the grass to avoid being seen. His head had been partly exposed, but he didn't think the driver noticed.

The truck rattled toward them, kicking up dust the length of the road, and with it a surge of hope that it would speed on its way and leave them be. After it left, they could collect the car, rescue the boy and find the others. Then get the hell out of there. A magnificent plan.

But when the truck was across from them, the man slammed on the brakes. The screech was as deafening as it was terrifying. Smoke spewed from the tailpipe as it idled in the road directly in front of them.

Jessica reached out and squeezed Cole's hand.

He saw us.

The truck idled louder; its frame vibrated. Sweat trickled down the side of Cole's face.

We're fucked. He saw us.

He could see the gruesome face of the man poking out of the hood—his robe back on—staring through the front windshield; something had caught his attention. The man swiped the hood of his robe back.

He knows we're here.

But he didn't know where they were. Instead, he had spotted their car on the other side of the road. The man's face calmly turned toward the church.

Gears ground, and the truck pulled into the church parking lot. The driver kept the engine running while he got out and walked to Cole's Accord. His robe billowed like a sail, catching the breeze, much like a skull pirate crossing the bow of his ship. He circled the car and examined its frame and the area surrounding it. He clomped to the back of the church, searching for the trespassers. When he returned, he opened the hood of Cole's car. Jessie and Cole couldn't see what he was doing, but after three minutes, the man closed the hood and returned to the truck.

His face, still painted with skeletal makeup, somehow looked distressed to Jessie. *He's not angry at us, he's in pain. Perhaps he's got OCD and we've disrupted his routine.*

The truck stormed back onto the road and sped away, vomiting great clouds of dust and smoke in its wake. They watched until it was out of sight and the sound of its engine long gone. In the distance, a swamp loon complained at the disturbance.

"Now!" Cole yelled, leaping to his feet and yanking Jessie with him. "Get to the car!"

They crossed the dirt road and bolted over the

gravel of the church lot. Their hands separated as Cole rushed to the driver's side and Jessie scrambled for the passenger door; both had been left unlocked. They slid inside, and Cole fumbled his keys into the ignition. He turned the key. Nothing happened. The engine didn't turn over. He turned the key again to no result. Soundless and stubborn, the car would not react.

"What's wrong?" Jessie asked. She glanced through the window to see if anyone was coming.

"No idea." He checked the gauge; plenty of gas. "He did something to the car."

Cole popped the hood and ran to check it out. A few seconds later, he closed the hood and pounded a fist on its metal surface, immediately regretting the noise it made. He whirled around, sure someone had heard and would be there, attacking from the rear. No one was there, but he couldn't shake the feeling of being watched.

Jessie got out of the car. "What's wrong with it?"

"He took the distributor cap and a spark plug."

"Can you fix it?"

"No, Jessie, I can't fix it! He took them. Do you have a distributor cap on you?"

She flinched but didn't take it personally. Her boyfriend shouted when he got frustrated. A gentle soul, he didn't mean it.

"Okay. So, what now?"

"I don't know, Jessie! Let me think." He punched 9-1-1 on his phone, but there was no signal. Pointless, he knew, but he couldn't resist trying. He hit AAA on his contacts, but nothing happened. The phone was as useless as the car right now.

The late afternoon sun had never felt so hot. Sweat coursed down his neck. He breathed hard as he shielded his eyes with a hand and scanned the grounds around the church. The flowers swayed in the breeze, but nothing else moved. They were alone. For now.

"Maybe he threw them on the ground to slow us down. Help me check." As he walked, he ruffled the grass and violets with his shoe to kick up anything that didn't belong there—preferably their car parts.

"Okay. What do they look like?" Jessie asked. She wanted to help.

"They look like a spark plug and a distributor cap, Jessie! They look like car parts. Exactly like car parts. Just tell me if you see anything that doesn't belong on the ground. Anything metal or... anything not grass or weeds."

His frustration was growing by the second, but she knew it wouldn't last. It would fizzle out and wind into an apology, eventually.

Five minutes of kicking through the grass along the sides and back of the church led them back to the gravel lot. Cole already knew it would be futile; he knew the man had taken the parts. The man didn't want the four of them leaving. He needed to strand them here until he got back. They had seen what he did. They knew his secret, and secrets are only kept by killing the witnesses.

"We're stuck here, Jessie. And I think that guy, that

freak, is gonna come back for us." *Come back to kill us.*

She had already guessed that. "I figured that much. We saw him bury a kid, Cole. He can't let us leave to tell the cops."

And then it hit both of them.

"Cole! That kid is still buried. We need to dig him up. He was alive, maybe he'll... I don't know, can people breathe underground?"

"Not for long. We need to go fast. You stay here with the car. I'll go try to dig him up."

"No way!" Jessie huffed, tired of his attitude. "I'm not staying here all alone. I *can* help."

"What if Zach and Pelt come back?"

"They know to stay with the car. If I'm here, it won't make a difference, but you might need my help to dig."

He glanced at her painted fingernails.

She noticed. "Yeah, asshole, they're pretty but they can dig dirt. Come on. We don't have much time. That weirdo might come back any minute."

"Fine. Fine. We'll stick close to the trees."

They held hands again and ran behind the church, into the back row of trees that stretched behind the house and joined with more at the end of the road. But the trees grew increasingly bare and dying the further they went from the church, and were completely dead behind the house. That might be a problem.

Dead trees provide poor cover.

CHAPTER 7

Zach and Pelt took a few steps away from the mud and the source of the tremolo loon calls. They tried to stay on dry land but didn't want to meet the gravedigger. They crouched and listened, stole a few more steps toward the road, crouched and waited more. Finally, Zach poked his head above the reeds and scouted the land.

Pelt yanked him back down by the arm. "You crazy? He might see you."

"No one saw me."

"What did you see? Anything?"

"I think so. Hold on."

Zach stood up again. "Give me your camera. I need to zoom in."

Pelt wasn't about to give over his precious camera. Instead he stood and looked through the lens himself. They were farther from the road than he'd thought. Through the zoom lens he saw the man in the brown robe again, and the shovel, both in motion.

"He's back across the street. Digging, I think. He's

near the truck."

"Good." Zach flicked a bug off his arm. "Let's go that way toward the car. That's where Cole and Jessie will go."

Pelt lowered himself to the grass line and zoomed in closer with the camera lens. He put a hand on Zach's shoulder. "He's burying the kid again."

"Fuck!" Zach knelt back down. He had to think. "We have to save him. We can't go to the car yet. We gotta help that kid."

Pelt snapped a photo, then squatted down. "Dammit. I knew you'd say that."

"You can stay here, if you want."

"No. No way. You'll need my help. But that guy is huge. He'll break us both in half. What can we do?"

Zach looked around, as if weapons might magically materialize from the mud or grass. Between the two of them, they didn't even have a knife.

"Maybe we can throw rocks and distract him. Get him to walk into the woods while we… well, we dig up the kid." Seeing it hadn't landed, he added, "I can throw pretty far."

Pelt furrowed his brow. "I think that only works in the movies. But we can try."

They slunk through the weeds, keeping low to the ground, and closed the distance to the road. It seemed much more difficult walking back than it had been running away. Their adrenaline was still high, but it had ratcheted down two notches. Now they noticed things they hadn't before, like the tiny nicks on their arms from the sharp grass and the vibrant insect life. And the heat! The oppressive heat felt like breathing sand.

Pelt stopped to tie his shoe—worn knock-offs—and noticed Zach's white Nikes soiled with mud. There would be a howl of anguish and pain when Zach realized that. Or maybe he already had but was holding his angst inside. Misunderstanding his look, Zach paused.

"You okay?"

Pelt nodded as they crept forward again.

Near the edge of the grass, they peeked through the screen of weeds at the mysterious set of graves. The gravedigger, back in his ceremonial robe, finished his burial task. He waved a hand over the grave he'd just covered and crossed himself, then scattered more white crystals over the top. The act complete, he threw the shovel into the back of the truck.

"I need a big rock," Zach said. "Something that'll make a lot of noise. Maybe I can even break a window in that house."

They searched for rocks or stones, but none were in the swamp grass—only mud and clods of loose earth. The closest rocks of any size lay scattered on the other side of the road near the truck. The lone tree, the only willow on this side, provided nothing, either. At least an oak would have had acorns.

Then madame luck gifted them with an opportunity. The gravedigger got into his rusted truck and started it up. Zach and Pelt could have cheered but settled for a fist bump. This was great! Better than they could've hoped. If the man drove away, they could rescue the kid, find Jessie and Cole, and escape in their car.

The truck convulsed like an aging freighter, but it held together and rambled up the road. The guys poised ready on their hands and knees, hanging on the edge of their grass asylum like runners at a starting line, anxious for the truck to leave the road. But it didn't leave. It stopped in front of the church.

"Shit!" Zach hung his head. "He found the car."

"So?"

"So, he might not leave now. It tells him we're still here. He probably assumed that, but now he knows for sure."

They counted the seconds until, at last, the truck revved its engine and pulled into the church lot. That put them out of its line of sight.

"C'mon!"

Zach left the shelter of the grass and sprinted across the road. Pelt followed with one hand steadying his camera from battering his chest. They skidded to the ground behind dead bushes at the road's edge and waited, ears to the ground. The truck still knocked and sputtered loudly; they could hear it but not see it. The man still might see them from the church. They didn't know how acute his vision was.

Zach ran to the kid's grave and began clawing at the fresh dirt with both hands. It seemed hopeless; he looked around for a shovel—anything he could use. There was nothing. Even the porch to the house was empty. He dove back in with both hands.

Pelt joined him; their four hands tore furiously into the soil. Though the dirt was loose, the job was grueling. They worried the kid might suffocate before they could get to him. Zach locked his hands together and dragged chunks of dirt toward him. On their knees, bent close to the ground, they shoveled handful after handful from the grave.

The hole got deeper as they worked, making it harder to reach the bottom from where they knelt; loose soil slipped back down. It would have been easier for one of them to jump inside and dig from there, but they didn't want to stand on the kid.

Heat sent sweat stains through their t-shirts, soaked front and back. The sun seemed to grow more merciless as it moved west, and the dead leafless saplings near the graveyard did nothing to help. But the falling sun meant the afternoon was losing, and dusk would soon win its place for a few hours. They raced to beat both the gravedigger and the night.

The engine of the truck revved again at the church. They stopped digging and waited to see if it was coming back. But instead, it headed up the road and vanished. The engine faded until, mercifully, it was gone. They thrust their hands into the dirt with more zeal than ever. When dirt started cascading back into the hole, Zach groaned and pushed his mound away from the opening.

"What is this white stuff?" Pelt wondered. His face was red and dripping sweat.

Zach examined the white pellets intermixed with the soil. Tentatively, he stuck out his tongue and tasted one. "It's salt. It's rock salt, like what you put on the streets in winter."

"Why?"

"I don't know, man. Why would you bury someone alive by the road? Why any of this?"

He bent over the hole and scooped up clods of earth, now one handful at a time, while his other hand steadied him and kept him from falling in.

A foul stench began to rise from the grave.

Finally, his fingers touched burlap. When he pulled on it, the kid underneath twisted and wriggled. Zach grabbed the burlap blanket and tugged it upward, but he couldn't get a good grip, and the kid was too heavy at this angle. Both he and the kid struggled. A muzzled cry escaped the cloth.

"Fuck it."

Zach jumped into the hole, keeping his feet as far apart as possible to avoid crushing the kid. He reached down and yanked on the burlap. The kid came up with it. Zach leaned him against the side of the grave and ripped the burlap off him. He peeled the duct tape off the boy's mouth and winced, imagining how it must hurt. He folded the tape on itself and tossed it. Pelt brushed dirt and salt off the boy, who gasped and fought for air. He coughed and shielded his eyes from the sun with his small hands.

"It's okay, kid," Zach said. "Take a minute to catch

your breath."

He untied the rope from the kid's hands and feet and tossed the strands aside with the duct tape. The boy swatted Zach's hands away and withdrew from him, terrified. He tried to climb out of the hole but couldn't.

Hoping to help, Pelt stood and blocked the sun with his body. "He needs to get used to the light. Kid, we're here to rescue you. We're trying to save you."

He looked like any normal kid in his young teens. Blue jeans, sneakers, and a Houston Astros t-shirt, dirty and stained. He might have thrown up on himself, and he had certainly pissed his pants. Maybe more than that; he stank of everything bad. His fingernails were encrusted with dirt, and small burn marks streaked his hands and forearms. His brown sweat-soaked hair, long for his age, matted against his face.

"We're not going to hurt you." Zach held up his hands and backed away. "I'm going to lift you out of the hole. Is that okay?"

The boy's eyes began to focus. He looked up at Pelt and Zach. Hesitantly, he nodded. Zach lifted him out of the hole and sat him on the edge. The boy scrambled away from the grave, and they thought he might bolt, but he stopped three yards away. In the sparse shade provided by the dead brush, he sat and gasped for air. He stared at the hole.

Zach approached him slowly, and the boy backed away, scrambling across the dirt.

"Easy, easy. We're not gonna hurt you, kid. We're not

with that guy."

"I know this is traumatic," Pelt said to the kid. "But we don't have much time. That man who took you, he might be back soon." He knelt down and extended a hand, not too close. "Come on. We'll help you get out of here."

The kid looked at Pelt, then at Zach, then at the house behind the graveyard. He cocked his eye at it.

"He's not there anymore," Zach said. "He left in the pick-up, the truck that brought you here. But I don't know when he'll be back, so we need to go now."

"We have a car not far from here," Pelt explained. "We can take you away in it."

"We need to get to it fast and find our friends. The clock's ticking, kid."

The boy gawked up at Zach as if examining an alien creature. He narrowed his eyes in mistrust. They wondered if his mind was already too far gone, and could only guess what trauma he had experienced before reaching this awful grave. From the looks of the burns, bruises and piss stains, nothing good had come his way today. Or maybe this whole week.

"Let's start with your name," Pelt said. "This is Zach, and they call me Pelt. What is your name?"

The boy hesitated, then answered in a weak voice, barely audible. "Andras… Andy."

"Okay, great, great. We want to help you, but we need to get away from here first."

Zach knelt down closer to the boy and gently pulled

the kid's hair back from his eyes. "Easy. I'm not going to hurt you. We want to find out what happened to you, but first we need to get somewhere safe."

"Away from here," Pelt clarified. Was none of this getting through? "We have to get off this road. Do you understand?"

"Right. We need to get you away from this place. And we have friends… somewhere." Zach glanced at the marsh.

"Can you walk?"

The boy nodded.

"How old are you?"

He croaked what sounded like *eleven* in a tiny high-pitched voice

"I can carry you if you can't walk," Zach said.

The boy shook his head and stood up. His legs were shaky, but he was able to walk. He touched Zach's hand with a finger, perhaps to see if his rescuer was real or a dream.

"We need to get him some water."

"We have a few bottles in the car," Pelt said. "We can also get him a clean pair of underwear. I've got spares; they might fit close enough." Pelt was skinny. He bought his swimsuits in the 12-16 boys department.

"Good, but we need to move *now*," Zach urged. "You sure you can walk, kid? Andy?"

Andy nodded.

They scouted a path back to the car and helped

Andy to his feet. They stood on either side of him, ready in case he fell, and started for the church.

But it was too late.

They heard the familiar roar of an engine.

The truck had returned. It rumbled toward them.

CHAPTER 8

When Cole and Jessie arrived at the woods behind the house, the truck was parked where it had been before, next to the graves. They had heard it coming down the road and ducked deeper into the cluster of dead trees. Now they crouched and canvassed the land as the sun moved closer to setting. The house was quiet until a dog barked. They saw it bounce in and out of view around the front and side of the house, occasionally growling at the graves.

After two minutes, three figures circled the house and entered it through the back door: the gravedigger with a woman and a dog. The gravedigger, in overalls, had shed his robe and shovel. The woman with him had long black hair, almost to her waist, and a spattering of white skull makeup on her face, but not complete. She looked like she had been interrupted in the middle of its application. She wore a wide-brimmed hat, a rainbow-colored v-neck shirt and tie-died bell-bottom pants. She could have been thirty or fifty years old; the makeup made her age hard to pin down. Trailing them was a black dog that resembled a rottweiler, but bigger than any rottweiler they'd ever seen. It was hard to see details from this distance.

The dog barked again, and the woman admonished it. "Quiet, Seph. Get inside."

The three vanished into the house. More barking could be heard from within its shell, then muted growling. Now in need of a new plan, Jessie and Cole could only bide their time and stay in hiding. Time moved like cold molasses.

A few minutes later, the woman and dog came out, and this time she held a shotgun in her arms. She led the dog around the side to the front of the house. Cole strained to see what they were doing. It looked like they were scouring the edge of the tall grass for something. The dog sniffed, then darted into the weeds.

"They're looking for us. All of us. Zach and Pelt," Cole whispered. "Shit. That dog might smell them."

"Maybe not. Swamps have a lot of smells."

"Dogs know the difference, babe. But I hope you're right. I hope." He bit his lower lip. "Where do you think they are?"

"They took off in the other direction when we ran into the grass. They might be in deeper. Maybe in the swamp? Is that good or bad?"

"I'm guessing: bad."

The screen door flew open again, and the gravedigger stormed outside with a machete in his hand, his skull face-paint intact. The screen slammed shut behind him as he surveyed the back woods. Cole slipped to his stomach and pulled Jessie down with him. They laid on the ground, praying the trees and shade would hide them.

The man took a few steps towards the woods, stopped, listened intently, then sniffed the air. He scrutinized every branch of every tree for seven or eight minutes; it seemed interminable. Cole held his breath. A fly landed on his face. He blinked an eye, and the fly moved on. He felt Jessie twitch and held her hand tighter. Suddenly, the man swung left and charged in the direction of the church. His legs took amazingly long strides. Halfway there, he paused again to listen, then continued on.

Cole got up on his knees and spied on the house. To the right, across the road, he saw the dog come out of the weeds, then the woman and her dog entered the swamp together. The weeds hid the dog, but he could see the woman's hat bobbing above the green, the end of her shotgun poking up. She tracked the dog deeper and deeper into the marsh.

Jessie lifted herself to her knees and tried to follow the man as he made his way to the church. She noticed the look on Cole's face. He touched his cap.

"We need to get our car parts," he said. "I bet they're in the truck. Or in the house."

"You want to go in that house? Are you crazy?"

"We can't save the kid anymore, Jess. But we can drive for help."

The man was no longer in view. He had shifted into

the woods or the church, or maybe he had joined the search in the swamp.

"You stay here. I'll be back in a minute."

"No."

"Only for a minute. I'm going to look in that house. But first, the truck. I bet our car parts are on the dash of that truck." He removed his cap, then adjusted it back on his head. It was a nervous habit he'd never break.

"I'm going with you."

"I can run faster without you."

"Don't be such an asshole." She loosened her blouse. "We don't have time for this. I'll check the house while you check the car."

"That's a terrible idea. We go together to the truck first, since I think that's where our stuff is, then together into the house. If we need to. Only if we need to. I don't really want to know what's inside the Munsters' house of horrors."

"I don't either."

"Maybe there are guns in the house, though. Or at least a knife. Gotta have kitchen knives, right? We could use a weapon right now."

"I guess so."

Cole stood up. Without asking if Jessie was ready, he ran. He was hoping she'd lose her nerve and stay in the woods, but it didn't work. She followed a few feet behind. They crossed the craggy dirt to the side of the house and then the front, always one eye peeled for the return of the strange man.

Cole reached the truck first and looked through the window. Nothing but a pair of work gloves on the dash and a jar of salt on the passenger seat. The truck bed only contained the shovel.

Jessie opened the passenger door and its rusted hinges complained much louder than expected. She made an apologetic face and opened the glove compartment. Nothing inside except papers and a crinkled map. She felt under the seat for the car parts, but it was bare. Cole yanked her out of the cab and shut the door as softly as he could. It still creaked shrilly.

"That's why I didn't open it!"

"Sorry. We had to check."

"The parts aren't here." Cole checked the driver's side through the window. No keys in the ignition, so they couldn't steal the truck. And their distributor cap wasn't anywhere in sight.

"Dammit," Cole swore and resisted the urge to punch the truck. "We'll have to check the house."

"Cole. Look. Look!" Jessie ran to the empty grave. "The kid got out."

"Holy shit. You think he dug himself out?"

"I don't know." She looked at around and tucked her damp, sweaty hair behind her ear. "Is that possible?"

"I don't think so. And the truck was only back a few minutes. Not sure that's long enough for the freaks to dig him up."

"You think… you don't think Zach and Pelt got to him?" She whipped her head around, checking all directions until the barking dog drew her attention, now a hundred yards into the marsh. The lady's hat couldn't be seen anymore. "Cole, if they got him and went back into the swamp, they might be… I mean, that dog will find them."

"Fuck. We gotta help them."

"How?" She bit her lower lip, thinking.

"Distraction. We need to get that dog back here. And the woman with him."

"And the man?"

"We know they didn't go to the church. We would have passed them. So, I think the man isn't the biggest problem right now. We need to get the damn dog out of the grass."

"The house? Let's check it first. There might be guns, you think?"

Cole nodded and ran along the side of the house to the back door. He hoped there was another shotgun or a knife inside; he desperately wanted a weapon. Most of all, he wanted their car parts back. Jessie entered two steps behind him.

The house was sparsely furnished and clean—as clean as an old shack can be. Their first impression was that no one lived here. This wasn't a home; it was a building used for something else. A simple metal folding table took up most of the small kitchen space. Cole opened the cabinets one by one, all empty. Nothing in the utensil drawers either—no knives. Corrosion stained the sink, and there was no refrigerator. Yet, very little dust covered any of the surfaces. The kitchen was empty but clean. And old. Very old. It smelled rank and musty, the same rotting smell of the church. The floors, constructed of scuffed boards, had never been painted or tiled. Or maybe they had been, a hundred years ago.

"This place is cold," Jessie said.

"It's not my grandma's home, that's for sure."

"I mean, it's… cold. It's not hot like outside."

She was right. The temperature had dropped fifteen degrees when they entered. But surely this shack didn't even have electricity, let alone a fan or air conditioning.

"Air con?"

"Are you kidding? I'd be surprised if it has any power at all."

He felt a chill.

The living room had the same look—wood floors and bare shelves—with an old leather couch by the front window and two folding chairs next to a square mirror on the wall. A crude staircase led upstairs, but its stairs slanted badly and looked unsafe. The wall leading up had a long crack in it.

"Doubt those stairs would hold us," Cole said. He looked at the ceiling. "I wonder if the upstairs would, either. Floors up there might be rotted."

A recessed door was fitted under the staircase. At one time it had been painted red; now pink residue peeled off in many places. To the right was a door to a closet, cracked open two inches. Cole nudged it open further. Completely bare.

"Nothing," Jessie said, relieved. She had half-expected a monster to come screaming out.

Cole was disappointed; he had hoped for a gun rack. He tried the other door. The knob was rusted and groaned as he turned it.

"Don't," Jessie begged.

They both feared what might be behind it, but he felt a burning need to see. Dead bodies? Dead animals? Whatever lay beyond the door was putrid. Already they could smell it.

Cole swung the door open and held his breath—partly from fear, mostly from the smell—and peeked in. It was a staircase to the basement. The stairs were as poorly maintained as those leading up to the second floor. Something down there was rotting; he nearly gagged and pulled up his shirt again to cover his nose. Slivers of light from a cellar window showed jars of salt along the wall at the bottom of the stairs. The rest was dark.

"Cole. Let's get out of here." She clutched the back of his shirt.

Cole froze, peering into the cellar. If any guns existed in this house, they'd be stored in the basement. He was sure of it. Country folk always had guns in the basement. Yet, he couldn't force his legs to move in that direction.

Guns and dead things. Country folk. They got 'em all downstairs. I bet it's all down there.

But he was afraid to go down.

Then something stepped into the light at the bottom of the stairs, and a defiant face stared up at him. Cole stifled a scream.

CHAPTER 9

The truck's engine revved. Zach and Pelt didn't know what to do, but Andy did. He ran to the house and onto the front porch, jumping over a tripwire that was guarding it. He waved and pointed to the wire to make sure Zach and Pelt both saw it. Then he ran inside. The screen door slammed behind him with such force it sounded like a bomb.

How did he know about the tripwire?

And what does it trigger?

Zach and Pelt didn't have time to wonder; they followed Andy into the house, careful to avoid the wire. Again, the door slammed behind them, but the noise didn't matter anymore; the truck engine drowned out all other sounds on the road, like a Sherman tank out of tune.

Andy had been in the house before; that much was clear. He didn't hesitate but went straight for the door to the basement and flung it open.

"We can hide down there," he croaked. His voice was still hoarse.

This was the first ounce of trust he had shown in

Zach and Pelt. His fear of the gravedigger outweighed his fear of his rescuers. He motioned for them to go downstairs and allowed each to pass through the doorway before closing the door tight; then he pressed his skinny shoulder against it to test it was secure.

In the basement, they receded to the corner farthest from the stairs. There they waited and listened. It was dark, except for a few splinters of light coming from a small window well. Dust particles danced in their rays. The stench of mold was strong but could not mask the overwhelming smell of Andy. The confined space of the cellar only exacerbated his stench.

Jars of rock salt lined one wall, and a shelf unit held jars of nails and screws along another. A non-functioning water heater sat rusting in the opposite corner. Water stained the floor in a trail to a sunken drain. Otherwise, the cellar was vacant. The gray stone walls were contaminated with fungus and mold. Rainwater had leaked in and left a pattern around the boiler.

They heard the truck pull in and park; its tailpipe backfired before it shut down. And then the sound of two truck doors slamming. A dog barked.

"Hezekiah," said Andy. He urged them closer to the wall, into the shadows.

Zach tried not to gag from the smell or the thought of the boy's soiled pants brushing against his. "What?"

"His name."

"You know him?"

"He kept me and my mom for two days." He thought about it. "Three days. Then I got away."

"Why?"

"He hates us." Andy's voice was weak. He coughed, then put a hand over his mouth to stifle it.

Zach and Pelt shared a look. If the kid coughed again, they'd be found. And then dead. But later they wanted the whole story about the kid and his mom.

"He'll kill you, too, now. If you saw him," the boy squeaked. "Did he see you?"

"Shh." Pelt put a finger on his lips. "Don't talk. Be quiet."

Above them, the back door opened. A dog scuttled inside and clattered its paws across the floorboard accompanied by heavy work boots and another set of shoes. A woman's voice spoke, but the words were muffled through the ceiling. The sound of rummaging through cabinets. The couch scraped across the floor.

Andy made a gun with his thumb and forefinger. "Gun under the couch," he mouthed.

Eyes wide, Pelt looked at Zach.

They have guns now.

Then the dog started scratching at the door to the cellar. It barked and snarled, trying to claw its way in.

Oh shit! We've been found.

The dog continued barking, agitated by the unfamiliar smells; it knew strangers were here. As it assaulted the door, it howled.

We're dead if that door opens.

Zach explored the cellar for anything he could use as a weapon. His only thought was to break a salt jar and use the glass as a knife. Pelt thought of the nails on the other side of the room but couldn't form a realistic plan for how to use them. He searched in vain for a nail gun.

The dog growled.

That one, that's a demon from hell.

Cole knew bad dogs. He knew some were not pets and would never be pets. Some dogs were bred to kill. Some, even worse.

Dogs that growl that way, they're bad to the bone.

Finally, the woman yelled for the dog to follow her, and it scampered away from the door. They could hear it chase her through the kitchen, then it barked outside. The woman said something, and the dog took off. It sounded like they were headed for the road; their sounds diminished as seconds ticked by.

But above their heads, the floorboards still creaked. A footfall lumbered over them. Then another. Slow and deliberate. The gravedigger was still in the house. Something scraped along the table above them. A knife or a tool. He didn't linger, but to the boys it seemed he might never leave. At long last, they heard the screen door slam. The man had left the house.

They heard nothing after that. They had no idea if he had followed the woman or still stood at the back door. How far had he walked? Even now he might be standing right outside the door, guarding the house.

Several minutes passed.

Pelt felt he might puke—part from fear, part from the smell—and he held his breath. He closed his eyes. The basement was cooler, at least.

"What should we do?"

"I don't know," Zach said. "We can't stay down here forever. Andy, are there other weapons in the house? Anything we can use?"

Andy shook his head. "Only the gun and big knife."

"And let me guess, they have them both."

The boy nodded.

They weren't sure how much time had passed when the back door to the kitchen opened again. Two sets of feet shuffled overhead, softer. Muted voices spoke back and forth.

That got Andy's attention. He looked at Zach and Pelt, then shook his head, confusion knitted across his brow.

"What? What is it?" Pelt asked.

"Hezekiah does not speak."

Pelt understood. The two voices upstairs were not the gravedigger and his companion. These were different people. Two voices were speaking, and there was no dog. The footsteps crossed into the living room. The voices were closer now, and the cellar doorknob squeaked. Whoever they were, they were coming in. The door swung open and, inexplicably, Andy ran to the bottom of the staircase and looked up. Absurdly, he thought it was his mom coming back from the grave to save him.

But it wasn't.

"Holy cow," a voice said. "It's a kid."

"Cole?" Zach recognized his voice and ran to stand behind Andy. "Oh shit! Am I glad to see you? Kid, we know them."

He half-pushed, half-carried Andy up the stairs.

They regrouped in the living room and quickly exchanged abbreviated stories of what had happened to them. Andy listened intently. Soon it would be his turn to explain.

"So, the woman and dog are in the swamp?" Zach asked. "Looking for us?"

"And the gravedigger is at the church," Cole said. "But I don't know for how long. And we can't use the car. Kid, do you know where the keys are to that truck out there?"

Andy pointed to his jeans pocket. "Yes. Hezekiah. In his pocket."

"And our car parts?"

Andy shrugged.

"That's his name? Hezaka ka?"

"Hezekiah. And his sister is Hannah. The dog is Sepharin. Seph. They call it Seph."

"Is it a cult or something?" Jessie asked. "You said they kidnapped you and your mom together. Where's your mom now?"

Andy's face darkened. He pointed outside at the

graveyard with the make-shift crosses.

"They killed her? Buried her?"

He nodded.

"When?"

"Yesterday. Or two days ago, I think."

So, there was no chance of rescuing her. Two days underground, buried under dirt, would kill anyone. They didn't ask if she was dead before the man buried her. No need to rake the boy across those coals again.

And now was not the time.

"Either of those lunatics could come back at any minute," Cole reminded them. "We need to get outta this house."

"And go where?" Jessie asked.

"They'll expect us to go back to the car," Cole said. "So we can't go there. Besides, the man is at the church now. That's where he went last."

"The road is open," Zach said. "Too easy to spot us. That doesn't leave many choices. It's the woods or the swamp."

Andy pointed to the tall grass.

Cole shook his head. "The dog and the woman are there. Kid, they'll find us."

"No choice. Only place," Andy said. "The woods are booby-trapped. Easy to get killed."

"Oh shit, are you serious?" Cole looked at Jessie. "We were just in the woods."

"Lucky," Andy said. "Traps are like all over." He

moved to the front door and opened it. "Fast, before Hannah is coming back. And… look at the wire."

"There's a trip wire on the front porch," Zach told Cole and Jessie. "Be careful."

They filed outside and ran past the graves. At the side of the road, they stopped to make sure no one was on it. Then Andy ran across and trampled his way into the tall grass. The weeds ate him and he was instantly gone.

The others chased after him, but the thick weeds fought back. Visibility was as difficult as running, every step awkward and demanding. This trek seemed much harder than earlier. The advance of darkness only added to the confusion. The sun melted into the horizon, disintegrating by the minute. With no streetlights on this road, darkness—when it came—would be absolute.

Dusk bled the last of the colors from the sky.

It was as if the swamp had a life and a will of its own, and it didn't want them together. It came alive at night and moved to guide them in one direction or another, herding them to different spots.

The five became separated.

Alone, they were stranded.

CHAPTER 10

The swamp is not haunted, Cole told himself over and over as he thrashed through the brush, knocking past reeds and blades of grass in his frantic attempt to reconnect with Jessie.

It doesn't think, it isn't haunted, and it didn't tear her from me.

Yet all evidence pointed to the contrary. He had been holding her hand, and then he wasn't. As if ripped from him by a force, the swamp had taken her and towed her in another direction. Now he stopped running and listened. An orchestra of crickets joined frogs and the occasional buzz of dragonflies as they zipped past his head. The dog no longer barked, which meant it could be anywhere. Cole had been moving south, away from the sound of the barking, while the dog moved north toward the weeds across from the church.

He stood still, hoping to hear one of the others winnowing through the weeds, but he couldn't be sure what he was hearing. Every time the breeze shifted the grass, he thought it was a person. He walked a few more steps, winding through the morass. Mosquitoes nipped at him endlessly, their swarms thicker than ever. That meant he was getting close to water.

Cole had lost his baseball cap, too. It had flown off in the grass, but he wasn't sure where. He wasn't aware it was missing until now. After a feeble attempt to backtrack and find it, he accepted that the cap was as lost as he was. The swamp was hopeless. He ran a hand through his hair, damp with sweat.

Night intensified the sweltering heat, an illogical paradox of the South. How could night be hotter than day? And with no sun, darkness consumed all. He welcomed a swarm of fireflies as a tiny source of light and walked toward them until they buzzed away.

"Jessie," he whispered.

Nothing.

"Zach, Pelt. Where are you?"

He raised his voice and repeated their names. If he wanted to make noise, it would have to be now. That dog might be near enough to hear him in minutes. And the woman. That devilish woman. Sure, he might hear the gravedigger coming; the hulk was large and his presence thunderous. But the woman might slip nearby unheard. Likely he'd hear the dog, too, but once the dog smelled him, it would be too late.

Run all you want. It'll catch you.

Soon his sneakers sank into mud. It got worse the further he walked in this direction. The sound of his shoes plucking off the wet ground worried him. It only got louder and messier as he walked. Then one shoe sloshed into six inches of water. He feared the splash was a dinner bell in the night.

He crouched down and rested, waiting. Nothing happened, so he ventured another foot forward, trying hard to avoid the water in the dark. No luck, there was wet mud and water everywhere now. He had found the edge of the marsh. Standing in seven inches of water, his shoes soaked, he squinted into the darkness. Nothing was visible beyond a few feet in front of him. Frustrated, he clapped a mosquito on his arm and then another.

That was also too loud.

Dammit.

It was like clapping one's hands. He cursed his stupidity and stopped moving. His legs were tired, but he dared not sit in the water. He was sure leeches and other insects were already salivating over his presence, and snakes couldn't be disregarded.

Something rustled the weeds ahead. It sounded human. It was someone walking, for sure, not a dog or other animal. It was one of his friends! One of them crept toward him.

He stood to call out, when a hand clamped over his mouth and strong arms yanked him down into the muddy water. He started to struggle but a voice in his ear made him stop. "Shhh." He went limp and listened.

The figure ahead moved closer and sang out. "Come here, little birdies, come to mama."

It was the woman. She was alone, battering the weeds with the barrel of her shotgun. The dog barked now, at least a hundred yards away.

"Come here, little birdies. Mama gonna bring you all home. Time to rest. Time to sleep."

Cole tried to breathe through his nose. A hand still covered his mouth and held him down firmly. His jeans were getting wet.

Something got spooked a dozen yards away and disturbed the grass. A loon took to the air. The woman cocked her shotgun and fired in its direction. She cocked it again and held it ready. A splash of water this time, and a creature—or a person—dove into the swamp. She chased after it.

When the sound of her movements landed far enough away, Cole wrenched the hand from his mouth and turned to face his attacker. It was Zach.

"Holy shit!" he whispered. "I'm so glad it's you. I say this with a staunch record of heterosexuality. I could kiss you right now."

"Rain check on that," Zach whispered back. "Where's Jessie?"

"No idea. We got separated. And Pelt?"

"I don't know. He and the kid disappeared after they hit the weeds. Fuckin' swamp, man. It's tricky as hell to get through it. Like a damn maze."

"Yeah. It's a bitch."

"This side leads to a lake," Zach said, "but there's another house, and I think I saw a light on inside it. For a few seconds, anyway."

"Really? A house?"

"Yeah, but we'll need to wade through the lake to get to it, or maybe even swim to get across. I know, it'll suck, but I don't think we have a choice. There might be a phone in the house."

"I really hate walking in this shit."

"You're not gonna like swimming in it, either. It'll suck like hell, but we might have to."

Cole was not a fan of swimming. A fit athlete and baseball player, but an advocate of staying on dry land. He also feared lakes. His dad said it was the *Jaws syndrome*, fear of what might be in the water. The sea creatures might be imaginary, but his fear was real.

The reeds grew sparser and the water deeper as Zach led him to the lake. They waded in muck and water until it reached above their knees; then the lake appeared. Most of the clouds had moved on, allowing the full moon to reflect off the surface of the water. The lake was placid but alive. Crickets and frogs sang a deafening chorus, more intense here than anywhere, and occasional splashes peppered the water's surface. That only served to further unnerve Cole. He dipped a nervous hand in the water, testing it. Nothing swam to bite his fingers, so he waded in deeper.

"Where's the house?"

Zach pointed. "Over there. See?"

The moon's light glinted off a metal awning and a square window sitting on an island at least a hundred yards out in the middle of the lake. But it wasn't actually a house, it was a shack even smaller than the house back at the graveyard.

"Dude, you didn't say it was on an island. There's no phone there! It's probably just a hunting station."

"Maybe there is, maybe there isn't a phone. There could be a radio, and I bet we can find some weapons in there. A knife? Everyone out here has guns."

"Shit." Zach was right, but he hated to admit it.

"You can do this."

"I know I can do this," Cole whined. "I just don't *want* to. But you're right. I can do this. I can... Let's get this over with."

"Take your phone out and hold it above the water." Zach had a Ziploc bag he always carried in case it rained. He already had his phone sealed up but knew Cole didn't have protection for his.

"You brought a phone condom?"

"I always do. In case it rains." Zach's shoes and phone were his prized possessions. The shoes were ruined by now, but there was still hope for his phone.

They waded deeper until the water lapped at their belts. Something splashed into the water a yard off and swam away. A frog or a lizard or a rat.

"Was that a gator?" Cole asked.

"No. Gators and snakes don't make noise when they swim."

"What? Is that supposed to make me feel better? Jeez fuckin Louise!"

"Relax. It was a frog. I saw it." He hadn't.

"I don't think I can do this, man," Cole said. He was shaking. His fear of darkness, snakes and water were coming together in a perfect stew to paralyze him. A trifecta of horrors. He was starting to lose his nerve.

"Cole, look at me." Zach held his friend's face in his hands. "There are no snakes out here. Only you and me. Just follow me and we'll be fine. We'll get to the house and call for help."

"I know."

"You're the strongest one of us. You're the all-star player. If I can swim this, you can."

"Why aren't you afraid?"

"Because I'm too busy being pissed off. My new Nikes are ruined. Fuckin' swamp!"

That almost made Cole laugh.

"Listen to me, Cole. Glide through the water. Don't splash. Any noise will attract the dog or that woman." *Or gators or other predators, but don't tell him that.* "It's not a pool at the gym. Slip through the water with slow breast strokes. No butterfly strokes."

Cole's face said he was petrified, but his mouth said, "Okay."

Zach let go of his face. "Look, man, I'd do it alone, but I can't leave you here. I might never find you again. We need to stick together. Also... I might need you at the house. We don't know who we'll meet there."

"I understand. No, I'm fine. You go first. I'll be behind you, I promise."

"No. You have to swim next to me. Slow and easy. I

need to be able to see you, in case..." *in case an anaconda drags you down, down under the water* "...your foot gets snagged on something or you panic. And keep an eye on me, too. Keep up, swim right next to me."

"Got it."

Zach started to move forward, then stopped. Something occurred to him. "Oh, and don't let your head go below the water. I don't know how safe it is. You know, bacteria and shit."

"Right."

The water was cool. It felt good and provided much-needed relief from the mosquitoes. It got colder the deeper they went. They continued to walk into the lake until it was no longer possible; the water now licked their chests. The island was still eighty yards away. Zach squeezed his friend's shoulder, then slipped into the lake and propelled himself slowly and quietly with smooth breast strokes, combing the water aside. Cole did the same and stayed close to him, matching his speed and position. He held his phone above the water, which made for an awkward swim. They glided forward almost soundlessly.

Cole's free hand brushed a lily pad, and he jerked it back, sure it was a snake or barracuda. That threw him off balance, and his right hand plunged into the water to keep him afloat. His phone slipped from his fingers and vanished to the depths. He cursed the splash he'd made.

"Dammit! My phone! It fell in."

"Leave it," Zach said.

"But it's my phone!"

"You want to swim down there in the dark and feel around for it?"

Cole imagined all sorts of spiny creatures foraging on the lake bottom. "No."

"Then forget it and keep swimming."

It belongs to the eels and fish down there now. And the six-foot catfish that's under your feet.

"This is bullshit." The fear in Cole now had a little anger to keep it company. He loathed the water and what was in it. He didn't care about his phone anymore, he just wanted to be out of this liquid hell. "I keep thinking of *The Creature from the Black Lagoon*. Why can't I get it out of my head?"

That scene, where it paws at the woman's foot.

He shuddered.

"You need to focus on shore, man. Get to the island. Nothing's in this water but us. It's a lake, not the ocean. Jaws isn't down there. Trust me."

"It's a swamp lake, man. Swamps are even scarier." He panted as he swam. "Tons of small shit with sharp teeth and needles and whatever. I really hate this."

"I know. We're almost there."

Zach felt something brush against his foot but didn't react. He didn't tell Cole. *It's only a fish*, he hoped. He kept an eye on Cole to make sure he was making good stride with smooth breast strokes and not lost to panic or hysteria. *People drown that way.* He paddled forward; the lake seemed endless, the swim harrowing. An intrepid fish nibbled at his jeans, testing it for food.

Eventually, his hand touched mud. They had reached the shallows. *Thank God!* They crawled onto the island's soggy shore until they found grass. There they lay on their backs and rested, out of breath from the swim. They inhaled fresh air and tuned in to their surroundings. Nothing on the lake seemed disturbed by their presence; they hadn't awakened a kraken or alligator—as far as they knew. Nothing except for a large bullfrog on shore. It took umbrage at their intrusion and plopped into the water to snub them.

"I have to tell you something," Zach said. Still on his back, he contemplated the shape of the moon and wiped his face with a hand. "I kept a secret from you. We said we'd never do that."

"What secret?"

"A couple months ago, when you went to see your sister's new baby, and there was that party… Tommy Wallace and Jessie… he kissed her."

"I know," said Cole.

"By *kiss* her, I mean they—"

"I know, man. I already know. I've known for awhile."

Zach leaned up on one elbow. "Seriously? How?"

"I just did. Don't worry about it."

"I don't think he forced her or anything—"

"No kidding," Cole laughed. "No one forces Jessie to do anything she doesn't want to do."

"Are you mad? Because I didn't tell you?"

"At you? No. It's okay."

"They were both drunk, and I was drunk at the same party. And… I guess I'm making stupid excuses. But I was really drunk."

"Stop." Now Cole leaned up on his elbow. "Jessie and I have our own problems. They've got nothing to do with you. It's fine."

"I should've told you sooner. I'm a bad friend."

"The worst!" Cole grinned. "You're more like family. A real pain in the ass but always there."

"True that," Zach said. "True that."

"Why are you telling me this now? Is it because you think we might die tonight?"

Yes. That's exactly it.

"No! No way. This is the first time we've been alone in awhile, that's all."

"Promise me something, Zach. Promise me the group will stay together forever, even if Jess and I break up. Don't start saying it's awkward or some bullshit. You have to promise me we'll stick together."

"Sure. I promise. No worries."

Cole lay back again. "Cool. Cool." After a minute, reflecting on the dark sky, he said, "I have a confession to make, too."

"Yeah?"

"I peed in the lake."

Zach smiled. "C'mon, we've got a shed to crack open."

They pulled themselves to their feet and dripped water all the way to the shack.

The structure was dark. Made of simple wood, it had only two windows facing north and south. It looked straighter and of better construction than the house, not as old. They circled it and found a rickety wooden footbridge that led to the other shore, sixty yards off. That was good; at least they wouldn't need to swim back.

Cole took his shirt off and squeezed water onto the grass, then put it back on. Their wet shoes and socks squished when they walked. Cole tried the door, but it was locked. He threw his shoulder against it. Though it didn't give, it bent inward more than he expected due to wood rot around the jamb. Zach and Cole worked together and slammed their shoulders hard into the wood. The frame shook, and the door splintered around the knob. One more hard shove and it opened, splintering small slivers of wood outward from the latch. Zach sucked in his gut and shimmied past to avoid getting poked; Cole did likewise.

Inside, their feet shuffled onto a concrete floor that appeared to shift and move. The two windows cast moonlight onto swarms of large cockroaches—palmetto bugs—racing for cover. Zach squashed one with his shoe. One crawled up Cole's jeans. The others scattered into hiding.

"Lovely," Cole muttered and brushed it off.

A row of rectangular drawers rose along one wall, each two feet wide. The boys counted forty-five drawers: nine rows of five. They were deep, extending at least five or six feet to the back wall. Cole rapped the wood with his knuckles. Hard teak, well-built and sturdy. Thirty of the drawers were padlocked.

Cole slid open the first unlocked drawer; it rolled smoothly on casters and sent a cloud of dust into the air. He sneezed. A dozen cockroaches scuttled out; one ran over his hand. He yelped and flicked it across the room. After the roaches vanished into unseen cracks, the drawer was empty. He continued to check the other drawers while Zach scanned the room.

Zach's phone served as a nifty flashlight. He removed it from its plastic bag and dimmed it to its lowest setting to save the battery. Tools and fishing gear lined shelves on the opposite wall. Some tools he didn't recognize; they looked to him like dental instruments. Cobwebs draped over two corners of the shelf unit, but no bugs crawled on this side. He counted ten boxes of gauze on a shelf. One box was open, so he reached in and rubbed the material with his fingers. Though it was linen, it felt a bit like snakeskin to him. Five bottles of a blue liquid and a jar of yellow grease lay on the floor below the shelves, along with the skeletal remains of an animal. It might have been a raccoon; he wasn't sure.

Their clothes dripped lake water onto the concrete slab, forming small puddles at their feet. This would later betray them, but for now it wasn't given a single thought. There was too much to take in. This shack was a mystery of its own, hatching new questions about the people chasing them.

Except for roach nests, Cole came up empty on all

the unlocked drawers. Now he wanted to know what treasures the locked ones contained. With any luck, they held guns or hunting knives. If explosives were stored inside, it would make his day.

He picked up a piece of metal that lay next to the shelves, admired its weight, and used it as a crowbar on the first locked drawer. He tried to work quietly, but breaking padlocks is a noisy job.

"Shh. Don't be so loud," Zach complained. "What are you trying to do, anyway?"

"I wanna see what's inside. It's probably guns. What else could it be? This is a hunting area. They'd lock up guns or traps, right? Right?"

"I guess that's possible. But do it quietly. You sound like a bulldozer breaking china."

"You mean a bull. A bull in a china shop—"

"Shh. Can you please be quiet?"

"Sorry," Cole mouthed.

He splintered the wood around the first drawer's lock. Unlike the rotting door and walls of the shack, the box's wood was well-maintained, treated against termites and moisture. It wasn't easy to break. A second latch held the drawer in place; he yanked hard but couldn't get it to open. He applied the crowbar again.

Zach reviewed the peculiar assortment of tools and gauze. It didn't make sense. He tried to imagine what all these materials were for or why this shack was here. No useful weapons were stored on the shelves, and the fishing gear was poor, but in the corner he found a small toolbox that held a shiny collection of surgical scalpels—small but sharp. One of these could serve as a handy concealed weapon.

Cole grunted and continued fighting with the drawer. Another piece of its front split off. The lock mechanism dangled. A good twist of the crowbar sent it clanging to the floor. He winced at the noise it made.

Then, for Zach, the clues fit together, and he realized where they were. He figured out what the drawers meant, the supplies, the tools, what this shack was built for. Zach spun around as Cole slid the drawer open.

"Don't…"

The drawer was already open, and Cole looked inside.

"What the hell…"

CHAPTER 11

Pelt lay in the grass and closed his eyes. He had fallen and couldn't find his glasses. His hands sifted through the reeds and mud, scrambling to get his precious sight back.

Alone, he would be dead without his glasses. Beyond a few feet, his vision was bad, really bad. Add that to the darkness and he might as well give up. No way for him to find the car again, let alone escape the psychos chasing after them. He felt helpless.

Sweat trickled down his cheek. He needed to think. His glasses would have fallen forward, in front of him. Unless they ricocheted off a reed or got tangled in the weeds.

Oh shit. They could be anywhere.

He ran his hands over his camera, still hanging from the lanyard around his neck. Was it intact? Broken? Maybe the macro lens could help him see the ground. He hit a button to activate the light and aimed it at the ground. The lens magnified terrain in front of him but didn't show any sign of his glasses. He rotated it left and right, then ahead, left and right. There! The light glinted off a glass lens. He reached out and felt the familiar form of the plastic frames. He snatched them from the weeds, then doused the light. After wiping the lenses on his shirt, he replanted them on his nose. One lens had cracked, and the alignment was off.

Dammit.

At least he could see, sort of. Darkness and heat still suffocated the night. The tiny slip of moonlight did little to help. He clawed handfuls of mud and plastered it all over his arms and neck. The mudpack would cool him down and keep the mosquitoes off. It might even mask his scent from the dog.

Where is that damn dog?

Barking faded in and out, as the dog cut across large swatches of swamp. At times it sounded near, minutes later it was far off. Now it barked a good distance away. Cricket song was constant.

"Zach. Are you there?"

Something disturbed the grass close to him. He crouched lower and held still. The changes in the grass were too smooth to be a dog or human. But maybe a snake?

Is that Cole or Zach, or did I call a python to me?

Something hissed at him. It was a snake.

No, it was a person.

"Shh." Andy erupted from the grass and plopped down in the mud next to him. "Keep your damn mouth shut."

It's the kid! I'm amazed he's still alive.

"And don't turn on that dumb light again," Andy whispered.

"It was my camera."

"It was dumb."

"Sorry. I needed my glasses."

"I could see it all the way over there. I was in the grass. Over there."

No shit. We're all in the grass, kid!

"Good," said Pelt. "It helped you find me."

"It also helps the bad people find you. Find us. So, keep it off. It's dumb."

"Fair enough."

"Why do you got mud on you all over?"

"It's cool. And it keeps the mosquitoes off. Here, let me help you."

He started to smear mud on Andy's arms and neck, but the kid pushed him away. "Cut it out! C'mon, this way."

They duck-walked low in the weeds for ten minutes. The grass grew thinner and mud became water, which started creeping over their shoes. Andy led him to an inlet of water three feet deep.

"Why are we here?"

"Hold on," Andy said.

He pulled off his shoes and socks and tossed them higher up in the grass, next joined by his jeans. He threw his shirt into the water. Finally, he stripped off his soiled underwear and tossed them farther in the other direction;

he didn't want those back. Quietly he slipped into the water. He dunked his head below the surface and vanished for a few seconds.

"I'm not sure that's safe…" Pelt said. "…oh, oh, don't drink any of that."

Bubbles popped to the surface, then Andy's head reappeared. He spat a mouthful of water and shoved a finger in each ear to clear them.

"Kid, that's not safe for drinking. Or bathing."

"I was gross."

Fair enough. You smelled like a garbage truck.

Andy went under again and came back with his shirt. "This is better."

"Maybe. Yes."

"I don't think this cleaned it, but it's not so bad now." He sniffed it. "Kinda."

The young pre-teen was calmer than he was. It astonished Pelt how anyone could be concerned with his smell when they were inches from death. But after being buried alive, maybe nothing else can faze a person. The kid seemed to Pelt to be disconnected.

"Here." Pelt fished a wet wipe from his pocket. He always had one. "Wipe this on you. It's scented. Roses or lilacs, I think."

"Thanks."

It did little to cast a rose scent, but the combination of the wipe and the bath did clean most of the stench off the kid. He seemed happier for it.

"You okay, kid? Andy?"

Pelt watched him pull his jeans back on without the underwear. Though his jeans fit loose, he was content to be a little bit cleaner and zipped up.

"I'm hungry. Starving."

"We need to find my friends," Pelt whispered.

"We're already dead," Andy said.

"What?"

"What?" Andy hadn't meant to say that out loud, but it was out there now. "Seph will find us. He'll kill us. Only a matter of time."

"Who? You mean the dog?"

"He'll find them all. They have no chance. Same as us. He's good at finding."

"I'd like to try to escape, if you don't mind."

Andy shrugged and pulled his wet shirt over his head. "I don't mind. Do you have any food?" After adjusting his shirt, he sat down and slipped into his socks and shoes.

"Yes. Back at the car."

"Nothing on you?" Andy ran a hand through his long, wet hair and swiped it away from his face. He tried to comb it with his fingers.

"On me? You think I keep a deli in my back pocket? No. We have food at the car."

"I thought maybe a candy bar."

"Even if I did, it'd be melted and disgusting by now. But no, I haven't got anything." He considered where to go next. "You said you were a prisoner here before. Do you know where the church is? It's up the road."

"Yeah. I saw it before."

"Can you get us there? That's where our car is."

"You have food there?"

"Yes, we have food there, in the car trunk. But more importantly, we have a flare gun. I can use it to get help. Or as a weapon against that man and his friend."

"His sister."

"Whatever. And I have another pair of glasses in the car. Also, I think it's where Zach and the others will go. I need to get back together with them."

"You can drive the car?"

"Yeah. But my friends said that man took some parts out. It won't run."

Andy nodded. "Sure. He does that."

"You act like you know him."

"I told you, he tied me all up. He put my mom in the grave hole. Two or three days ago. I heard them talking a lot."

"You didn't answer me. Can you get me back to the church or not?"

Andy contemplated the question. "Sure. I can get you there."

"Alive?"

"Maybe."

"Wonderful. What's your plan? It's that direction, right? We'd have to walk right by that damn dog."

"We can trick it."

"How?"

"Follow me. Gotta stay close. The grass will make us go apart. It's good at that."

Andy reentered the tall grass and beat a path back toward the road. Pelt glued himself to the kid and even held onto his shirt a few times. Andy didn't seem to mind. He was right about getting separated in the grass, but Pelt was determined not to get stranded alone again, especially with hampered vision. He eventually grabbed onto a loop on Andy's belt.

The grass will make us go apart.

What the hell did that mean?

It's good at that.

Pelt wondered about the kid but didn't doubt his wisdom on the grass. It had its own agenda.

They crawled forward for ten minutes before Andy halted. The dog was getting closer. It had ceased barking. An eerie quiet followed, save for the mosquitoes buzzing around their ears.

"That's bad," Andy said. "He stops barking when he finds something. Sometimes it's something to bite."

Weeds rustled. The dog sniffed. It bared its teeth and tore through the blades on its way to Andy and Pelt.

CHAPTER 12

Separated from the others, Jessie panicked. She lowered her head, slapped the grass away from her eyes and ran forward without a plan. When she felt her shoes sink into mud, she turned around and ran back the way she had come. Every blade of grass confused her. Afraid to stand or even look up, she bent forward and moved ahead. Knowing that this made little sense did nothing to save her from going in circles.

When she stopped to rest, she thought she had run for an hour, but it had been only a few minutes. Time has no measure during confusion and chaos. Her breathing labored, she could feel her heartbeat in her ears.

Weeds crinkled. Something moved near her, but she had no idea from which direction. Should she run toward it or away from it?

"Cole? Cole, is that you?" she called out softly. Her voice strained to find him without alerting the wrong person, or thing. "Cole, where are you?"

A reed broke.

It's not Cole. It's that man.

That awful man.

A whimper escaped her. She remained as motionless as possible, breathless, and listened to the secret whispers of the grass, as its blades caressed each other. She prayed it was only a breeze. Prayed it was the sound of nature; but knew it wasn't. There was little wind, and the noise was too deliberate.

Another reed crinkled.

They're coming for you.

And you can't hide.

She thought of the movie Cole had made her watch last Halloween, *Night of the Living Dead*. She had hated it, but it stuck in her head. The cemetery where Barbara was chased. It wouldn't leave her be.

They're coming to get you, Barbara.

She squatted and wrapped her arms around her knees, locking her fingers together to stay them from trembling. On the ground near her feet, a one-inch beetle migrated down a clump of dirt and lumbered onto another, its back shiny and iridescent. Another wobbled up a stalk of grass. She closed her eyes. If she didn't look, no one could catch her.

That's how it works, right?

Close your eyes and the monsters go away.

The grass whispered more, and another reed broke. Was it the wind, or a body moving through the blades? Something stalked her. Someone. No animal could be this noiseless, this discreet. But the scary man couldn't either, could he? And the dog. It wouldn't be this stealthy. Or would it? She imagined it leaping from the bush and clamping its jaws into her leg. Or worse, her neck. It would drag her back to the house, breaking down weeds and leaving a long trail of blood along the way. Cole would only find her bloody trail, nothing more.

A blade of grass bent under a cat-like step. A shoe fell against the ground and crushed a twig. The stillness around her, barely perceptible sounds, rattled her nerves. She peeked through slits in her eyes as a shadow fell. Something blocked the sun from her cowering form. Why don't they speak or move? Had they not seen her? Their silence made them even more frightening. She stifled a cry and clasped her hands ever tighter until they turned white. The slits in her eyes narrowed and shut.

Make it go away.

Please send the boogeyman away.

Suddenly a bag dropped over her head and covered her face. Her eyes sprang open. An acrid smell inside the bag hit her hard. Her nostrils burned, and her eyes watered. The bag was tightening around her neck. She fought against two arms holding her down. Slender arms. This wasn't the burly gravedigger. It was someone else.

The world buzzed and shifted to its side. She felt the violent shock of a boat riding hard to port. The water lapped hard at the bow and rolled the boat over. Her stomach felt queasy, her arms stiffened. She couldn't move them, couldn't fight the slender arms any longer. She was paralyzed. Her vision blurred.

Her world went dark.

Cast into the water, she allowed herself to drown.

CHAPTER 13

Cole stared down at a body wrapped in strips of linen. Though fully encased in the material, its shape was undeniable: a human body resting with its arms folded over its stomach, sealed from head to toe. Even the face was enclosed in linen gauze. A mummy. These drawers were for storing mummies.

"We're in a mausoleum," Zach said. "This isn't gauze, it's mummy wrap… or whatever you call it. And I bet those jars of blue crap are embalming fluid."

"Fuck me," Cole breathed. "These are dead people. Dead fuckin' people. You think that's what's in all of these drawers?"

"Yeah. I think so."

"There's thirty of 'em locked, man." Cole stepped away from the drawers. "Thirty dead bodies."

"And fifteen are still empty. These aren't boxes or drawers; they're caskets. Not all of them are filled, which means they left room for more." Zach tapped an empty drawer. "Same as the graves, man. They plan to kill more."

"This just gets better and better. And weirder." Cole

wiped the sweat from the back of his neck, then fanned his shirt. "They bury some people out in that little cemetery but put some in here. Why? What's the reason for all this shit?"

"Religion?" Zach shrugged. "Some religions prefer to bury their people above ground."

"I don't think those freaks ask before they kill you. You think they asked that kid, Andy, before they buried him? *Kid, you want a grave, or you prefer an above-ground drawer?* I don't think they had that conversation, man. Do you?"

"No, I guess not. I wonder how they decide who goes where. Something strange is definitely going on here, but…"

"What?"

"Nothing. We just haven't figured it out yet. It's some kind of cult, right? It has to be. The cops are gonna have a field day with this one."

"Assuming we get to any."

"Don't you think it's weird that no one else ever found this shack before. Wouldn't someone notice a stack of dead bodies?"

"Maybe they did." Cole pointed to the coffin drawers. "Maybe everyone who found this place is dead and stashed in there."

"So, are some of these drawers for us? These four here?" Zach opened one of the empties and poked his nose inside. "There was room for more graves, too. Are we gonna be above-ground or below?"

"Why the hell would you say that?" Cole rubbed his eyes. He felt miserable standing there in wet clothes, his arms itching from mosquito bites. And nothing made any sense. "Don't even joke like that."

"Sorry. That's not what I meant. I mean, why do they put some victims in graves and some in this piss-poor mausoleum? What's the reason?"

Cole gave an exaggerated shrug. "I don't know. Mood of the day? They draw lots?"

"It's not random."

"How do you know?"

"It wouldn't be," Zach said. "It just… it wouldn't be. Nothing here is random. They're doing this for a reason."

"Maybe. Or maybe the reason is insanity."

"And another thing, he put crosses over the graves. Remember? And look, there are crosses here, too."

Zach shined his phone above their heads. Cole hadn't noticed them until now. Nine crosses were attached to the wall, one above each row of caskets. Unlike the crude tree-branch crosses at the gravesite, these were nicely carved from teak. Ornate and beautiful. They belonged in a cathedral.

"What's your point?"

"It's not a devil cult," Zach said. "They're not satanic. It's almost like they're… Christian. Religious ones, real ones; not the fake conservative talk-show kind. How many serial killers do you know who'd put crosses over their victims? And these crosses have been cleaned, dusted, kept in good shape."

"Thankfully, I don't know any serial killers."

"But you see what I'm saying, right?"

"Yeah. I see it. But how does that help us?"

"I don't know yet, Cole. But you gotta help me think. And you need to stitch it together, man." He could see his friend starting to get spooked again. The mummies had flustered them both. Cole would be useless if he started to panic. "Don't think about the bodies. We're gonna walk across that bridge and get back to the car soon. See? Bright side already; we don't have to swim the pee lake again."

"Yeah. That is good news. But my phone is still at the bottom with the fish. Bastard lake."

"Don't think—"

"Oh shit! Look!"

A flash of white caught his eye through the dirty window. Something pale moved in their direction. It was the gravedigger's white-colored skull, and he was marching across the ground toward the footbridge. A large machete swung from his right hand. Anyone could have seen Zach's phone through the same window, and it was a safe bet the gravedigger had seen it.

"Fuck! We're fucked," Cole yelled. "What do we do? There's nowhere to hide, man."

"We can swim the lake again," Zach suggested. "Take the back way."

"It's too late. He'll see us. He'll find us. That woman might be on the other side of the lake right now. And the damn dog!"

Zach looked around the room. "Shit. There's nowhere to hide except…" He slid one of the bottom drawers open on an empty row. "Get inside. I'll push it shut when you're in."

"That's a stupid idea. And what about you? You can't close the drawer from the inside."

"I think I can. There's a hook inside, see?" His fingers ran over a hook and a grooved mechanism for holding the lock. "I think I can close it."

"Fuck me. This is the worst idea ever, Zach. What if he checks the drawers?"

"Why would he?"

"Why *wouldn't* he?"

"Our choices are slim, dude. Get in!"

The gravedigger stomped onto the first plank of the footbridge. Zach had killed his phone light so he and Cole wouldn't be seen, but the man already knew they were there. And in one minute he'd be inside the mausoleum. The window showed his white skull bobbing toward them.

The dog started barking in fits. This caused the man to stall and look in its direction. That only bought them another thirty seconds. They had to act fast. Zach's mind raced.

The coffin drawers seemed the only option. He had other ideas but none of them were good.

We could slip into the water. Hold our breath. Stay under. Maybe breathe through a reed? Does that really work?

Or we could drown.

Or get eaten by an alligator.

"Cole, I need you to move fast. We don't have time to argue. Can you do exactly as I say?"

The man turned away from the dog and resumed his march across the bridge. His boots hammered on the loose planks. Every step was a clap of thunder, a death knell. Frogs took off into the water. The dog had found something to terrorize and was growling, but distant, no longer near.

The man's boots shook one plank after another.

Thud. Thud.

The gravedigger had crossed the bridge.

CHAPTER 14

When they were ten years old, Zach and Cole came up with a brilliant plan to climb the water tower in Schaler Township. It had all the points needed for a day planned by ten-year-old boys: it was dangerous, illegal and stupid. Check, check and check. The objective was to spray-paint a face of Charlie Brown on the side of the water tank and add their initials. This was a lofty goal in their eyes, equal to the moon landing.

For this mission, they would also need their new friend, Milton Peltner, who had moved in down the street that summer. He wouldn't get the "Pelt" moniker for another year. The new kid had to come along since only he could draw a proper Charlie Brown head. This was witnessed many times in class; he drew them on his books, papers and even the chalkboard when opportunity arose. That, and a triceratops. He couldn't do a good T-Rex but his triceratops was first-rate. And his CB was "straight fire," in Cole's own words.

While Cole was afraid of water, Zach had a fear of heights, which only added to the excitement of the operation. Peltner wasn't afraid of anything *per se*—no phobias—but he was afraid of almost everything to some extent. Hiking along the creek was fine with him, but climbing an unsteady ladder sixty feet into the air… that didn't fit into his definition of fun. However, he wanted to be a part of the cool gang in his new school, so he was easily swayed. Especially after they explained it would be "easy peezy lemon squeezy." They said that a lot back then.

One Saturday morning after *Dino Squad* and reruns of *Jonny Quest* and *Land of the Lost*, the three set out on their bikes for the old water tower. It was twelve miles, most of it on paved streets, until they hit the dirt path that ran through a sparse wood and half a mile through a cow field. The cows did not mind.

They ditched their bikes and began their long climb in mid-afternoon. Cole went first, then Zach, and Peltner last. A ladder extended from midway to the top. Scaling the first section posed no problem for three boys; they could climb anything with joints.

The ascent succeeded without incident. Peltner painted the Charlie Brown head in black spray paint and applauded his artistic work with pride—not unlike they imagined Michelangelo did after he painted the Sistine Chapel—then each boy penned his initials with the same can of Satin Black No. 54.

Mission accomplished!

This was their flag on the moon.

After reveling in the view and each taking the time to spit over the side and watch it land, they began to descend the ladder. No one had told them it was harder to climb down than up. These are the lessons we pick up along the way, sometimes the hard way. They descended in reverse order, Peltner first. Halfway down, Zach's sneaker slipped on the rung and kicked Peltner's hand. The new kid yelped and lost his grip.

And he fell.

Thirty feet to the ground.

He landed on his back. Zach and Cole rabbited down to him and felt sure he was dead. He wasn't moving.

"He's not breathing!" Cole shouted. "He's dead! He's not breathing!" But he had no idea how to tell if someone was breathing or not. Unconscious meant dead to his young mind.

Zach put his ear to Peltner's chest and heard a heartbeat. It was actually his own heartbeat, thumping timpani. "He's alive! We gotta get him to a doctor."

"How?"

"We gotta carry him."

"It's too far, Zach. How… how can we?" Panic is a cruel companion, but it sticks like glue. Cole lifted his baseball cap and clawed at his hair. "Oh Jeez!"

"I'll go for help. You stay with him, okay? I'll go as fast as I can."

"Where to?"

"Saint John's."

"Shit, Zach. That's a hundred miles."

"No it ain't. I think twenty-five."

"No. No, don't leave."

"Wait up, wait up. I know. I'll go to a house and call the cops. I'll call a'mergency."

"Yeah, yeah. That's a good idea. A couple blocks over I saw a house."

It takes kids a while to sort their way to the exit, but they get there eventually. Zach pedaled like the devil was on him, three blocks to a row of small houses, and got to a phone after pounding on two doors. A young woman called 9-1-1, and Zach flew back to his friends. The ambulance arrived half an hour later.

Milton Peltner was never in any real danger. The paramedics said he cracked a rib and got the wind knocked out of him. But to his mind, and for years to come, it was the closest he had come to death. Same with Zach and Cole.

It would be almost fifteen years before the three of them faced off again with the grim reaper and his harvest scythe.

* * *

Andy pulled up a root and tied it in a knot. He wrapped grass stalks around it and tied them, as well. Next, he unzipped his pants and urinated all over it.

"Save yours for the next one," he said. "We gotta do it a few more times."

"What in the hell are you doing, kid?" Pelt squinted

through his cracked glasses. "Look out! You're getting it all over."

"I'm trying to pee on the grass. The dog will follow the smell."

The dog was growling and getting closer, sniffing through the weeds and trouncing the underbrush as it moved, relentless in its hunt for the five humans.

Andy zipped up his pants and held out the urine-soaked weeds with satisfaction. He grabbed the smallest end of the root and flung it into the air as high and far as he could. Piss splattered them as it sailed, but sail it did, landing twenty yards away. The dog stopped for a second, barked, then chased after it with gusto. It loved the chase.

"Good arm, kid."

"C'mon," Andy said. "You're too slow. Go faster. This way."

After a few minutes crawling, running and then crawling again, Andy made another root-weed bomb. This one was bigger and heavier. It would go far if properly thrown.

"Your turn," he said.

"My turn what?"

"Hurry up. Pee on it."

Pelt groaned. "Fine."

He unzipped and aimed a stream onto the end of the root. "I really don't think this helps, you know. I mean we're leaving piss all over the place. Won't it smell that, too?"

ON GRAVEDIGGER ROAD

"We're confusing it. That's all that matters."

Pelt zipped back up.

"Okay, carry that. We don't use it until we have to."

"Carry it? It's got piss on it. It's dripping."

"I know it's gross. You gotta."

Andy didn't wait for an answer. He began crawling forward again. Pelt gave in and grabbed the smallest end of the root. He dragged it behind him.

Ten minutes later, the dog found its way back to them. When it sounded like it was getting too close, Andy gave the signal to throw the root. Pelt swung it around twice and tossed it a few yards away.

"Are you kidding me?" Andy asked. "You throw like a little girl. Wait here."

The dog got closer. Andy disappeared through the grass. A noise in the darkness sent the dog in another direction, off on a new hunt and a fresh barking spree. Andy crawled back to Pelt.

"Was that you?" Pelt asked. "Did you find it?"

Andy didn't answer but motioned for Pelt to follow him. They slunk across the swamp, occasionally running a few yards, then ducking down to crawl again. When they had achieved a safe distance, they stood up. On his tiptoes, Andy was barely tall enough to see over the grass, but Pelt spotted the house with a light on inside. Far across the road and behind the graves, the lamp shone dimly through a window.

"There's a light on. I can see it in the window of the house. Does that mean anything?"

"Hannah," Andy said. "She lit a lamp. That doesn't mean nothin' but maybe she's there. Or they could all be out here hunting us. But she lit a lamp for a reason. She does everything for a reason."

"What does that mean?"

Andy shrugged. "She does."

"We're close to the road."

"I know. That's the point. We gotta stay in the grass close to the road. Too easy to get lost out here in the dark. We need to get back to your car."

"It's a long walk." Pelt lifted his camera to his eye. Nothing to see through the window, but a shadow flickered on a wall.

"You said your car was at the church, right?"

"Yeah."

"We can get there. Stay close to me."

"How do you know the way so well?"

"My second time. I ran away before." The kid bent down and tied both his sneakers tighter. "Can you be more quieter? Stay close."

They duck-walked for a dozen yards and then rose a bit to walk faster. The car mirror glinted ahead but still seemed miles away to Pelt. He felt weak, following a child to safety. But Pelt wasn't cut out for things like this. He considered himself neither brave nor athletic. That was Zach and Cole. And, apparently, Andy. Not him. Adrenaline was all that was keeping him going at this point.

Andy was the opposite, fearless, and quickened his

pace.

Pelt bent forward and ran in Andy's path to keep up. Seconds later, something hit Pelt's head and sent him crashing to the ground. He had collided with a pole, bruising his forehead. When he looked up, he found himself under a skull suspended on the end of a spike. It appeared to be laughing. It held Pelt's stare for several seconds, and then it giggled again. The laughter may have been Pelt's imagination, but the skull was all too real.

"Come on," Andy urged. "Put your arms in front of you. Stick behind me."

As they advanced, they saw more skulls on spikes, lining the road like guardians of the night. Pelt wondered where they came from. These hadn't been here when they arrived that afternoon. He would have remembered such horrors. Had someone put them here after nightfall? Or had they materialized on their own? To him, they looked animated enough to have sprouted up from the ground of their own accord. But that was just the wind, tenderly nudging them to and fro, their jaws wobbling, furthering the illusion of laughter.

It's funny, the way you run from us.

There's nowhere to run.

We always see you.

But Andy seemed unfazed by them and was already yards ahead of Pelt. Deep in the swamp, the dog yapped and a loon took flight. Both sounded so far away, but Pelt knew the beast could be on them in minutes. It seemed to navigate the swamp like a razor through a soft melon. Pelt ran to catch up and grabbed the back of Andy's shirt.

"Hold up. Hold up, kid. What's the plan?"

"The plan? What do you think? The car's the plan. You said you have food and water there. You do, don't you? And your friends'll be there."

"I said they *might* go there. Really I have no idea where the hell they are."

"But you got food. Right?"

"Yeah. We have food and water. And juice, but I don't think that'll save us. How can you be hungry at a time like this?"

Andy frowned. "Follow me and don't drag. I don't want to lose you, too."

"Me *too?* Who else did we lose?"

"My mother! Those bastards took her and buried her, remember? I'm all alone out here if you go away. I was alone before. I don't like it."

"Oh, yeah. Sorry. I'll stay close."

They skirted the edge of the swamp near the road, careful to steer clear of the line of skulls. While the skulls didn't appear to frighten Andy, he made it a point not to approach them. He kept one eye on them as they walked. He didn't fear them, but didn't like them, either.

The dog snarled and yipped, closer this time, and Andy fell to his stomach. Pelt joined him. They lay still and listened. The sound of it barreling through the weeds was mixed with crickets, loons, toads and indiscernible growls. Alive with life, the swamp cared little for the new intruders. Something would catch them if they stayed too long.

The dog zigzagged, chasing shadows.

They waited.

CHAPTER 15

The world spun circles around Jessie. Her head felt heavy enough to drop off. She imagined herself a marionette with a giant head that sagged. The last thing she remembered was running from the hound. It had her, its jaws locked onto her pants. Then something grabbed her face, and she blacked out.

Was that real?

No. That didn't happen. What did happen? How did I get here?

She opened her eyes. A bleary flame dabbed shadows at a wall before her. She blinked and found herself back in the house. A single lantern lit the room from a shelf on the wall opposite her. It hadn't been there before. Pressure against her wrists told her she was tied to something. As her senses returned, she became aware that her hands were tied behind her and looped onto the chair she sat in—one of the folding chairs she had seen earlier, now in the center of the room.

She blinked her eyes; the blur receded and the room no longer gyrated. An image came into focus in front of her. It was the woman, her long black hair shiny under the lamp. She was in the other chair, facing the wall mirror and applying makeup to her face.

When the woman heard Jessie stir, she said, "Don't fret, honey. A side effect of the chloroform, that's all. It'll wear off. Give it time."

"You… you drugged me?" It came out more like: you youdruck mit.

"Sit still, dear. You'll give yourself a headache if you try to talk too soon. Let it wear off."

The woman turned around and smiled an awful smile. She had applied skeletal makeup to match her brother's, except hers extended down her neck. The flesh paint depicted a line of bones trailing to her chest. She held the smile an arguably long time, then turned back to the mirror to continue applying her makeup.

Jessie's focus sharpened, and the room's elements became clearer. She took inventory of the rope around her hands, the chair, the furniture. The man wasn't there, nor was the dog. They were hunting her friends, she assumed. She had so many questions.

"Where are my friends?"

The woman was now applying eyeliner; she gestured toward the window with the tiny brush. "Out there, dear, where you left them. Hiding like little field mice."

"What do you want with us?"

"Want with you?"

"Yes. What do you want?"

"Why, nothing, dear. We don't want you at all. We want Andras."

"Who? You mean Andy? You mean the little boy?"

"I do indeed." She finished her makeup detail and stopped to admire her work in the mirror, insufferably pleased with herself.

"Why?" Jessie asked. "Why do you want him?"

"Because," the woman said as she ran a comb through her long silky hair, "he is the devil."

"What?"

The woman swiveled to face Jessie and continued brushing her hair. Her face was something from a Friday night creature feature. With Jessie's blurred vision cleared, she could see the intricate details in the face painting. It was impressive. Any other day, she would have marveled at the artwork on the skin, but now she only recoiled from it.

"Well, not *the* devil," the woman said. "*A* devil. A demon. And it's my brother's job to put demons away."

"You mean bury them."

"Exactly. You're smart, you catch on quick." She put the brush away and rested her hands on her lap. Her long fingernails were painted black and attracted attention. "My name is Hannah."

"I'm... I'm Jessica. Jessie."

"How lovely to meet you, Jessica."

"Why am I tied up?"

"Well, for a number of reasons. To keep you here, first and foremost, and second, to lure your friends here and eventually to get Andras back. You can scream for help, if you like; it will only bring them in faster."

Jessica considered it but declined; she might scream later, she thought.

Hannah smiled again. It was the most disquieting smile Jessie had ever seen. It reminded her of the way the cheerleaders smiled before dumping baby oil on her back in high school gym class, or getting her shirt wet before class so her top became see-through.

Hannah is a mean girl. A mean girl with a gun.

"What the hell's wrong with you?" Jessie asked.

"I'm not the bad guy, sweetie. Neither is my brother. This world would be a dangerous place without Hezekiah."

"The world still is a dangerous place."

"It would be more dangerous, trust me, if not for me and Hezekiah."

"Heza…"

"My brother, Hezekiah. He's a demon hunter. Well, he's also a demon. But that's beside the point. Now he hunts them."

"And I suppose your dog is a hell-hound?"

Hannah laughed. "That's a good one."

"You're insane, lady."

I was wrong. She's not a mean girl. She's the psycho who kills the mean girls.

"Seph is the opposite of a hell-hound. Well, yes, technically Sepharin is a hell-hound—again, these are mere semantics—but he helps us put demons in the ground."

"So, you work for heaven?" The sarcasm in Jessie's voice was running thick. It was also starting to annoy her captor.

"No. Not at all." Hannah kept a calm tone, but her patience wasn't endless. "We work for both sides now. There are demons even hell doesn't want roaming on earth."

"You're…" *a psychopath, a raving lunatic.* "… never letting us go, are you?"

"I might. After we get Andras back."

"We saw you bury that kid. Andy. We're witnesses. You won't let us go. I know it."

Hannah put a long finger on her chin. "I would consider it, letting you go, if Hezekiah agrees. But you must help me fetch that awful Andras."

"Andy isn't some demon. He's a kid. Why do you think he's dangerous?"

"His mother was a witch, dear. He's the spawn of a witch. We buried her a few days ago. Right out there." She tipped her head to indicate the graveyard outside. "We buried her with salt. Same as we buried Andras. He was dealt with, *fait accompli*, until your friends interfered. They dug him up. Can you imagine? Digging up a demon and letting it loose on the world? Your friends, no, we won't let them go free. They're already dead to us. But you, dear, I might consider letting you go. Unless…"

Jessie cocked her head. "Unless what?"

"Unless you'd care to join us? We could use another

crusader."

"No thanks. I like my crazy in a padded cell."

"Suit yourself."

"You put salt in the graves to keep the demons in," Jessie said. It made sense; this was a cult steeped in mythology. "That's why all the jars of rock salt are in the basement."

Hannah's eyes widened. "Sweet Azriel, you are smart! You're right. We can't actually kill the demons. They won't die, not by our hand, anyway. But we can keep them from leaving their graves. Demons can't pass salt. A line of salt is a wall to them. If we put salt on the dirt, they can't dig themselves out. Clever girl, you figured that out all by yourself."

"I'm a history major. I know my mythology."

"Some myths have their origins in truth."

"Maybe." Jessie shrugged. "Maybe not. Can I ask you a couple things?"

Hannah held out a slender hand. "You can ask me many things, dear. Anything you want."

"Why the makeup and costumes? It makes you and your… brother… look like demons. But you claim to fight demons. That makes no sense."

Hannah snorted. "In many ways, demons are like anyone else, sweetie. They can be scared same as you and me. We dress this way to scare them. They don't like it. It frightens them. Or at least it unsettles them. Even the name of this road is meant to unnerve our enemies and break their spirit."

"That's the craziest thing you've said yet, and the bar is pretty high today. Isn't it usually the bad guys who dress up like weird creatures, like something… scary?"

"Not always, dear. You never heard of a wolf in sheep's clothing? Some of the most dangerous creatures on the planet look like ordinary men. Some even pose as ministers or senators. Don't be fooled by norms, dear. Covers are just that: covers."

"In my experience, bad people look like you. Good people look like me."

Hannah smiled, amused. "Why do you dress up on Halloween?"

"I don't."

"Yes, but others do," Hannah said. "And you did as a child. Why do it? It's to scare the ghosts and spirits away on that night, the one night they can roam free, supposedly. Truth be told, they can roam free any night or day they want. But we need to scare them from our homes. That's why we carve intricate jack-o'-lanterns with saw-toothed grins and place them on the porch. It's to scare the beasties away." She drew a breath and tapped her chin. "That's why I could never understand children dressing up like nurses or football players. What's scary about that?"

She stared at Jessie.

"Oh! You're asking me?" Jessie smirked. "I've no fucking clue."

"I guess they've all forgotten what Halloween is really about. Sad, isn't it?"

"I think we'll live. Even without the true meaning of Halloween."

"No. No, you won't." Suddenly, Hannah was cold and serious. "Not unless you get Andras back for me. You must put thinks right again."

"I'm not playing your game."

Hannah picked up a small knife from the cosmetic table. She rose and took measured steps to Jessie's chair. She lifted Jessie's chin with the dull edge of the blade, forcing her to look up. Their eyes locked.

"This is no game, Jessica. If it were, I'd have already won. I will get Andras back, one way or another. Your only chance to live is for you to assist me. But with or without you, he's going back in that grave."

Jessie pulled her chin away from the tiny blade. She looked out the window. Hannah's reflection in the glass was spooky. The woman looked like a ghost; the face paint only heightened the illusion. Jessie tried to look past, to see anything else outside, but it was too dark.

Wherever you are, guys, don't get caught. These people are crazy. More than we could have dreamed.

In our worst nightmares.

Hannah put the knife back on the cosmetics table and clapped her hands together. The sudden sound startled Jessie.

"I'm going to open some wine. Would you like some, dear?"

"Yeah. I would. Bring the whole damn bottle."

CHAPTER 16

Zach and Cole closed their eyes and tried not to breathe; each struggled to make not even the tiniest sound. They listened to the gravedigger trudge along the side of the shack with slow plodding steps, as if every footfall had meaning. He scraped his machete along the outside wall. It created a horrific sound, worse than fingernails on a chalkboard, tormenting the old planks.

He ran the blade along the entire length of the shack, marring the wall and announcing his presence.

Then he started to whistle. That sound was worse even than the scraping of the machete. He whistled a familiar childhood tune. It taunted them.

Mary had a little lamb...
Little lamb, little lamb...

The crickets had stopped chirping. Were even they afraid of this man? Their silence left a vacuum that amplified his discordant whistling.

Gently, the gravedigger pushed the broken door open. Its hinges screeched long and slow. He stood in the doorway, but no footsteps landed inside yet. They could hear him breathing heavily but not moving.

Again, he whistled.

... and everywhere that Mary went ...

Finally, the sound of a boot on concrete.

... the lamb was sure to go.

He entered the make-shift mausoleum and stopped whistling. The puddles of water and wet footprints showed there had been intruders. He ran a boot over a puddle and spread the water.

He noticed the drawer that had been breached. He opened it wide and issued a strange sound—half whimper and half cry of pain. His strained breathing rose to fill the shack. The broken drawer had saddened as much as angered him, and he cried out again. The sound was inhuman; it was feral. To him, this was a cruel act of desecration. It hurt him.

The odd sound made Zach and Cole tremble. Had this tomb belonged to a friend of his?

If you hurt a madman... what does he do to you?

When he had finished mourning, he pounded the machete hard on the drawer. The wall of caskets shook. Both his fists came down on the drawers, and the walls shook. This man's strength was fierce, and now he was more motivated than ever to find those who had broken the seal of the dead. He scraped the blade along the front of the caskets.

Zach noticed water dripping off him.

Shit! That could give us away.

Cole closed his eyes tighter and listened to the callous scratches of the blade. From the sounds, he imagined the man's every movement. He had felt the shaking of the walls and wondered how long he could stay in this uncomfortable, precarious position. It was hard not to move; he wanted to shift his weight but dared not.

Worse than the whistling, the gravedigger's raspy breathing rattled from his chest. He stood without moving and let seconds tick by. Now he was angry. It might have been a job to complete before, but now it was personal. He wouldn't toy with the interlopers any longer. He would kill them. He breathed heavily and pounded the blade twice more on the drawers. He was sending them a message.

He opened the first of the unlocked caskets on the top row. He slid them out, one at a time with methodical care, taking great pains to ensure their fronts lined up perfectly when re-closed. He was in no hurry. The offenders were trapped.

Zach listened to the dull glide of the drawers' casters not far away. His leg cramped but moving it would be suicide. Silence was vital, but this position was untenable; he couldn't stay twisted this way for much longer. He prayed this ordeal would end soon. He wondered what would make the man angrier, finding them or not finding them. Soon they would know.

The second row. The man checked each drawer with the same care. He continued with the third and fourth until he came to the bottom. There was nowhere else to hide inside this room. The trespassers would be in the bottom row, the easiest to climb into. He could lock the caskets now and seal their fate. But he was incensed and motivated to shed blood tonight.

A roach crawled across Cole's neck. He flicked it off, disgusted. *Did that make a noise?* He breathed shallowly, certain even one breath was too loud. The gravedigger continued opening drawers.

Four drawers left. He jerked one open. Empty. He tapped the bottom with his blade.

Next drawer. Same.

Two drawers left.

Had they gone in feet-first, their heads would be at the top. One slice would cut their throats.

Cole held his breath and listened, eyes shut. His hand that held the rail trembled; he pressed hard to steady it. Zach was only two feet away. He wondered if he was half as scared.

The man yanked hard and slammed his machete inside as soon as the drawer opened. He expected to impale either a head or foot, but the drawer was empty.

Both were in the same drawer.

Now he really did want to lock them in. They'd suffocate within a day, both using up what little air lay inside the box. But he wanted blood. After that, a ritual would be performed to reseal the mausoleum.

The door flew open. The blade came down hard. He let out a sound that resembled the eerie scream of a child's doll when deflated. It wasn't natural. The gravedigger did not have the same vocal chords as normal people. As Andy had said, *he does not speak.*

The empty drawer confused him. He stood and spun around the room. The raccoon skull laughed at him. The tools and supplies sat idle. He tapped the shelf unit with his blade. It vibrated but held.

The trespassers had left. They must have swum the lake while he was searching the shack. Furious, the gravedigger marched outside and stood at the shoreline, breathing heavily, scanning the water for any disruption. Insects skipped above the surface. Frogs croaked; one leaped in. On the opposite shore, nothing agitated the grass except for a light breeze. If they had made it that far, they would be crawling away from the lake. Maybe back to their car.

He whirled into motion, rounded the shack and pounded across the rickety footbridge. Each step was powerful and angry. He stomped the grass before him, not caring what tracks he made, and circled back toward the road.

Zach opened his eyes. He waited a minute to be sure they were alone before he tried to move. The crickets had returned in song, which meant the man was off the island.

He and Cole had climbed onto the roof while the gravedigger was punishing the wall on the other side with his blade, and now they clung to a slim rail on the roof tiles in a sprawling spider-like position. The cramp in Zach's calf was painful. He tried to work his legs to climb back down, and the cramp threatened to throw him over.

Cole let go and scampered off the roof like a monkey and scanned the darkness. He pulled his shirt over his head and shook it out, then swatted his back and arms. It felt like bugs were still on him. He put his shirt back on and looked up at his friend, now hanging over the edge. The drop was only twelve feet.

"What's wrong?"

"Leg cramp."

"Damn. Just fall. I'll catch you, bro."

That was already happening without his consent. Zach tried to scale down the wall, but his leg gave out and he fell on Cole. They tumbled onto the wet grass. Cole listened to see if anyone had heard them, while Zach massaged the cramp out of his leg.

"I thought we were dead when the water started dripping off my jeans again," Zach said, finally able to stretch his leg out. "Wasn't sure how secure the roof was. If that water came dripping on his head, we'd be dead now."

Cole looked at the roof. "I mean, it protects the bodies from rain. I don't think that was a problem."

"Still worried me. Shit. That guy's pissed now."

They recovered and stood up. Zach leaned against the shack and worked his leg back and forth. It was almost back to normal.

"I don't think it matters that he's pissed off."

"It might."

"C'mon. We need weapons."

They reentered the shack, this time only using moonlight for guidance. Zach took a scalpel from the toolbox. He cut a piece of linen and wrapped it around the blade, then slipped it carefully into his back jeans pocket. Next, he wrapped his arms in the same linen gauze, then shoved an extra wad of it into his front pocket. He noticed a hammer and snatched it up.

Cole chose a fishnet on a pole; he wanted a stick or bat. He was about to break the net off when he saw something better: a pole with a hook on the end. He dropped the net and took the hook instead. He held it in both hands, felt the weight, and whirled it twice around. It sang through the air.

"Oh, yeah. This'll do."

"Easy, Captain Hook! You almost poked me."

"What the hell is on your arms?" Cole asked. He ran a finger along the gauze that covered Zach from shoulder to wrist. "Is that the mummy cloth?"

"To keep mosquitoes off."

"Dude, these mosquitoes are the size of rats. I don't think that'll stop 'em."

"I'm wearing it, anyway. Let's go."

They headed back outside. This time they would use the footbridge and were thankful for it. Still not dry from their swim, they didn't relish another dip in the fetid lake. And it was best not to tempt fate with its creatures; the low growl of an alligator continually plagued the night. From its sound, it wasn't far off.

They stepped around the shack to the bridge. Cole was first to test the planks with a foot. It didn't feel steady, but the gravedigger—a larger man than either of them—had just crossed it, so it must be able to hold their weight. Cole placed a foot on the first plank. Wobbly, but the plank held, so he took two more steps onto the bridge. He was ready to venture a crossing when the dog barked again.

"Shit! Look." Zach held Cole by the shoulder.

The dog charged from the grass and stood its ground on the other side of the footbridge. Its barking turned into a growl, and it looked angry enough to tear them apart with its teeth. Saliva dripped from its jaws. It blocked their way and paced impatiently at the mouth of the bridge.

"Crap. Cujo is back. What now?" Cole asked.

"We gotta shut that thing up. It'll bring the other two freaks back here. And then we *will* be trapped."

The dog pawed the first plank. It looked ready to cross the bridge any second now.

"How? How can we make it stop barking?"

Cole picked up a rock and threw it at the dog. That only made it madder. It snarled and put both paws on the bridge. Soon it would race across and sink its teeth into them. Even if they escaped its bite, the barking would surely attract unwanted attention. More than the crazed man with the machete, other creatures might wake up.

Zach saw some of that unwanted attention already, in the shallows near the shore. The moon's dim light reflected off two shiny eyes at the water's surface, drifting toward the bridge. The commotion had caught the attention of an alligator, and this was no baby. If the swish of the water was its tail, it was over twelve feet long. A behemoth. It would be their death or their salvation.

He shared his plan with Cole.

The dog padded farther out onto the bridge.

The gator moved toward them.

"You can do this. Pretend it's a baseball and hit a home run," Zach said. "Don't be scared, Cole."

"That's like telling me not to be six-feet tall. I'm scared as hell. But..." He didn't finish the thought. Instead, he walked a third of the way across the bridge. The planks shifted under his weight.

The dog growled and came closer to the middle.

Cole swung the hooked pole around, so the dull end faced front. He tapped the planks in front of him and challenged the dog to come get him. He stared into the eyes of the hellhound.

The alligator was almost at the bridge.

"Come on, you piece of crap," he goaded the animal. "Come bite me, you pansy." He barked back at the dog, crudely imitating it. He ran toward the middle, and that set the dog off.

The hound bared its teeth and raced toward Cole. Saliva flew from its jowls, and its snarls turned into one last bark before it reached Cole. They collided in the middle of the bridge. The dog snapped its jaws at Cole's leg, but Cole struck first with the stick, putting all his weight into it while kicking with one foot. And it worked. The dog flew off the bridge and into the water with a heavy splash. It went under, then came up and paddled frantically toward the island.

The alligator dove under and took its prey from beneath. It seized the dog in its jaws and twisted its body into a death roll, its colossal tail flailing violently. The water roiled and churned black.

Zach and Cole could only make out a great thrashing on the water, the flash of a reptilian tail, and then both the gator and the dog went under. Ripples widened across the lake for a moment, then no more. Both were gone.

The lake settled back into its nightly routine, unconcerned by the little battles in its world. Except that a thin fog crept out from the opposite shore and inched over the water, smothering each soundless quiver from the bugs that skittered on its skin. But the gator did not resurface. That was the last of the hound from hell. Its barking had been muzzled for good.

"Shit. Godzilla versus the devil dog," Zach said, not without a bit of respect. "That thing was huge."

"We swam in there, dude. That damn dinosaur was in there! That dog could've been us. Gator chow."

"Doesn't matter now," Zach said. "Let's go."

"Damn. Wonder how many more there are out here, their beady eyes on us."

He couldn't wrest his eyes from the water—now

consumed in fog—until Zach nudged him with a hand to his back. They crossed the bridge to the shore and scurried into the grass, as far from the scene as possible. Cole led the way, batting the grass aside with his pole.

"You know," said Zach as they zig-zagged toward the road. "If he was angry we opened one of his caskets, imagine how steamed he's gonna be when he finds out we killed his dog."

"The gator killed his dog. We didn't."

"I don't think that'll matter."

"He was never gonna let us live, anyway. And stop trying to scare me. I'm already there. I almost pissed my pants back there."

"You did good, Cole." Zach patted Cole's shoulder and squeezed it. "You did great. But let's lie low and see what happens. My guess is that shack's about to get another visit from the candyman. You have any idea where we are?"

"None."

They crouched in the grass and took a beat. Passing the swamp from this side of the lake had disoriented them. It wasn't clear where the road was from here or which direction they should head. For the moment, they rested in the grass and listened for footfalls. Or a machete cutting the weeds. At least now the threat of the dog had been eliminated. Without its help, the man would actually need to find them, see them. That would be harder.

"You sure they're human?" Cole asked. "Maybe they

can sniff us out. Same as the dog."

"What do you mean?"

"I mean, what if they have some voodoo spell to find us? Or supernatural powers. What if they can smell us?"

"Then they would have found us already. They're only people, man. Crazy fucking people. Now they got to find us on their own without that stupid mutt sniffing around."

"So, what's the plan?" Cole asked. He kept grabbing for his baseball cap that wasn't there. His fingers swiped his hair. "I told you there was no phone in that shack of death. All we got was a lousy spear and a hammer. But no guns. What now?"

The night sweltered. Their cool dip in the lake only made the air feel worse now. The humidity swallowed them whole, as did the mosquitoes. And yet, that thin layer of fog glided further into the swamp and now tickled their shoes, an element out of place.

"I'm parched. I could use a drink," Zach said. "Anything. Water, iced tea…"

"Beer."

"Even that. Yeah," Zach said, gazing up at the round moon. Clouds had moved across it and blocked half its light. If they got any thicker, this night would be too dark to navigate.

"We have bottles of water and juice at the car… if we can find it. That's where we should head. The others might be there already."

"Yeah, but where the hell is it?" Zach adjusted the gauze on his arms.

"Not sure. That way, I think. Is that mummy cloth really working?"

Zach swatted a mosquito on his neck. "Not entirely. There are trees across from the graveyard and along the road to the church. You stand up and see if you can find the road. You're taller."

"I'm six feet one. You're five-eleven. I don't think that makes me taller."

Zach blinked sweat from his eyes. "That's exactly what it means." He wiped his brow. "Fine. We'll both look."

They stood up and peered over the grass. Torchlight drew their attention to the right, where four tiki torches blazed brightly in the distance, casting burnt shadows in front of the small house. The flames guarded the graveyard and danced a tango of orange and yellow in the breeze. It might have looked festive if not for the dead they guarded.

In their glow, the costumed gravedigger loomed over the graves, dressed again in his brown robe. He glared directly at them—the eyes of a tiger piercing the night, two yellow pupils gleaming in the shadow of the hood—and Cole felt a chill.

"Holy Moses. He can see us."

"He can't see us, Cole. We can barely see him. He's looking at the swamp, but he doesn't see us. We're in the dark here. Too far away."

The man put his hands together. He looked to be praying. When he bent his head down and the hood hid his face, he could easily have been mistaken for a simple monk. The torches around him created a focal point in the darkness, a compass to guide them north, away from their glow. Behind the torches, a lamp flickered through the front window of the house.

"At least we know where we are now," Cole said.

"That way. Back to the church and the car."

The sky turned dark, the clouds now fully obscuring the moon. They relied on the distant amber of the flames to lead their way. After a hundred yards, Zach glanced back and saw the torches now burned alone; the gravedigger had stolen into the shadows.

CHAPTER 17

Reaching the car felt like coming home, a familiar object and place. Pelt rummaged through the trunk for two bottles of water. He gave one to Andy, who drank it immediately, then he gave him another.

"Save half of this. We don't know when we'll get back here, and we can't carry too much if we need to sneak around." Next, he opened a box of snacks. "We've got power bars and granola bars and one Snickers. It's melted, I think."

Andy snatched the Snickers from Pelt's hand and tore it open with his teeth. He devoured it instantly and did the same with a yogurt bar, while stuffing an extra one in his pocket.

Pelt unzipped the small suitcase he'd packed and retrieved his spare pair of glasses. They felt clunky on his face. He wasn't used to this pair, but at least he could see again. He fished out a pair of boxer shorts. Pelt was skinny, so they would almost fit the kid.

"Here. Put these on."

With a second yogurt bar sticking out of his mouth, Andy shucked his jeans and put his legs through the shorts. He hopped to keep balance and pulled them up all the way. They sagged on his hips but did the job.

Pelt felt around his suitcase and found the bag he was looking for. It contained a blue t-shirt with a cartoon alligator and *Bud's Gator Farm* emblazoned on the front. He handed it to Andy.

"Put this on, too. It's clean."

Andy wriggled out of his filthy wet shirt and threw it on the ground. The new one fit him almost perfectly with only a little baggage in the shoulders. He put his jeans and sneakers back on and shoved a granola bar in his mouth.

"Who did you buy this for?" Andy asked between bites. "It's not for you. It would be bigger."

"The shirt? For my nephew. A souvenir."

Andy stopped chewing and touched Pelt's shoulder in an oddly adult manner, a strange gesture of sympathy. "Don't be sad. You'll get back to him. I'm sure."

The words threw Pelt off balance. He turned away and zipped his suitcase.

I never doubted we would get back. Should I?

At the rear of the trunk was an automobile emergency kit with a flare gun, two flares and four glow sticks. He took the gun and flares and shoved two of the glow sticks in his back pocket. He closed the trunk, gently pushing it down until it latched with a soft click.

"Okay, kid, we gotta leave." Pelt picked up Andy's dirty wet shirt and thought about putting it in their laundry bag, but it still smelled rank. He shoved it under the car, out of sight.

"Where?" Andy drank three quarters of the second water and twisted the cap back on. "We should stay at the car. It's safe." Lightning cracked the far sky. "And be dry if it rains. And if your friends come back."

"The car is where that crazy man will come to look for us first. Don't you think? Psycho clown and his crazy partner."

"His sister. Hezekiah and his sister, Hannah. I told you before."

Pelt looked around. He could see the flickering of the torches down the road at the graveyard, but nothing else. A drum roll of thunder swept their way, closer each time. Hiding in the church was risky. Dry, but not safe. He scanned the three weeping willows that towered over the driveway from the road, giant wardens of the church. Their willows swayed wildly in the breeze that was fast becoming a storm wind.

"We need to climb one of those and stay out of sight. Hopefully the boogeyman won't see us, but we'll see if Zach or my other friends come back."

"Okay." Andy started to climb the one next to the car, using the door as a foothold.

"Not that one. Too close to the car. It's too easy to see us or hear us. The middle one, behind it. Its branches are thickest, the most hidden."

Pelt boosted Andy into its lowest branch, and the kid took off like a spider monkey. He scaled the branches effortlessly and was high in the center branches in seconds, obscured from view. Pelt grabbed a low branch with both hands and used his feet to climb the trunk. He stood on the branch and clambered up to the next one. The branches sagged from his weight but seemed sturdy enough to hold him. He found Andy deep in the boughs twenty feet up and settled on a branch opposite him. His camera swayed on the lanyard around his neck.

"Why do you still have that?" Andy asked. "The picture machine."

"You mean my camera? Never heard it called a picture machine before." *How far in the sticks is this kid from?* "Do you even have the internet where you live?"

Andy shrugged. "Why don't you get rid of it? It slows you down."

Pelt considered the question as he slid a granola bar from his pocket. "I don't know. I guess I always carry it. You never know when the perfect photo is right in front of you."

"You like it," Andy said. "You like making pictures of everything. What do you like better for pictures: things or people?"

"I guess I like capturing people. If you snap a smile that a girl doesn't know you saw, or an expression on a child he doesn't even know he made. An old man with memories on his face. Still… sometimes a thing can be wonderful. A pair of tennis shoes that's been hanging from a telephone wire all summer. Or this church—"

"What about it? What about the church?"

"It's wonderful, don't you think?"

"No."

"So old. People long ago, already dead today… they used to worship here." Pelt bit into the granola and put the wrapper in his pocket. "Someone might have met here to argue the upcoming civil war, years before it happened. A ton of history in every board. Don't you think?"

"I don't like it. I don't want to go inside."

"We won't. It's the last place we want to be, 'cause it's the first place they'll look."

"Hezekiah goes in there. If he finds me, he'll kill me. He hates me."

"Chill out. I told you, we won't go in there. Why do you think he hates you? Didn't he just randomly capture you? It could've been any kid. Most serial killers are creatures of opportunity. Like spiders, they catch what comes near their web. You were in the wrong place at the wrong time, I'm guessing."

"What's a cereal killer? Like, breakfast?"

"No. Not like breakfast. It means he kills a lot of people. And maybe he's crazy, too. That's a serial killer."

"He hates me because of my mother." Andy subconsciously looked toward the torches, toward the grave where she was buried. "He thinks she's a witch or a demon or something."

"He kidnapped you and your mother together?"

"Yeah. They did. He and Hannah came. I live in Texas. They came and got us at night."

"They hauled you all the way from Texas?" Pelt

shifted himself on the branch. There was no way to get comfortable. "That's a very specific serial killer. And he brought you both back here to kill you? Why here?"

"Because that's where his special grave is. And he didn't kill my mom or me. He *buried* us."

"I think one leads to the other, but... okay. Technically, he brought you here to bury you. Why? Why here and why you?"

"I tol' you already. He hates my mom. She reads tarot cards at the carnivals. They think she's a demon. It's stupid. They're stupid."

Thunder boomed straight overhead. Pelt felt a drop of rain on his arm. Seconds later, he heard more drops peppering the willow branches. They'd get wet in this tree—he didn't mind that—but if the storm turned out to have lightning, it would be too dangerous to stay up here. If the kid wouldn't go in the church, and the car was unsafe, where else could they go? Pelt was tired and couldn't think. He wanted to sleep.

"I got out this morning. Escaped," Andy said.

"Really? Where did you go?"

"Over there, past the fields. The swamp takes you to the big road that way." He pointed into darkness. "But he found me and hit me with a shovel. He brought me back and tried to bury me, same as my mom."

"I know. We saw it. My friends and I saw it happen. That's why we dug you up."

Andy looked at Pelt with the giant eyes of a doe, wide and curious, as if that concept only now dawned on him. "Oh yeah. Thanks." He rubbed his chin. "That was cool. But weren't you scared?"

"Hell yes, we were scared. Well, I was, I'm not sure anything scares Zach. He's better at this than me."

"Better at what?"

Pelt waved an arm through the air. "All this. Being outdoors, saving people. Solving problems. I'm just as happy staying home in my room and editing photos on the computer. I'm not cut out for swamps and shit. The irony is, to get a good photograph, you need to go out and explore the world. I'm not an explorer."

"Hmm." Andy held out a hand and caught a few raindrops. "Can't you stay home and take pictures of models? Like a fashion show?"

Pelt laughed. "I guess so. Only if you're famous, though. I don't think that's in my future."

"Do you want to be famous?" The rain started falling harder; Andy held out his tongue and tried to catch some.

"Not really."

Then Andy asked him something that caught him off guard. "Is Zach your boyfriend?"

"What? No! No, I like girls. He does, too. I think. We both like girls. Why would you ask that?"

Andy shrugged. "I don't care if he is. The way you talk about him, I think you love him."

"Kid, you're freaking me out. You talk like an adult. Where the hell are you from? Venus?"

"Janus, Texas. I tol' you already."

"Well, for your information, Zach is not my boyfriend. Maybe I look up to him the way I look up to Andy Warhol or John Carpenter... or Luke Skywalker! But that's it."

"Okay. I just asked." Andy didn't seem to care either way. He had moved on to examining the tree, making sure nothing else was sharing it with them. He occasionally tasted the rain again.

Pelt was getting antsy. "We need to find the others. Cole and Jessie, too. Any ideas how to do that?"

Andy shook his head. "You said they'll come back here to the car, right?"

"That would make sense. But what if they're stuck somewhere? What if they're in that house behind the graves? I saw a light on in there."

"Yeah. Hannah and Hezekiah made me stay there. I was a *prizner*. Maybe they caught your friends. The dog stopped barking."

"What does that mean? The dog not barking."

"It means they pro'ly took him inside. In the house. So they have some of your friends there, maybe. They found them. That's why Hezekiah lit the torches. He thinks he's guarding the dead."

"No shit?"

"He's crazy."

"No argument there."

"So's Hannah, but she's smart."

"If you say so." Pelt shifted again on the branch, then stood, straddling two branches. "My butt hurts."

"Yeah. You're too big for trees."

The rain came down a little harder, not yet a full rainstorm but considerably more than mere drops. The willow provided thin shelter, less efficient than a leafy maple. Most of the rain eventually trickled down to them, and they started to get wet. At first, it felt good; it washed off the sweat and cooled the night. But as the storm thickened, it became a hindrance. Pelt almost slipped off his branch. He caught himself and held on tight.

"So much for dry clothes." Pelt lamented the wasted effort. Andy only got to wear dry clothes for twenty minutes. "At least you smell better. They're clean, at least."

"I'm okay. Thanks again for the shirt and underwear. And for saving me."

The rain increased intensity. Thunder grumbled but discharged no lightning yet. They saw two of the four torches go out at the gravesite. It didn't matter, but there was little else to notice. They sat on their branches, listening to the rain. Thunder again, closer this time. And then they saw a shadow flicker underneath the tree and disappear under the car.

"Something just ran under the car," Andy said. "Something big."

"Like what?"

"I don't know. It's not a cat or raccoon. Bigger I think." He hugged the tree closer for protection. It gave him small comfort.

"Maybe the dog."

"The dog barks," Andy said. "It won't be quiet."

"It can't be the man, can it?"

"Hezekiah moves fast, but I think he's too big for under the car. It was black and scary."

"It's dark," Pelt pointed out. He kept his voice low but there was no need; the rain had become a deafening sound screen of its own. "Everything is black and scary."

They were at a bad angle to see the car through the willow branches. Something had run under them and taken refuge under the car. What would do that?

"Can gators move that fast?"

"They like rain," Andy said, "and water. They won't hide from it. Maybe a lizard? A big one?"

"Don't lizards and snakes like water, too?"

"Oh, yeah." Andy thought a moment. He wiped the rain from his face with one small hand. "Maybe it's Hannah. She goes fast, too. And she's skinny. She can go under the car."

"That man's sister?" That was a sobering thought. She had a shotgun. Pelt felt his back pocket to make sure the flare gun was still there. He pulled it out and held it in his hands. It was getting wet. Would it work wet? He had no idea.

Unexpectedly, Andy swiped the flare gun from him and checked to see if it was loaded.

"Easy," said Pelt. "Don't shoot yourself. Do you even know how to use it?"

"I'm from Texas. I know how to use guns." Andy looked through the sight and aimed at the car.

"Hey, that goes up. Aim at the sky when the storm ends. I want to get someone's attention. Call for help."

"That won't work." Andy lowered the gun from his eye and held it cradled in one hand. "No one's around for a long, long way. And the cops don't care. They don't care about us."

"We have to try."

"It's a waste if we use it at the sky. We can shoot Hezekiah in the face. That's how we end this."

Jeez! This kid is cold. What the hell else has he been through? He's like an adult in a child's body. Like a bitter old man with a grudge. Who knows how to use a gun!

"I'm going down to the car," Andy said. He climbed down to the next branch. "I'm gonna shoot what's under it."

"Don't do that! What if it's some lizard, after all? Or a raccoon? I only have two flares. Don't waste one."

"I think it's her. Down there."

"Don't—" Pelt started, but instantly the kid was out of reach.

Agile as only young boys are, Andy moved like silk; he swung down from branch to branch and jumped the last four feet to the ground. He crouched there a moment, trying to see under the car. Then he took small steps in its direction. The gravel crunched under his sneakers, scarcely heard above the rain.

From his perch, Pelt anxiously followed the kid's

progress. At last, lightning came. Its flash illuminated the landscape for a split second. Pelt looked around and saw the gravedigger. The man was leaving the graves and torches behind. Something was slung over his shoulder as he walked in their direction. Still a good way off, but he was powering large strides that would bring him to the car in minutes.

"Andy!" Pelt tried to get the kid's attention. The boy was almost at the car. "Andy! It's the man. Hezeka. He's coming."

Andy looked back at the tree, and Pelt pointed toward the gravedigger, now invisible in the darkness. A new flash of lightning showed Pelt waving and pointing. Andy looked toward the graves; the man was only visible for an instant. He was already a third of the way here. A glint of steel—the machete!

Damn he walks fast!

Andy looked between the car, the tree and the remote graves. Then, in an eye blink, the boy fell and vanished. Something from under the car had grabbed his ankles and pulled him under. His body raked against the gravel; he was helpless to stop his fate.

Pelt watched in horror. He heard a yelp from Andy and then nothing. Lightning showed a quick image below him—the empty lot and the flare gun abandoned near the car's wheel. Andy had lost his grip on it going down. Now rain formed puddles around it, and Andy was no more.

Rain pummeled the tree. Pelt clung to the branches

without feeling, numb to the surrounding terrors. He thought he heard footsteps but was blinded by the storm around him. Darkness blanketed everything. He shrank into the tree's barbed embrace.

Whistling competed with the storm's rage, but he couldn't be sure if it was imagined or real. It got closer and louder until he was sure someone was whistling a song near the car. Then it stopped.

Moments ticked by.

When the next lightning flashed, the gravedigger was standing under the tree, directly below him. He carried a body slung over his left shoulder, the machete in his right hand. At first, the man scanned the yard in front of the church, around the car, the road. And then he looked up, straight at Pelt. Despite the rain, the gravedigger's ghostly makeup held; a hair-raising image to look down on. More lightning lit the sky, and Pelt was discovered. A white t-shirt and pale skin was hard to miss.

He saw me. He fucking saw me!

The gravedigger pounded his machete against the tree trunk, and the giant tree quaked, its willows trembled. It shook again and Pelt shook with it. The ghoulish man dropped the body to the ground and grabbed a willow branch.

CHAPTER 18

Spinning the green shawl through the air, Hannah draped it ceremoniously around Jessica's shoulders and plucked at the corners to let it settle into place. She adjusted it the way a mother would a daughter's gown before a recital.

"To keep you from the chill, my dear."

"Thanks," Jessica mumbled. "Rain didn't cool it down. Just made it more humid."

Hannah dipped a coffee mug into a large plastic container filled with water. "The tap water is brown," she explained. "We haul our own. Here. Drink."

She held it to Jessie's lips. When the mug was empty, Hannah refilled it with red wine from a bottle. This time she only allowed Jessie two sips, then put the mug on the floor. Hannah herself drank two gulps straight from the bottle.

Through the window, they both watched Hezekiah light the torches on the four corners of the small cemetery. Jessie couldn't see what he did after that.

"Who's buried out there?"

"I told you," Hannah said, flipping her long hair

back. "Demons we've captured. Unclean beings that never belonged in this world."

Jessie swallowed. "And my friends? You have graves for them, too?"

"No. Not at all. Your friends are not evil, not monsters. They are pure, for the most part. I promise you they will not be put in those awful graves."

"But you'll kill them, anyway."

"Yes, we will kill them, but we'd never bury them on tainted soil. They won't have to share land with the monsters from hell. Never."

"Is that supposed to make me feel better?"

"It should. This ground is poisoned by the demons in its bosom. The soil is rotten. The infected souls we captured over the years… they've spoiled the land. Even trees no longer grow here." Her expression said she thought that was a shame. "It's a bad place. I don't know how my brother can stand it."

"If you won't bury them, where will you put them? Dump them by the side of the road?"

"Don't be foolish. We take good care of those in our charge. On the rare occasion we must kill someone who gets in the way—like your friends—we put them above ground. In a proper, holy place where they can rest in peace." She paused, serious. "We guard them. To us, they are sacred."

"And me. You intend to kill me," Jessie said. "So, why should I help you? I'm dead already, so do it already. But don't do me any favors by guarding my body or putting me in some holy shrine. I don't need your charity."

"Child." Hannah knelt down next to Jessie. Her eyes were soft and warm. "It's not charity, it's love. We love and cherish the sacrifice your friends must make. Don't ever mistake that for anything less. And as for you... I don't intend to kill you. I'd rather not. But that's up to you, isn't it? If you don't force me, I won't."

"Why?"

"You're different. I can see something in you. The world would be a better place with you in it. A more interesting place. You could help us. I could speak with Hezekiah. You could be a part of this."

"A part of what? What the hell are you talking about? Inviting me into a cult? No thanks. I didn't drink the Kool-aid." Her eyes landed on the wine. "Oh wait. Maybe I did. Is the wine—?"

"No, dear. I didn't poison you. The wine is fine."

"Still... No thanks. I'm not joining a cult. Not on my bucket list, thanks."

"You could help us put demons in the ground." Hannah stabbed a long finger at her. "You could unwind yourself from the trappings of the world and help make it a better place. Yes, more than one devil child would trust a sweet girl like you."

"I'm not seducing boys into your death trap. Forget it. I'm not helping you."

"That's not what we do." Hannah tilted her head; she looked at her captive sadly. "The pain in you goes back far. A long strain. I could smell it on you the moment I saw you. Not the others; they're not like you. You've experienced pain deeper than any. It's souls like you who make for good allies in our work. The demons, they don't get much from ones like you. You're already broken."

Thanks. I taste sour to a demon. Big whoop.

But she chose her words carefully. Best not to antagonize the woman. "Tell me more. Why is it only you who can catch these demons?"

Hannah shed her smile briefly and looked at the girl sidelong. "Are you mocking me?"

"No. I want to know."

Hannah looked out the window. "There are things even devils fear, things that cause dark spirits and foul creatures to tremble in the night. One of those things lives on Gravedigger Road."

"What is that?"

"My brother, Hezekiah. He's only half-human. Not like the demons, he can be killed. But he can't be killed so easily."

"The demons can't be killed?"

"Not really. But they can be sent back down. We bury them with salt so they cannot leave their graves. After so many years, their bodies rot. Eventually, the vessel isn't able to stand. It becomes useless, and they have no choice but to return to the underworld. We rid our home of them. This world of the living gets cleaner for every beast we bury."

"Your brother lives here?"

"He lives upstairs."

Hannah regarded Jessie and studied her eyes, which seemed to continually scan the room. Hannah noticed every twitch of her face, the pace of her breathing. It fascinated the woman.

"You don't believe me. You're only humoring me until you see your chance to escape. But it doesn't matter. Belief or disbelief doesn't make something less real. If I don't believe that butterflies come from caterpillars, does that make caterpillars less real?"

"I guess not."

Hannah crossed the room and unfolded a small table, only two feet high. She placed it next to the couch, then sat on the floor in front of it and began shuffling a stack of cards. She shuffled for several seconds, humming, taking her time. Next, she dealt six cards from the top, two rows of three.

"Jessica. Let's play a game, shall we?"

"No, thanks."

"Oh, come now. Play a game with me."

"Stick it up your ass." *So much for not antagonizing her.*

"Jessica." Hannah's expression turned hard. She wasn't asking. "Play a game with me, Jessica."

Jessie thought this might end badly if she declined. Reluctantly, she conceded. "Fine. Whatever. What's the game?"

"Excellent!" Hannah shouted and clapped her

hands. She gathered the cards back into the stack and reshuffled them.

"What is that, solitaire?"

"This? No. This is how I'm going to find Andras. Maybe even your friends. The cards will tell me." She laid out another six cards, two rows of three, stared at their backs for a second, then looked up at Jessie. "But first, I want to find out about you. Why you carry so much pain."

"From the cards? Like tarot cards?"

Hannah cast her a derisive look. "No. Not like tarot. Now choose a card."

"How? I'm tied up."

"Fair point. Top row or bottom."

Jessie breathed and kept her thoughts to herself. She'd need to play along to gain this woman's trust. "Top row."

"Which card. One, two or three?"

"Two."

Hannah raised an eyebrow. "Interesting choice. You always choose the middle?"

"I guess. I don't know."

Hannah flipped the card over. These were not normal playing cards; they bore photos of animals and scenery. The card face-up had the image of a bear.

"Choose one more card, dear."

"Bottom row, I guess. I don't know. Middle."

Slowly Hannah turned the card over, displaying a

lake with one purple lotus flower floating on its surface. "Oh. Oh, now I see. It's not only pain that runs through you. It's anger. You're angry. Who are you angry at, Jessica?"

"At the moment, you."

"Tell me, Jessica. I want to know." The tone in Hannah's voice said this was more than a game to her. It was something she needed to know. "It's a family member. Not a sibling. Hmm. You're angry at mummy or daddy, is that right?"

"Not at all."

Hannah shuffled the cards again. This time, she lay out nine cards in one row. Her eyes never left Jessie as she dealt the cards. Meanwhile, Jessie stared out the window. She would play the silly game to appease the crazy woman but refused to look at the cards.

"Pick a card." Hannah instructed. "Tell me."

"Whatever. Third."

"And now another."

"It doesn't matter. Any… I don't care. Fifth."

As Hannah's long fingers flipped the cards face-up, her fingernails grazed the corners and made an ugly scratching sound. The first card was a gold crown; the second a red bull. She drew in a satisfied breath and tapped the first card's face.

"I see. It's your father. And I was right; you're not scared of him. You're angry at him. So that means… what? He didn't abuse you? No, I think not. No midnight trips to your bedroom for a game of tickle. That doesn't fit."

"No. He never touched me." She was quick to defend him on that. "Never."

"But he did do something terrible, didn't he? Something to your mother? Or to both of you? It was bad, whatever it was."

"I have no idea what you're talking about. He was a good father."

Hannah's eyes pierced the girl. "But you do. You know exactly what I want to know."

Jessie bit her lower lip. She didn't like this game. It was making her believe the crazy woman might be less crazy and more soothsayer. It would be a tremendous burden to accept such a thing as true. If anything were true here on this haunted road, it might mean these horrible people weren't insane. Sanity was a harder pill to swallow than insanity. Accepting that sane people might do all this…

But none of it is true. She's just guessing.

And she is insane.

"You're wrong. I love my father."

"Oh, that's interesting," Hannah said. She tapped her chin. "He's not your dad; he's your *father*. Words are sometimes better than the cards."

"What does that mean?"

"I was right. You hate him. You hate your father, and it's a weight you've carried with you for years. I want to know why. Every detail." Hannah leaned back as if to watch a movie, ready to hear a tale that would enthrall her. She was giddy with excitement.

"I'm not here to amuse you with my life's story," Jessie spat. "You can go to hell."

"Been there. It's not what it's cracked up to be. No, I'd rather be here, listening to your story! Oh, I've got goosebumps! Haven't you?"

"No."

"Oh, you must, dear. I have a feeling your story will be intoxicating!"

"I'm not as excited about this as you."

"But think about it! You can finally free your heart, child. You can tell me *anything*. How often do you get an offer that good? It's thrilling, is it not?"

"No."

But it did sound appealing. To bare her soul to a complete stranger who didn't matter, who didn't know her or her family. Strangers keep the best secrets. It was tempting.

"Oh, please," Hannah begged. She did not seem angry by the rebuke. "I'm asking you nicely. After all, you agreed to play the game."

"I don't want to talk anymore. Or play any games. Kill me or let me go."

"I'll make you a deal," Hannah said, rising from the floor. She moved to the couch and sat with one arm draped across the back. "You tell me your story. The part you know I want to hear. And I'll let you go."

"Really?"

"I promise."

"Simple as that?" Jessica didn't believe her for a second, which spurred more sarcasm. "I tell you why I'm angry at *Daddy*, and you untie me and let me go. Easy and simple as that?"

"Simple as that," Hannah said.

Something in her tone rang true. Jessie thought it might be possible to believe her, oddly. It was a strange request. And even stranger that it would get her free, but there was no guile in Hannah's face. She might actually keep her promise. Unless there was a trick at the end of it all.

"You're not going to let me go just to have your brother waiting outside with a meat cleaver, are you?"

"No, dear. What would be the point to that? To set you free means exactly that. You'd be free to leave this road. You'll find I don't play games with words. But I want the whole story with all the gory details. Leave nothing out." Then she added, "And don't lie to me. I'll know."

What have I got to lose?

My mind.

"Fine. I'll tell you. And then, you let me go. Car parts and all."

Hannah wagged her finger. "Uh-uh. I said nothing about car parts or your friends leaving here. But I promise I will let *you* go. You, Jessica."

Fucking tricks. I knew it.

But I'll take what I can get. One step at a time. I

need to get out of here.

"Fine. I'll tell you my story. I'll tell you, and then you'll let me go free."

Hannah beamed. "Excellent."

Jessica took a deep breath and started. "This is my dark and ugly story. And it's got no happy ending."

CHAPTER 19

As Pelt had earlier, Cole smacked into a skull—the first of many skulls on pikes lining the road—and fell backward. He regained his balance, then stood with his hooked pole ready to engage it in battle. Zach cast a burst of light from his phone for one second to see it wasn't a living being, only a human skull on a pole, likely meant to frighten off any intruders. Six feet further, another one.

"What the—"

"Yeah, creepy, but not a threat," Zach said. *Or are they?* He squinted closer. "At least, I don't think they're dangerous."

It was starting to rain. The wind caused the skulls to sway a few inches backward and forward, which seemed to give them life. Ghosts of past victims. They counted six along the path, but more might exist beyond the scope of the phone light. Would their own heads someday be on pikes like these? Or mummified in the shack of the dead? The skull heads shook as if to say: *Not this way, guys. Go back.*

The skull sentries were new. They hadn't been there

before. But how they got there, where they came from, was a riddle. The road had secrets. How many more were yet to come?

Maybe they come alive every night, thought Cole.

"Where the hell did these jokers come from?"

"No clue," Zach said. "Could be more people are working with the two wackos. The two number-one Kiss fans have a whole pit crew, I bet. Maybe little people jump up and plant these here at night."

"Right. Unlikely."

"My point is, we're not alone out here, man."

"Thanks. Because I'm not freaked out enough."

"Just keep your eyes open."

The rain grew heavier. Soon they'd be drenched again. Quietly, they pushed past the skull sentries, fell to their hands and knees and crawled to the roadside. They waited on their stomachs in the grass to make sure the road was clear. The car was somewhere across the road, but they couldn't see it. Darkness consumed all. Zach put his phone in his pocket. Any more light from it might alert others to their presence.

Other bad things.

Then lightning struck and lit the church lot; the car sat directly across from them. Perfect.

"I'm going over."

"No. The first place they'll look for us is the car. As soon as you open the door, that light comes on and we're cooked."

"We can hide under the car," Cole urged. "It'll keep us dry from the rain, and when the time is right, we'll get what we need from the trunk. When the rain stops, I'll crawl in through the back seat and pop it. I don't think the light goes on when the trunk opens. I think."

"I think it does." Zach looked at the dark road. "And that's a long way with no cover, no place to hide. Whoever put these skulls up is still out here. They might be watching the road right now."

"I'll run fast and slide under. It'll be just like sliding into home plate."

"Yeah. I doubt that."

The clouds burst and released the full weight of the storm they'd been hauling across the land. Rain showered the swamp. Another lightning flash showed the car, and Cole focused solely on it.

Not wanting to waste time on more discussion, he stood up and launched himself across the road. He sprinted as if the World Series depended on it. When he hit the car, he slid under as planned. Aside from small pieces of gravel that scooped into his jeans leg and scraped his stomach, it went smoothly.

Zach couldn't see if Cole had made it, but the next lightning flash showed no one on the road or at the car. He assumed, hoped, his friend was under the car. The pole with the hook was still in the grass; Cole had abandoned it for speed. Zach got to his knees and lifted it in his left hand. He considered whether to keep the hammer or the hook. Weapons were too few in their group. He dropped the hammer and traded up. The hook felt good in his two hands.

Something caught his eye across the road. A shape dropped from the tree behind the car. Too big to be a squirrel or cat, he wondered if it might be a body dropping from the boughs. This place was rife with them. Then lightning revealed the shape of a small boy. It was Andy.

He saw Andy walk toward the car. He heard a voice from the tree and thought he heard whistling in the distance. Rain continued to batter his face as he tried to see what was happening. At the next flash of lightning, Andy was gone.

* * *

Andy hadn't heard Pelt's warning, but Cole had. He saw the legs of the gravedigger from his vantage point under the car. They were being hunted again. He acted fast and pulled the kid down with him. Together they lay on the gravel underneath the car, Cole's hand over Andy's mouth to prevent him from crying out.

His eyes tracked the boots marching over the ground and onto the church lot. Heavy boots. It was the gravedigger he had seen coming their way. He motioned for Andy to be quiet and lifted his hand from the kid's mouth.

"Hezekiah," Andy whispered.

* * *

Zach watched the man trudge around the car and under the tree. The rain didn't seem to ruin his ghoulish face paint—he wondered if it was tattooed on—but he had abandoned his robe. His overalls were soaked, but he clearly didn't mind. What was he carrying?

Is that a person? Is that a body?
Could that be Jessica? Or Pelt?
Who's in the tree?

The man stood there, unaffected by the storm, as if it didn't exist in his world. He appeared to be scanning the church grounds, looking for something. Looking for them, perhaps. Then he glanced up and saw the person in the tree. He dropped the body and hacked at the tree with his blade. Finally, he grabbed a branch to climb.

He's gonna kill someone!

Determined to save the person lying on the ground and help the stranger in the tree, he made a rash decision. The hooked pole gripped firmly in both hands, Zach stood up and barreled across the road. His sneakers pounded through puddles of rain.

Screaming into the storm, Zach rammed into the gravedigger with the pole held up and shoved the man back. Zach was impressive in a good run, and he threw his full force into it. Any lesser figure would have fallen to the ground, but this man only staggered three steps backward. The look on his ghoulish face was frightening, but Zach didn't back down. He stood his ground and swung the hook. It stabbed into the man's side; he pulled it back for another attack.

Seemingly unhurt, feeling no pain, the man stepped forward and swung his machete. Zach held up the pole and caught the blade; the force nearly knocked him down. The man swung again, and again Zach pivoted and caught the blade on his pole, but this time it splintered in the middle. The third strike cracked it in two. The bottom end fell to the ground, bounced and rolled toward the car. Zach held the small end with the hook, but he knew it would be inadequate. The other man was too strong, his blows too powerful. He raised his machete to split Zach's skull.

At that moment, Pelt jumped from the tree onto the man's shoulders and tried to choke him. But Pelt was too weak. The man flung him to the ground as if tossing a bag of oranges aside. Pelt hit the gravel hard; his camera flew off him and skipped across the lot. The man slashed at Pelt with his machete, slicing into his left leg. The next blow was aimed at his head but didn't land. The distraction was enough for Zach to get another hook in the man, this time in his shoulder. He yanked the man back hard, away from Pelt. A sinew tore.

The man ground his teeth.

That one he felt; a piece of flesh was ripped from his shoulder. Enraged, he turned on Zach to slice him in two. But Cole and Andy had crawled from under the car and now joined the fight. Cole picked up the dull end of the pole and used it as a bat. He beat it against the gravedigger's back and head. The man whirled around, ready to face Cole, now with two enemies in front and back.

Andy picked up a handful of gravel and flung it at the man's face. It temporarily blinded him. Cole and Zach charged the man together with hook and bat and knocked him to the ground. Zach drove the hook into the man's leg so deep it wouldn't come out. He abandoned it and fumbled in his pocket for the scalpel. Twice he stabbed the man in the back with the small blade until it also wouldn't come out. When he tried to pull it free, the blade flew from his hands and disappeared in a puddle. The man growled and got to his hands and knees. He wrested the hook from his leg and prepared to stand, but he didn't make it. Andy snatched up the scalpel, then rushed in and jumped on the man's back. In one swift cut, he slashed the man's throat. Hezekiah dropped to the ground, bleeding out amid the pools of rainwater forming on the lot. Andy stuck the scalpel in the man's shoulder and scrambled away from his body.

This kid is cold, thought Pelt, not for the first time.

The kid was still a mystery. Pelt wondered what had happened to him to make him so rough and hardened, less frightened than any of them. At the moment, they were grateful he could do what they could not.

He killed the boogeyman.

Zach turned over the body that had been carried here on the gravedigger's shoulders. It wasn't Jessica; it was an unknown man in his thirties. A quick check of his pulse confirmed he was dead. They would have been surprised if he were still alive.

"Why was he carrying a body?" Cole asked. "Where was he taking him?"

"In there." Andy pointed to the church. "They all meet in there and do bad things to the bodies. Then they put them in places no one can find."

"Yeah, I think we found one of those places," Cole said. "You wouldn't like it."

"Pelt! You're bleeding!" Zach grimaced at the blood gushing from the wound in Pelt's leg, soaking his ripped jeans. It was a deep cut. "Let's get you into the church and bandage that up."

Cole and Zach supported Pelt and helped him limp to the front door of the church, but Andy lingered at the car. He didn't want to go inside.

"They do bad things in there. If they come back, that's where they'll go first. They'll find us."

"We have to get out of the rain," Cole shouted through the storm. "And we need to patch up Pelt's leg or he'll bleed to death."

"We'll go in for a few minutes," Zach promised Andy. "We won't stay long. Cross my heart."

Pelt limped between them to the church door. They nearly carried him the last few steps.

Inside, Andy drifted along the wall next to the door and crouched down in the nearest corner. Curled up in a ball, shivering, this child hardly seemed capable of slashing a man's throat. And yet he had done just that, right before their eyes. Andy was an enigma hard to unravel. Perhaps being buried alive does that to a kid. Or something else does.

They laid Pelt on a pew at the back of the sanctuary, and Zach lit his phone to get a better look at the wound. Cole ran to get the first aid kit from the car, while Zach unraveled the gauze he had in his pocket. When Cole returned, they doused the wound with iodine—only a tiny bottle came with the first aid kit—and Zach wrapped Pelt's leg tight with the wad of gauze he had stolen from the shack of death. A small spool of bandage tape in the kit was inadequate to keep the wrapping tight. Cole fetched a roll of masking tape that —for some inexplicable reason—was in the trunk, and they made a tourniquet for Pelt's leg. Finally, they splashed a little alcohol on the entire wrapping, half of the bottle provided with their first aid kit.

"Cole. Your arm."

Zach examined a six-inch cut the machete had made glancing off Cole's forearm.

"It's nothing," Cole said.

Zach ignored him and unwrapped the mosquito-protecting gauze from his own right arm. He dripped the rest of the alcohol on Cole's cut—to a wail of pain from Cole—and wrapped his forearm with the linen gauze. He spun the masking tape around it twice, finishing the roll.

"Well, that's it," Zach said. "Any more wounds and we're out of luck. No more supplies left. Let's hope there's not a second machete murderer out there."

"His sister's out there still," Cole reminded him.

"And Jessica is out there somewhere. Can you stand up, Pelt?"

Pelt nodded. "Hurts like hell, but I'm okay. I can walk. Just not too fast."

"I'm not sure that won't get infected," Zach whispered, touching Pelt's wrapping and checking its hold.

They spoke in low tones, despite the racket of the storm. It was unlikely anyone could hear them, but they couldn't shake the feeling someone *was* outside listening. And the sanctuary magnified their voices, no matter how hushed they spoke. Every raindrop sounded like a creature clawing at the roof, eavesdropping, stalking them and waiting to get in.

"We need to get help soon," Zach said. "And it's not coming for us, so stop hoping for that. We need to go out and get it for ourselves. We need to help ourselves."

"What are you suggesting?" Cole asked.

"It's fifty miles to the highway, give or take. I can run it. If I go alone, I can get there by tomorrow and flag down help."

"That's crazy."

"It's our only hope."

"Are you mental? That's the worst idea ever."

"No, it isn't," Zach insisted. "Pelt needs medical help. And we all need to be rescued. No one's coming for us otherwise, man. You know I'm right."

"But it's so far." Cole combed a hand through his hair and flicked water over the pews.

"I might even get a phone signal, twenty or thirty miles out. I can try."

"How much battery do you got left?"

Zach checked. "Eighteen percent. It might be enough if I keep it off. I'll turn it back on after about twenty miles."

Pelt opened his phone. "Mine's at thirty-nine percent. Take mine instead."

Zach agreed. They unlocked their phones, exchanged passcodes and made the trade. But Cole wasn't sold yet. He tried to poke holes in the plan, even though he knew it was their best option.

"It's dangerous. And you can't run along the road. You'll have to stay hidden in the weeds in case one of the cult people is out there. Or their friends. You know how hard it'll be to run through that shit?"

"I can do it."

"Maybe I should go," Cole offered. "I'm the best athlete of all of us."

"Debatable. But I'm the track star. I can run faster. Besides, you're hurt."

"My fuckin' arm, not my leg! I can run! I can do this, Zach."

"No, man." Zach brushed his wet hair from his eyes. "It's me. I'm the only one of us who's run a 50K. Fifty miles is more than 50K, but I can still do it."

"Fuck." Cole wasn't happy about splitting up, but he also knew it was the only way to get help. "It'll take you a day. That's gonna be rough."

"Yeah. Depends on the terrain. The ground and swamp might be a bitch, but I can do it. I think by tomorrow afternoon, I should be able to hit the highway. I'll flag a car down or get a signal. One way or another, by tomorrow night this place will be swarming with cops."

"I hope you're right, man."

Pelt put a hand on Zach's shoulder. "Are you sure, dude? It's dangerous as hell out there. Giant gators could take you, even if the cult people don't. There are pythons in the swamp; some are bigger than cars."

"It'll be easy peezy lemon squeezy, just like that water tower back home." Zach slapped Pelt's cheek, then Cole's in a brotherly pat. "I ain't scared of no ghosts. Or snakes. You two ladies make sure to find Jessie. Get out of this church and stay away from the car, in case that woman comes after you with the shotgun." He lowered his voice. "And take care of Andy."

"Got it." Cole tapped a fist against Zach's chest. "We'll hide in the weeds and try to get a look in that house. Jessie can't be far. You… you travel safe."

"I will, I will. But I'll need two bottles of water from the car first."

As quickly as it had come, the storm passed. The rain slowed to a mere sprinkle. A gift from the sky, and they'd take it.

Pelt limped between them as they headed for the door. They saw Andy was sleeping in the corner and didn't wake him. The kid had been through more than any of them in the last two days.

Outside, the fog had thickened over the swamp, rising more than a foot off the ground, but it hadn't crossed the road yet. Near the car, Pelt scooped up the flare gun and put it in his waistband. Cole opened the hatch and fished out four waters, two for Zach and one for him and Pelt. Zach took a small sip.

"You want more?" Cole asked. "Six bottles left."

"No. Can't drink too much on a long run. And I need to travel light. I can't carry more than two. I'll drink a little along the way."

They closed the hatch. The moon peeked out from the fast-moving clouds, giving them a little illumination, enough to see the pain on everyone's face. Splitting up didn't feel right, but it was the only option.

The rain slowed even more. Save for a few drops, it had stopped. Like a speeding train, the storm had moved on to its next destination.

"Can someone get my camera?" Pelt asked. "It hurts to bend down."

Zach picked the camera off the gravel; he and Cole searched for the missing lens that had popped off. They found it and handed both to Pelt, who inspected the works and twisted the lens back on.

"The lens is cracked pretty bad. Might as well put it in the car." He said it like a father resigning himself to his son leaving home, letting go of something that's a part of him. "No more pics to take, anyway."

"No. No, keep it," Cole said. "We'll need the zoom

ON GRAVEDIGGER ROAD

lens to see into the house. Won't we? Will that work?"

"Yeah. Yeah, we can do that." Pelt slipped the lanyard around his neck and let the camera dangle over his chest. He felt whole again.

Seconds passed. There was nothing more to say.

"I'll go now while it's not storming," Zach said. "You guys find a spot to hide in. Stay out of sight till I get back."

Andy had slipped through the door and joined them like a silent breeze, an unfamiliar shadow in the dark. His high-pitched voice startled them. "Go that way. Cut across the edge of the swamp."

"Jeez, kid, you scared me," Cole said. "You okay?"

Andy ignored him and continued directing Zach. "There's dry land if you keep right. You'll hit a main road after a long time. I don't know the miles. Don't stop at any houses. They can't be trusted."

"Why can't they be trusted?"

"Can't trust no one out here. You stay low. Wait for the big road."

"The highway? Got it. Thanks, kid." Zach tapped Andy's shoulder with his fist. "Keep it together, little man. And keep an eye on my friends."

Zach met Andy's empty eyes. He was eleven going on fifty. Emotion had drained from him long ago. Now only practical survival tactics lay behind those juvenile eyes. Almost to the point of being creepy.

"Hide from strangers till the big road," Andy repeated. "The big road."

Zach nodded. There seemed nothing else to say. It was time to part ways. Time to run.

"Oh, shit!" Pelt yelled and pointed to the gravel lot under the trees.

The gravedigger was no longer there. A blood stain remained where he had been lying, but his body was missing. They glanced in all directions, expecting to see him limping away or someone else carrying his body, but there was no one.

"Come on," Andy said. "Fast."

He ran across the road to the high grass. They followed him, but much slower with Pelt's leg; Zach and Cole helped him limp across. They reached the grass and stood inside the line of skulls to avoid being seen. And to say goodbye.

"Go fast," Andy said. He cracked his knuckles and hopped from foot to foot like he had to pee. The kid was nervous. "Hezekiah isn't dead. There are others, too."

"He may be right," Cole said. "Stay hidden, keep low, in case he's out there. Or his friends. We'll stick to the weeds and try to see into that damn house."

"Hezekiah is out here," Andy said. His eyes darted around in all directions, then up at the sky. "You need to go now before the storm comes again."

Pelt handed the flare gun to Zach. "Take this, man. If anyone… or anything…"

"What?"

"Shoot it as a last resort. If anyone catches you, fire it into the sky. Maybe, if you're close enough to the highway, maybe someone will see it. And…"

"And what?"

"It… it will let us know you didn't make it."

"Shit," Cole said. "Don't say that. He'll make it. Of course, he'll make it."

"Yeah, I will," Zach said. "I'll make it and I'll get help, I promise. It may take a day, but I'll get the cops out here. I'll get the fuckin' National Guard if I have to."

There seemed nothing more to say, except *Don't Go*. But that wasn't an option. All of their lives depended on this plan. Thunder rumbled in the distance as if to remind them the clock was ticking. Time to move.

"God speed," Pelt said. "Get out of here. If we see the man, we'll distract him. And… good luck."

Zach and Pelt shook hands.

Cole pushed Zach's hand aside and hugged him for the first time in his life.

"Good luck, man. Stay frosty." It was a tight hug. Part of him still felt he should be the one to risk the run. He wanted to stay to find Jessie, but that was also the safer option. Running alone through the swamp, on the road, that was the riskier mission. He didn't want to let his friend do it. But someone had to.

Zach patted his friend's back twice, pulled from the embrace and winked at Andy. "I'll be back with help, little man. I promise. You take care of these two." As he walked away, he said, "Easy peezy!"

"Lemon squeezy," Cole whispered. "Good luck."

Zach walked backward and put on a reassuring

smile, then turned forward and jogged along the edge of the swamp. After fifty feet, he turned back and waved for a few seconds, a water bottle in each hand. Silently they returned the wave. He continued to jog faster and was soon swallowed by the darkness.

Pelt and Cole watched their best friend go and stared into the void for a minute after he had vanished.

They never saw him again.

PART II

"We shall see that at which the dogs howl in the dark, and that at which cats prick up their ears after midnight."
— H.P. Lovecraft

ROD LITTLE

CHAPTER 20

Passing the line of skulls, Cole and Andy helped Pelt limp down the road toward the graveyard and the house. They tried to bend below the grass line to be cloaked by the grass and weeds, but this proved too difficult for Pelt. Unable to crouch, he had to walk upright, and thus so did Cole to help him along. Andy was the only one short enough to be concealed by the weeds. He did his best to assist Pelt from the other side.

The rain had stopped completely, but the ground was now soggy, muddier than before. Thirty-five painful minutes of hobbling took them to the area opposite the cruel graveyard. Its four torches had been snuffed out by the rain. Beyond lay the crooked little house with one lamp still lighting its living room, the flame bobbing, shadows waltzing across the walls. The large front window was open with the curtains only a quarter drawn. They struggled to see through the opening to make out who was in the house.

"Can you see anything?" Cole asked.

Pelt brought the cracked telephoto lens to his eye. He focused it on the house. Someone came into view.

"Well? What do you see? Anything?"

"Two people. Wait. Get down." Pelt couldn't follow his own instructions. It hurt to bend below the weed line. "Someone... someone's coming."

All three saw her now. The woman came charging out the front door with such purpose in her stride, they were certain she had spotted them. She held a shotgun in her right hand and something else in her left. Matches; it was a box of long matches. She had come outside to relight the torches. One at a time, she set all four ablaze. The flames sent ghostly shadows across the graves. Her shadow was a creature all its own, her long hair swaying in the wind. The skull paint on her face stretched down her neck. In the torchlight it made her look unreal, a true ghost come back to life. That image would haunt them for the rest of their lives.

"Holy shit," Cole whispered. He swallowed hard. "She's one scary bitch."

"She'll kill you," Andy said flatly. For him, it was merely a matter of fact, a piece of practical advice. There was no hyperbole with this kid. "When she finds you, she'll kill you both."

"Then let's make sure she doesn't find us, kid."

"Check it out," Pelt said. The lens remained glued to his right eye; he strained to see past its spiderweb of cracks. "It's Jessie. I see her. She's in there. And she's alive."

"You sure? Let me see."

Cole snagged the camera from Pelt. He saw his

girlfriend moving her head around, searching for something in the room. Looking for an escape, he assumed. Though her hair was tangled, dark circles under her eyes, she didn't look injured. There was no way to be sure from here, but she seemed okay. Alive, at least. That was all they could be sure of.

"Well, that answered our first question," Cole said. "We know where Jesse is."

"And our second question?" Pelt asked.

"How the hell do we get her out?"

"No clue, man."

"And by 'we' I mean me and the kid. You're in no shape to help rescue anyone. No offense, Pelt-man, but you can't even walk."

"I'm sorry. I'm useless here."

"Not your fault man."

"Dropping down on that man was fuckin' stupid of me," Pelt apologized again. "I'm gonna be in the way, aren't I?"

"Like a chaperone on prom night." Cole returned the camera to him. "Don't sweat it, man. I didn't mean to blame you. We need to come up with a plan. At least it's just the woman in there."

"That's not *just* a woman," Pelt said. "It's a scary fuckin' devil woman with a shotgun and a mean-ass temper."

"I didn't say it was just a woman, I meant it's *only* the woman. Not the woman and man."

"Hezekiah is not dead," Andy reminded them. "He

walked away. And I don't think we can kill him easy."

"No, he's out," Cole said. "He may have stumbled away, but he was bleeding bad from the neck. Best case for him, he doesn't die before morning."

"No." Andy tugged on Cole's shirt. "He can heal fast. And he will be angry."

"Whoa, whoa, he's right." Pelt had been monitoring the front window again through his camera lens and now he sucked air through his teeth. "I can see him. He's in there with Jessie. Fuck! Cole, he doesn't look so hurt. There's a bandage on his neck." He looked away from the lens and met their stares. "He's walking again."

"Son of a bitch."

"I told you he was strong," said Andy.

In that moment, Cole saw what none of them had noticed before. When the torches were lit and you stood directly across from them, the shadows of the crosses formed the image of a face with "X's" for eyes and a frightening grin.

Shit, that's scary! I hope the others don't see it.

The three barely moved, hoping for the woman to leave or go back inside. She stayed behind the graves for several minutes more and scanned the swamp through the darkness. At one point, she raised the shotgun to her eye and aimed it across the road toward the field. If she fired, the bullet would come damn close to the three boys.

"She can see us," Pelt whispered.

"No," Cole said. "She's using it for the sights. It's

too dark on this side of the road. She can't see us."

"I hope you're right, man. I can't run."

Finally, she lowered the gun and went back inside.

Pelt breathed a sigh of relief. His leg throbbed, and he didn't think he could walk much farther before resting. He didn't want to burden the others, so he contemplated where he could lie low. Maybe he could recline in the mud and make a window in the grass to keep an eye on them. He wished he had a gun.

"That still doesn't solve our problem, though," Cole said. "Jessie is in there. How the hell do we get her out? Both psychos are in there with her."

Their ideas were few and flimsy. With no actual weapons, charging the house was out of the question. And Pelt wasn't going to be much help wounded.

"We don't have any weapons," Pelt said. "Or leverage. Nothing to negotiate her out."

"What's lebrage?" Andy asked.

"Leverage is something the other side wants. We don't have anything they need. Money won't impress them; they're not asking for ransom."

"These aren't criminals," Cole said. "We won't get anywhere thinking they are. They're part of a lunatic cult. So, how do you deal with crazy people?"

Pelt shrank back. "I don't think you do. They didn't negotiate out of Waco or Ruby Ridge. You can't deal with maniacs or mental cases. At least, not without casualties."

"You do have lebrage," Andy said. "You have me.

They want all of you dead, but most of all they want me. Me, mostly."

"What are you suggesting?"

"You can tell them to trade me for your girlfriend."

"That's brave, kid. But that's also nuts," Cole said. "They'll kill you. Or bury you again. Or both."

Pelt agreed. It was a bad idea. "We didn't rescue you just to give you back to them."

"I didn't mean they can keep me. We can make a plan to get me back."

"How is that better? Or any different from where we are now?" Pelt asked.

"I can fight good."

"Jessie can fight, too. She's not a powder-puff flower, you know. She's smart. If only we could get a signal to her. But I don't see how. We're really fucked, man."

"Well, we need to do something." Cole bit his lower lip, thinking. "I don't know how long they're willing to wait before they kill her. And then they'll come after us again."

"I think…" Andy started. He was squinting at the house. "I don't think they'll kill her."

"Why? What makes you say that?"

"They didn't kill her already." Andy shrugged. "Why not? They want her for something."

"They didn't kill you right away, either," Cole reminded him. "They held you for two days, you said."

"That's different. They think I'm special. They wanted to do a big thing, a rickshaw, and then bury me."

"Rickshaw? You mean ritual?"

"Yeah. But you people are normal. They kill normal people right away. But they didn't kill your girlfriend. I don't know why."

"To lure us in, maybe," Pelt said.

"I think they want her for something else." Andy wouldn't explain further. He seemed sure they never intended to kill Jessie. All he would say was, "I know these people. I know them."

The door to the house opened again, and Hezekiah stormed outside with a longbow in his hands. Bandages covered his neck, but he appeared unharmed. Unbelievable, but there he was in front of them, alive and walking. It was almost a miracle; a horrid miracle. Even his ghoulish makeup remained intact, despite the attack on him. He was the living incarnation of every knife-wielding movie trope that wouldn't die.

At the edge of the graveyard, he produced an arrow and dipped its end into one of the torches his sister had re-ignited. The arrow tip caught fire. Next, he walked to the edge of the road and scanned the swamp. His pupils seemed to glow in the dark.

"Help me sit down," Pelt whispered.

They eased him gently to the ground, safely below the weed line. It felt good to get the weight off his leg.

Hezekiah was too close for comfort. Only a dirt road and a curtain of grass lay between them and him.

Andy and Cole squatted low and eyed him through gaps in the slats of green.

Now Hezekiah raised the flaming arrow and nocked it in his bow. The arrow sailed across the road into the first of the skulls perched on pikes. The skull burst into flames. Seconds later, the other skulls lit up one by one, until all of them were ablaze. They counted fifteen, running up the road past the church.

"Shit. How did he do that?" Cole crouched lower. "How the hell did he do that? Are all the skulls connected somehow?"

"They lit them last night, too," Andy said. "I saw them. And the night before, when they brought my mom and me here."

"They're throwing one helluva light on the swamp," Pelt said. "He'll see us for sure if we try to run. If *you* try to run. Me, I'm stuck here."

"That is a lot of light," Cole agreed. "Dammit."

Hezekiah planted his feet in the middle of the road and looked out on the torch-lit swamp. His head did not move, nor any part of his body. Only his eyes shifted. Nothing was scarier to the boys than his dark figure in the glow of the torches, not moving at all; only his luminescent eyes shifting left and right. A zombie glued to the road, a vampire minding everything in his kingdom, lord of every shadow on Gravedigger Road. Watching for movement. Hovering with the patience of a spider at the edge of a web. Locked in place, he stood there for seven or eight minutes. They wondered if he would ever move again.

"Fuckin' freak show," Cole hissed. "How're we gonna get past him now?"

"We don't go that way, anyway," Andy whispered. "We're going to the house."

"How do you figure?"

"It's where your friend is."

Hezekiah's head tilted slightly. He was listening. Cole put a finger to his lips and gestured for them to shut their mouths. A new boom of thunder bowled miles away. That might help them if it rolled their way. Rain might chase the gravedigger away. Or empower him; it was hard to tell on a night like this.

Maybe that's what he hears. I hope so; rain would kill the flames.

They remained hidden in the weeds and did not speak or budge an inch. Hezekiah was equally silent and motionless in the road. It was a standoff to see who would break first, who would make a noise.

The standoff lasted a brutal twelve minutes.

Hezekiah broke first by whistling. He stood in the middle of the road and whistled a familiar tune.

"I'm not crazy, that is *Wish You Were Here*, right?" Cole whispered.

Pelt nodded. "The crazy bastard is whistling Pink Floyd. I think."

They listened.

"How I wish you were here…" Pelt mouthed the

words with no sound.

"It's weird," Cole mouthed back.

"What's Pink Freud?" Andy mouthed.

Pelt closed his eyes and made the sign of the cross. The vapid youth of today and their music was of constant concern to him. He laid a hand on Andy's chest and mouthed, "Quiet."

It was as if Hezekiah were saying he wished they were here with him. Taunting them to join him.

The whistling persisted.

Crouching in the weeds, they listened to the creepy song of the skull-painted Hezekiah. It lasted for two minutes. Then it stopped. Cole thought the whistling was as creepy as it could get, but he was wrong. The silence was much worse.

Hezekiah finally moved.

CHAPTER 21

As Jessie spoke, Hannah's attention was drawn to the back door. It slammed shut, and then came the shuffling of feet. The table barked over the floor. Hannah ran to meet the sounds. Muffled scraps of words crossed from the kitchen, but Jessie couldn't make them out or see what was happening. Hannah came back and ran past Jessica, up the stairs where more noises were heard. Scuffling, perhaps the opening of drawers. She returned and fled back into the kitchen with a box in her hands.

She's not special. This is just a cult. They can't see anything. She can't read cards or minds. They don't catch demons.

They're crazy. Fucking crazy bitch.

When I get out of here...

Hannah returned to the living room with her brother, the gravedigger, and helped him to the couch. She opened the front window, now that the rain had stopped. A heady breeze kicked in.

"Hezekiah is hurt. Don't disturb him." Then she spoke only to her brother. "Rest. There is still time to catch him. There is time, still. Ignore the girl."

He moved his hands in sign language, signing two words. She nodded and patted his arm.

"He doesn't speak?" Jessie asked.

"He doesn't need to. He sees more than any of us, and words are mortal instruments of distraction."

"Good for him."

"He is good at his job. He doesn't need to disturb the air with the spoken word."

Hannah had wrapped Hezekiah's neck with a large cloth bandage, and now he sat on the couch with his eyes closed. Hannah sat next to him and dabbed his forehead with a cold compress.

"That looks bad," Jessie said. "Is he going to die?"

Hannah turned from the cold compress and shot daggers at Jessie. "No. He'll meditate and heal. I told you, he can't be killed the way normal people can. It takes a lot to hurt him… to hurt him beyond healing."

"What happened to him?"

"This is the work of that foul Andras. That's a wicked one, maybe the worst we've had yet."

"Andy? The kid? I doubt that little boy did this to your brother."

"Are you saying your friends did this?"

Is she baiting me?

"They wouldn't do that either."

"You're right. I don't blame you… or them. Few people on this earth could kill a man with a knife. I doubt any of you could. But that little one has it in him. Hezekiah says it was him."

"I'm not sure. But you're trying to kill him, aren't you? Do you expect him to hand himself over without a fight?"

"To be fair," said Hannah, "we're trying to kill your friends. As for Andras, we're only going to bury him."

"Sure. That's not crazy."

"Excuse me a moment," Hannah said.

She signed a few words to her brother, then grabbed her shotgun and a long box of matches and left the house through the front door. When it slammed shut, Jessie flinched. She tried to look through the window to see what the woman was doing, but it meant staring over the head of Hezekiah, still resting on the couch. The man gave her the heebie-jeebies. She looked toward the kitchen instead. For the one hundredth time, she strained against the rope to see if any knots might loosen. They held firm.

Minutes later, Hannah returned and rested the shotgun in the far corner. Jessie eyed it hungrily; that's what she'd go for if she got loose. She assumed it was loaded, but she'd never shot one before. She prayed it was as easy as pointing and pulling the trigger.

Hannah signed to her brother and said, "Leave us, my brother. I need to talk to the child alone."

Hezekiah lumbered upstairs. Already he seemed more healed than possible.

"Have some more wine, child." She put the cup to the girl's lips. "Now, your story. And I will know if you're lying to me."

Hannah picked up the small knife and moved it between her fingers. "Don't mind this. I use it to relax me. And if you lie to me, I'll use it in other ways."

I don't doubt that, thought Jessie. She had no intention of lying. In fact, she had wanted for years to tell someone her dark secret. Who better than a psychopath she would never see again?

"It's a short story. Short and sad. Not much to tell."

"Nevertheless…" Hannah laid her palm out to say *proceed.*

Jessica gathered her thoughts.

"I was eight. I had a babysitter. A high-school girl. She was so beautiful, I thought she was a princess. Eight-year-old girls think that way, I guess. Hard to remember why."

She paused as the sound of heavy steps shook the stairs. Hezekiah came downstairs with a longbow in his hand and a quiver of arrows over his shoulder. He didn't look at the two women. Facing forward, he barreled through the front door and did not return.

Hannah only glanced in his direction. She scooted closer to the edge of the couch near Jessie and swigged from the wine bottle again. The knife twirled around her fingers. "You were saying, dear?"

"It was fifteen years ago, when I was eight. I idolized my babysitter, Cindy. Even her name sounded like a princess. I called her Cinderella."

"She was beautiful?"

"She was. Her hair was like a fountain of gold. She and I would wear princess tiaras and pretty dresses and have tea parties. Just the two of us."

"That sounds lovely." Hannah's eyes were lost in thought, imagining the scene. She closed them and brought the wine to her lips.

As she spoke, Jessie's eyes swam into the single flame of the oil lamp. In it she became free. She understood moths suddenly, to be drawn into something better than the darkness around you.

"Those were good times. Every child should have good times like that, I think."

"So, what happened? What spoiled it?"

"She was a whore," Jessie said abruptly, her tone instantly bitter. "Simple as that. She slept with every man she ever met. She wasn't a princess. She was a cow. A nymphomaniac."

Hannah blinked. "It can't be as simple as that. What happened? Tell me."

Jessie sighed and released her shadows. *Here it comes.*

"One night, my mom went to a PTA meeting, my father was at work, and I was left with Cindy. Same as it was week after week. Except that night was different; my father came home early. Really early, like right after mom left. He took Cindy to the bedroom and locked the door." She shifted her gaze from the flame to meet

Hannah's eyes. "Even an eight-year-old knows what happens behind closed doors. Did they think I was stupid? They told me to watch TV and stay quiet." She snorted. "They thought they got away with it. People think kids are stupid."

"How many times did this happen?"

"Only a few. A teenage boy moved in next door and I asked mom if he could babysit me instead. I pretended I thought he was great with kids, but he only played video games while I watched TV. He sucked. But he wasn't Cindy, and he wasn't some other girl. I never allowed a high-school girl to babysit me again."

Hannah sat back. She stopped twirling the knife. "I see. But… that's not the story you want to tell me. Is it, dear?"

How does she know?

Whistling filtered through the open window. It came from the road.

"You're right. It isn't. It's only the preamble. The real drama came years later. I was in high school with my very best friend in the world, Amelia. She and I grew up together. We had plans to be roommates in college."

"And did you?"

"Yeah," Jessie snapped. "It all ended happily ever after. And here I am on your dirt road of hell."

"So, what happened?" Hannah didn't mind the sarcasm; her patience was extraordinary if the promise of a payoff was coming. She knew it was. The gates were open now. No way to shut them. "Tell me, child. Tell me what happened."

"Amelia had an affair with my father. It lasted a year before I found out."

"Chrissakes, your dad must be a hottie. All the girls are on him like bees on honey, it seems."

"She had been lying to me for a year. That fucking skank. And my mother… my mom is the sweetest woman on the planet. I swear this to you now. You'll never find a nicer, kinder woman. She took care of me and my brother and my father. She deserved better."

"The denouement. Tell me. How did in unravel?"

"When my mom found out, they got a divorce and he moved away. That's that. He went away. And my mom is alone now."

Hannah studied Jessie for a moment without speaking. She tried to meet her eyes, but Jessie refused and only looked down at the ground, then closed her eyes.

"No," said Hannah. "You're lying to me."

Jessie's eyes shot open; she stiffened. Would she be stabbed? Where was the knife? There it was, on the couch next to the woman. Would she snatch it up and kill her for lying? And how did she know?

"You can't know that!" Jessie said. "Why do you think I'm lying?"

"It was true all the way up to the divorce," Hannah speculated. She narrowed her eyes, thinking, calculating how much truth was in the tale. "I think it went off the rails right before that. There was no divorce, was there?

That's too easy."

Jessica hung her head. "No."

"Did your mom even find out about the affair?"

"No. Never."

"And Daddy still lives at home? Life goes on at the *Leave it to Beaver* suburban household?"

"No. Not exactly."

Hannah leaned in. "I didn't think so. Well, what exactly happened, Jessica? I believe you about the babysitter. I believe your friend in high school fucked your dad. I'm sorry, your *father*. Or the other way around. And I believe your mom is the sweetest woman in the world. God knows mine isn't! I'll let yours take that ribbon. But the truth ends there. No divorce came to your house. There was no separation, was there? But Daddy doesn't live there anymore, right?"

Jessica nodded sullenly.

Hannah prodded. "What happened?"

The whistling faded. Hezekiah was moving farther up the road.

"I confronted him, and he moved away. Far away. I made him promise to never see mom again."

Hannah wagged a finger. "You're lying to me again. Jessica, that's no way to start a friendship."

Friendship? Is that what this is?

Tears welled in Jessica's eyes. "Please stop. I never told anyone before."

"You did confront your dad. That sounds right. But

he didn't agree to move away, did he?"

Tears now streamed down Jessie's face. She looked at the floor but didn't see it. Through blurry eyes she saw the world spin past her. Every person she ever loved, smeared into a collage, edited to exclude the one she loved most—her father. She had looked up to him, and he had let her down.

"You confronted him, Jessica. And then…"

"I told you enough. I told you. Please… let me go now."

Hannah shook her head. "It's too late, child. The cat's out of the bag. You can't stuff it back in. Time to let it go free. Tell me the rest. It will make you feel better. You know it will." She was savoring the girl's story, every morsel of it. This was fine theater to her.

Jessie spoke the next words for the first time in her life. They fell like poisoned food from her mouth.

"I killed him." Jessie felt as if she might black out.

Hannah reached out and touched her leg. The sympathy on her face somehow made it past the cruel Halloween makeup. She felt and appreciated the pain and anger in this young one.

"I killed him," Jessie repeated. Now that she said it aloud, she wanted to shout it over and over. But she whispered instead. "I killed him."

"I know you did, child." She had always known.

"I shoved a steak knife into his stomach. And again and again, I just kept stabbing him. Because he wouldn't stop seeing Amelia." Finally she looked at Hannah. Her vision was blurry. "I couldn't let him break mom's heart. You understand that, right?"

Hannah smiled wanly. "Dear, I might be the only person who truly does understand that. I do."

They sat in silence. Thunder resounded miles off, almost too far to be heard. The whistling no longer in earshot, the roaring silence of the room closed in on them. It threatened to strangle them until Hannah whispered.

"Can I ask you something?"

Jessie nodded. She couldn't stop crying.

"How did you get away with it?" Hannah took a tissue from the cosmetic desk and dabbed the girl's eyes. "It's not easy to get away with murder. Especially the murder of a loved one."

I'll tell you. Because I no longer care. When this is over, I'm turning myself in to the police.

"I lured him to a seedy hotel in town. I left him a perfumed message on his car's windshield, pretending to be Amelia. After I killed him, I took his wallet to make it look like a robbery and pushed his body out the window. It fell into the alley. I climbed down the fire escape and ran. Everyone thought he just got rolled." It was a fog to Jessie; she reassembled the pieces now. "Sure, they wondered why he was in that part of town, but that didn't stop the cops from sweeping it under the rug. It was a small town. The file was closed, mom got the insurance money, and she never knew her husband cheated on her."

She might have known, thought Hannah. *A wife often knows. But don't take that illusion from the child.*

"My Lord! The strength you must have had." Hannah admired the girl. "To accomplish such a deed and then to roll a body out a window. The physical strength alone would fail most, but the mental force needed… you astound me, Jessica. I am impressed." She leaned back. "Truly impressed."

"I don't care what you think." Or did she? Jessie found she wanted this woman's approval.

"You did good," Hannah told her. "You protected your mother. That's a good daughter. A good person. I knew I was right about you. Or… is that not the only reason you killed him?"

Jessie didn't want to answer that, so Hannah answered for her.

"He stole your best friend. That made you angry. You were jealous."

"He stole everyone from me! I was afraid to bring any friends home." She shook, her face red and puffy from crying. "Do you know what that's like? I couldn't trust him. I was afraid."

"I know, dear. I know."

The approval. She felt better for it.

"Can I have a drink now?" Jessie let out a rattled breath. She had never unloaded this to anyone before. It was her first and only confession.

"Certainly, dear. You've earned it." Hannah untied Jessie's right hand; her left hand and ankles were still tied to the chair. She handed her another tissue and the cup of wine. "Drink slowly. Not too fast. And you've earned much today."

"Like what?"

"My trust, for one. And that's no small thing."

Jessie blew her nose, then sipped the wine. She was surprised the woman had untied one hand. Did she really intend to fulfill her promise and let her go? Was it possible?

"Thank you," Hannah said. "Thank you for telling me that. And for not lying to me. It was the first time you told anyone, wasn't it?"

Jessie looked down and nodded.

"It takes a special person to kill for love. Or jealousy. You would be such a valuable asset to the cause." Hannah drew a breath and closed her eyes as if smelling a flower and getting high off it. "Thank you. I won't forget this."

Jessie wiped her face with the back of her hand. She stole another tissue. "So, you'll let me go now? You said you'd let me go if I told you."

"Yes. I will. I will let you go."

"Really?"

"Soon. But not yet," Hannah said. "First, you have to hear my story. I have one, too. And it's a good one."

CHAPTER 22

The reasoning behind the gravedigger's actions was never clear, but they thought they'd figured it out. The whistling, the listening, scanning the swamp patiently. Hezekiah was looking for his dog. He expected the whistling to bring the hellhound running home.

Hezekiah trudged into the weeds to the first skull and retrieved the flaming arrow. He nocked it again and shot it into the air. It soared like a firework through the sky and came streaking down in the swamp fifty feet behind where the three boys still hid. There it vanished, the wet ground killing the flame.

Hezekiah stepped back onto the road. He walked slowly up the center toward the church, pausing every few seconds to listen. The echo of his boots hitting the dirt pierced the night. The crickets had shut down their concert again. The swamp no longer made any sound. No frogs, birds, or night creatures. Only the scuffing of the man's boots on the empty road. The boys waited for him to reach the church before opening their mouths.

"He knows the dog is dead," Cole whispered. "He'll want revenge for that."

"How do you know his dog is dead?" Andy asked.

"Zach and I... we killed it."

"Really?" Pelt was surprised. "With what? That hook you had?" It seemed unlikely Cole or Zach could kill a dog.

"We fed it to a gator. It's a long story. Just be glad we got rid of it. It's good he's not sniffing us out. We'd have been found already if that mutt was still around."

"A gator?" Pelt grimaced at the thought of being eaten by an alligator, or even seeing something get eaten by an alligator.

"Was it gross?" Andy asked.

"I don't know. Can we focus on the house, please?" Cole popped his head up for a quick peek. "Pelt, give me your camera."

"Did you see it get eaten?" Andy persisted. "I bet it was gross."

Cole ignored him and took the camera from Pelt. He pressed it to his eye and hit the zoom button. The open window made for a small theater with occasional glimpses of the woman as she walked around the room, in an out of view. She kept talking, arms gesturing as if lecturing or explaining something.

What could they be talking about?

From this angle, he couldn't see Jessie's face, but he saw her hand lift a mug to drink.

She's not tied up? Why doesn't she run?

The two women were locked in conversation. It almost appeared to be a tea party. He could only assume

ON GRAVEDIGGER ROAD

Jessie was stalling for a chance to escape, and he wondered if a diversion would help her.

The world at this end of Gravedigger Road seemed too quiet to be real. If they sat still long enough, they could hear the crackling of the torches. Hezekiah's boots continued to plod up the road, way too loud for comfort. Wildlife teemed around them, but—unlike earlier in the night—not a single creature now let out a peep. This wasn't normal. It was unnatural. Almost supernatural. If the swamp creatures were in hiding, they were expecting something bad.

But crickets don't hide.

Why did they stop chirping?

"This place is cursed," Andy said, as if reading his thoughts. "Don't think about it too much."

"I don't believe in curses."

"You don't have to believe in 'em for it all to be real." Andy shrugged. "That's what my mom used to say. They don't care if you believe or not. They don't care. And it doesn't matter."

"You believe in Santa, too?"

"No," said Andy. "Santa is a story. Curses are real."

"I'm with the kid," Pelt said. "We've been cursed since we drove down this fucking road. I can't wait to get the hell out of here."

"I was being sarcastic," said Cole.

"I know," said Andy. "But you don't believe. And that's why you won't make it."

"Fuck. You think I won't make it?"

"Not if you don't believe. You're weak if you don't believe. And Hezekiah is already too strong."

"Fine, it's cursed." Cole continued to peer through the camera. "That isn't helpful, but I'll admit… wait… you really think I won't make it? You mean, I won't get out alive?"

Andy yawned. He was tired. "None of us will, unless we play smart."

"We're trying to be smart. We need to get Jessie out of there now, while Mr. Happy is up near the church."

"If we run inside fast, I can kill Hannah," Andy said. One minute he looked like a sweet innocent child, tired and in need of a nap. The next, he was the cold-blooded killer who slashed Hezekiah's throat and now was ready to kill again. His face was hard to read. "And you can get your girlfriend. But I need a weapon. You got one?"

Cole pointed to his pockets. "No. Do you see any weapons on me?"

"We shoulda kept the gun, the one your friend Zach took. We need it."

"That was a flare gun. Not a real gun."

"It's real if I shoot it in Hannah's face."

You're a real piece of work, kid.

"Well, we don't have it," Cole snapped. "Zach has it. So, shut up and start working on Plan B. Is there any way to get that woman to come outside now? If she does, you two can sneak inside from the back door and get Jessie."

"You can go to the front door and knock," said

Andy, sticking his chin out. "And then you run real fast. I'll get your girlfriend out the back way. If you run fast, maybe you don't get shot in the back."

"Helluva Plan B. No thanks."

"I can be sarcastic, too. You're not the only asshole here. But you'll be the dead one if you don't get smart."

"Easy, kid. I have a better plan," said Pelt. "We trade me for Jessie. I'm wounded, anyway. I'm no help out here."

"How is that a plan?" Cole asked. "That sucks. It's the same as his plan but worse."

"No. Because Jessie doesn't know where we are or what we're planning. I do; or, at least, I will. We'll trade me for her and when I'm inside, I'll get ready for you guys to attack. We'll make a plan for me to do something."

"Are you nuts?"

Andras shook his head. "They don't do that. They don't trade people. They only kept her alive so she can be bait for us. Trust me, sure, they'll kill you if you ask to trade for her. And then they'll kill her."

"He's right," Cole said. "This isn't a bank heist. We can't trade one hostage for another."

"Then I'm out of ideas, guys." Pelt's leg ached. He tried to bend it at the knee to avoid a cramp. Dried blood began to stiffen the jeans. "What can we do?"

"We need to stall until Zach can get help. He'll be back by tomorrow, right? We need to stay hidden until then. Andy, do you think they'll hurt Jessie?"

Andy shrugged. "I don't know. I don't think so. I think if they didn't kill her now already, they won't do it until they find us. They need to find us first. Mostly they need to find me. Mostly."

"So, the best plan is to hide and wait for Zach," Cole affirmed. "That makes sense, right? Hide and wait. Are we agreed?"

"I guess so."

"Sure," said Andy. "Hide. But where? Not in the church; it's not safe there."

"Any chance we can lie down here in the swamp? Stay low until Zach gets back?"

Andy shook his head. "No way. In the morning it'll be easy to find us. We need to go someplace they can't see us in daytime." Then he added, "And there are more gators out here."

"Crap. I know a place." Cole dreaded the next words before he even said them, but he had to suggest it. He knew it was the best place to hide. "I know a place we can go. I really don't want to go there. But we'd be out of sight."

"Where?"

"On an island in the lake. There's a small shack where we can hide. Zach and I found it. I don't think he'll check there again. He knows we were there and left already."

"Good."

"Not good. They keep dead bodies there."

CHAPTER 23

Exhausted from the emotional drain of the last two hours, Jessie blinked the haze from her eyes. The room came back into focus. She saw a shadow at the window, a dark figure blocking the lamp. A silhouette until it became Hannah. The woman stood at the window and gazed out, her hands folded behind her head. Was she thinking or boring into the darkness with her mystical voodoo eye?

Can she see Cole and the others? Does she really have special powers?

Hannah turned and sat on the couch. She picked up her deck of cards. Jessie watched her deal eight cards onto the couch cushion next to her in two rows of four. She flipped two of them face-up and smiled.

"Oh, those naughty boys." Hannah winked at Jessie. "They're hiding in the swamp. That can't be fun for them. Or safe. I hope nothing eats them before my brother finds that awful boy." She stroked her earlobe pensively. "He's with them, you know. They're protecting him."

"He's only a little boy."

"Is he?" Hannah twisted her mouth into a crooked smile. She gathered the cards into a stack and laid them aside. "We'll get to him later. First, my story. I need to tell you. One good confession deserves another."

Jessie nodded. Whatever was needed to get out of here. She could listen, if that's what it took.

"Well," said Hannah, reclining with both arms on the couch back, "my story starts much earlier. I was five, you see, living up north in the heartland. Indiana." She sneered. "A gawdawful place. You ever been?"

"No."

"Good for you, honey. Good for you. Oddly, Illinois is pretty nice. How can one place be so backward and its neighbor be so lovely? I mean, they're only a few miles apart, but they're like night and day. And they do not get along."

"Really? I never heard that."

"Never mind, I'm getting sidetracked. You see, at five years old, the mind takes in everything. I understood what was happening, but my parents assumed I was a lump of clay in the corner. I could have been a stuffed animal. Often they talked openly in front of me. They thought I didn't understand things like witchcraft or murder. But I did."

With her free hand, Jessie yanked the shawl from her shoulders. She was getting hot. The humidity stifled the room. She sipped her wine.

"My dad claimed to be a demon hunter. That wasn't his job—he worked nine to five as a machinist, you know

—but demon hunting was his passion. Every free moment he mapped out clues that he claimed led him to evil people. Creatures of ill intent, he called them. He spent his weekends going on trips to track them down. Never talked about them, but my mom begged him to stop. She thought he was taking down bad people, killers and thieves, but she never believed they were evil. She didn't believe in anything supernatural. That lack of belief didn't save her, though."

Hannah topped up Jessie's mug with wine then swigged twice from the bottle and continued. She played with the paring knife while she talked.

"One Saturday night while my dad was away, a man came to the door looking for him. When my mom said he was away, this man pushed into the apartment—we had a shoddy little second-floor apartment back then—and he attacked my mother. Straight away, no more words, no offer to talk about it. He only asked where my dad was. That was it. When he didn't get an answer, he beat my mom to death with his fists. I sat in the corner and watched."

"Shit," Jessie whispered. *To watch a person beaten to death! And her own mother!*

"Yes. It was shocking. You know, one thing I remember most was his eyes. They were yellow. They glowed like fire."

She looked over at the oil lamp. The knife twisted in her hand.

"Even at five, I knew eyes aren't supposed to look

like that. I comprehended what my mom never could; that my dad was right. He wasn't a fake or a flake. His work was genuine, the real deal."

"How awful," Jessie said. "You must have been so scared. Five years old. That's so young."

Hannah chuckled. "You have no idea. I crawled under the sofa and hid. And that's when I realized he hadn't even seen me. The man didn't know I was there."

"You were lucky."

"Hmm. Yes and no. Anyway, I heard him move my mom's body. And though I couldn't see much from under the sofa, I swear to you I heard three people whispering, and I saw three shadows." She looked back at Jessie. "But there was only one man."

Now Jessie felt goosebumps.

This wasn't a fairy tale. This happened. Hannah was many things, but a liar wasn't one of them. That much Jessie knew. Somehow, she knew this woman.

"Anyway." Hannah waved her hand in the air as if to make it all go away. "Fast forward. We moved to Peoria so my dad could work for Caterpillar. My dad and me, the two of us. We had a small house. I liked it. I liked the people there. We lived near the river and saw the Delta Queen and Julia Belle Swain race every year."

"What are those?"

"Steamboats! Oh, they were magnificent. Quite a show! We'd stand by the river and watch them tear through the water. Well, as a kid it seemed so; I think they actually moved quite slow. But lots of people lined the river to get a glimpse of them. Very exciting. And things went well for me in my new home until I turned ten. They say tragedy comes in even intervals. Do you believe that? For me, it was every five years. So, when I was ten, these creatures, the ones that look like men but with extra shadows… two of them came and took my dad from me. He was spirited away in the night. I assume they killed him, but… who knows? And then there was one. Only me."

"You were left all alone? What did you do?"

"The State put me in a foster home in Moretown. They were good people and treated me well. I had two foster brothers. One of them was Hezekiah."

"So, he's not your real brother?"

"Don't get caught up in words like *real* or *true*, dear. He's my brother in every sense." Swiftly, her tone changed and brightened. "Do you believe in fate?"

"I guess so."

"No, you don't. But it doesn't matter. Fate happens regardless. Hezekiah's real father was a demon, and his mother was human. That gave him special abilities. He heals quick, for one. And he knows how to find other demons. He knows."

"But he can't speak."

"I think he can. But he chooses not to. And he can hear, too. He signed long ago that nothing is worth saying anymore. I indulge him. His is such a pure soul. An angel without wings."

"Who murders innocent people." Jessie hid in her

cup. Maybe she shouldn't have said that.

"He chose to fight the good fight. He didn't have to. He *chose* to continue my dad's work. If an occasional human victim must be dispelled on the way, so be it. It's regrettable, and don't think we enjoy it! We don't relish killing anyone. But how many others do we save in the process?"

She believes all this. Jessica wondered how this type of brainwashing happened. It must have been drilled into her from a young age, or even from birth.

"You stayed with that family. Did they know? Did they know about your brother?"

"We stayed until he was eighteen and I turned sixteen. Then we went out on our own. We attended carnivals and fairs and trapped the demons and shifters as best we could. One day in some hollow in Montana, next at fair in Reno. We traveled a lot. He took care of me while I took care of him. Oh, that seems like centuries ago."

"It's just the two of you? And the dog?"

Hannah rested the knife between the couch cushions with its handle exposed, and glanced out the window.

"There are others of us, those who fight the good fight. Hundreds scattered across the land. Many right here in this area. We rely on them a great deal. We travel to find the evil things and bury them here. Then we guard them."

"You lost both your parents. And now you're trying

to… what? Revenge their loss? By capturing innocent people and burying them? I don't think that's a good way to honor their memory."

I should tread lightly here. Or I'll be dead instead of free.

"Because you don't believe me. And I'm okay with that. But I wanted you to know what we do here. We've saved countless lives. There are creatures that still roam the world. Some even have positions of power. Only we, our group, can take them down. And, by the way, it's *avenge,* not *revenge.*"

"If you say so."

"You can join us, Jessica." She scooted over and pulled in close to the girl. "You have something in you, a spark. You'd fit in magnificently."

"Anyone can wear scary makeup. Doesn't make them righteous demon hunters."

Hannah smiled. "No scary makeup for you. No. You could help us in so many other ways, exactly the way you are. You could bait them. Lure them in. And Hezekiah could bury them under a wall of salt. A little less hell on earth. A little less darkness."

"I can't."

"I don't extend the invitation lightly, Jessica. Not everyone has the strength to murder someone they love. That's rare. You would be such a powerful force on our side. I am offering you a chance to change the world. To save it."

"I think I'll pass." Jessica downed the rest of her

wine and stared into the mug's empty shell. "The world isn't worth saving. But... thank you for listening to me."

"It was my pleasure." Hannah drank from the bottle, then shook it to agitate the pool of red inside. She was fond of swishing the last of the wine around the bottle before finishing it. The tiny blood-red sea behind tinted glass always delighted her.

"What happens now?" Jessica asked. She noticed there was moisture in the corner of Hannah's eyes. The cosmetic base made it hard to be sure if she had shed a tear or not. For that brief moment, she felt sorry for the woman trapped in Hezekiah's world.

"What happens now?" Hannah placed the bottle on the floor and plucked the small knife from the cushions. She stood and blinked, recomposing herself. "Now, I keep my promise and let you go."

"Really?"

It can't be true.

Jessie eyed the shotgun again but would not go for it. She would not betray Hannah after all they had shared. If freed, she would only run. The best option was to trust the woman to keep her word. Oddly, that seemed to be the case.

Knife twirling deftly in her fingers, Hannah moved behind the girl and cut the rope to free her other arm. She crossed to the other side of the room, tossed the knife on a shelf, and examined several jars of salt—some round, some square, one shaped octagonal. As she passed them, she tapped their glass with a long black-painted fingernail.

"Untie your ankles and stand up. You'll need to stretch a bit. You've been sitting too long."

Quickly, in case her captor changed her mind, Jessie untied the rope around her feet and tossed the strands aside. Her hands shook as she fumbled herself loose. She stood up and swooned, steadying herself against the chair. Her legs had cramped from the long hours sitting, and she was still lightheaded. The wine wasn't helping.

"Careful, child." Hannah spoke with her back to the girl, a trusting act. She didn't fear any reprisals. "Stretch a bit, I said."

She chose a small round jar of salt and popped the lid to sniff it. Satisfied, she smelled it again and nodded. This one suited the occasion.

"You've stumbled into the middle of a blood feud, Jessica. Like the Hatfields and the McCoys, but so much older." She turned and looked at the girl. "And, as with any fight, with any war, it's important you land on the ride side of history."

Jessie flexed and stretched her back. She suspected she had bruises, maybe from the fall she suffered when she passed out. When Hannah crossed the room and closed the distance between them, Jessie instinctively took a step back. It was more reflex than fear.

"We'd make a good team, you and I," Hannah said. "Please think about it. We can't save the whales or the rain forest, or even the endangered lemur frog, but we can save people. We can save souls."

"I think… I don't—"

"Hold out your hand, dear."

The salt's potent smell now met Jessie; she wrinkled her nose and opened a trembling hand. Anxiously, she extended it. Hannah poured seven grains of rock salt into the girl's tender palm.

"You put this salt in the hand of young Andras," Hannah said, "and see what happens. When you don't like what you see, when you don't like his reaction, you come find me."

The certainty in the woman's voice and manner, combined with the absurd spectacle of her costume, sowed doubt in Jessica. Nothing felt certain.

Could she be telling the truth?

Surely not.

Hannah caressed Jessie's hair tenderly. "Promise me you'll do that, at least, my child."

"I will." Jessie's voice sounded small. She felt like a ten-year-old girl.

Hannah glanced out the window. "Morning will be up soon. An hour or two. 'No one knows till he has suffered from the night, how sweet and dear to his heart and eye the morning can be.' That's Bram Stoker, you know. Dracula."

"Oh," said Jessie.

Of course, she'd know that.

"You do as I say, child."

"I will," Jessie breathed.

"But the thing about Gravedigger Road," said Hannah, "is that it doesn't stay here forever. If you want my help, don't wait too long."

CHAPTER 24

Avoiding the light cast by the skulls, Andy and Cole walked on either side of Pelt to help him walk. They worked their way through the tall grass, deeper into the swamp toward the body of water they were calling a lake. It wasn't far, but they were at the wrong end.

"We have to go to the other side," Cole told them. "Sorry. The bridge is over there." He pointed into the darkness.

"How far?"

"Pretty far. Sorry."

"Don't you think that's the first place he'll look?" asked Pelt. "It's an obvious hiding spot."

"No. I don't know. Maybe." Cole was hungry and frustrated. "Look, he already checked there once. He knows we've been there. Why would we go back? He won't suspect it. Especially with all the dead bodies there. And roaches."

"Roaches?"

"Giant cockroaches, Pelt. My God! You've never seen such monsters. Thousands of them. They're creepy and disgusting."

"Lovely."

"But that's all the more reason he might not think we'd go there."

"It's not great," Andy grumbled. "It's not much to hope on, hoping he might not check there again."

"I don't have any other ideas!" Cole said a little louder than he had intended.

"Shhh. He's up the road, but he might hear us," Andy whispered. "His hearing is good."

They continued to wind through the weeds, supporting Pelt. The light from the flaming skulls reached far, much farther than expected. Even here they could see themselves in its glow. They would need to get away from the light.

"I'm starving like hell," Cole said. "Anyone have any food on you?"

"No. We've got power bars and granola bars at the car. Why didn't we take those? We should've."

"We had other things on our mind. I was so scared, I didn't realize how hungry I am."

"You're scared?" Andy asked.

"That's a big Yes, little man. You're not?"

"I am a little." Andy eyed the two older boys. "You get scared when you're big? I didn't think so."

"Trust me, kid. You can be a grandpa and still get scared. Age doesn't make you brave."

Pelt paused to rest his leg. He held up a finger. "For

the record, I am terrified. Fucking terrified." They looked at him. "In case you're keeping score."

Cole gave him a sour look and shook his head.

Don't frighten the kid.

"I think Pelt means he's worried," Cole said to clean it up. "Of course, he's not terrified. He's just hungry, too. We're all tired and hungry."

"No. No, I am full-on terrified. No point in lying to the boy. He was *buried* this morning. You don't think he can know how scared we are? I think he knows we're fucked."

"Yeah. Good point."

"But yes, I am also starving and tired as hell. And my leg is killing me." His shirt already stuck to him from sweat mixed with rain, and now his pants felt fused to his skin as the blood began to dry on both sides. "But Andy and I did take some yogurt and candy bars."

He wriggled a crushed yogurt bar from his pocket. "My last one. I'm sure it's mushy, but you can have it. I ate two already."

"Thanks." Cole tore it open and devoured it. He was still hungry but put on a brave face. "That did the trick." It hadn't.

"I ate all mine," Andy apologized.

"It's okay. That was perfect." Cole licked his fingers and looked down at Pelt's blood-caked jeans. It looked bad. Really bad. He didn't mention that. "Do you need to rest?"

"Maybe two more minutes." Pelt leaned a hand on

Cole's shoulder for support and took all the weight off his injured leg. "I don't like this plan, man. We're like fish dumped in an octopus tank. You ever see an octopus get a fish out of a jar? It works and works at it, man, and in the end it always gets its meal."

"That man is the octopus?"

"He knows this swamp better than we do. He has weapons. And time. He's got all night."

"They say an octopus can smell its prey from a mile away," Andy said. "I saw it on the Science Channel." Now he squatted and looked at the blood on Pelt's leg. It looked gruesome in the orange glow of the remote torches.

"A mile? I don't think so," Cole said.

"It can find it."

"Awesome. What's your point?"

"Hezekiah can find us." Andy continued examining the wound the way a child might study a bug. "He can sense where we are. Maybe not right away. But he can find us after some time."

Cole frowned down at the kid. "You know an awful lot about this guy and his cult. How did you learn so much in two days?"

"I know him."

"Yeah. You keep saying that. But how? You mean you knew him before all this?"

"No, of course not."

"You're an enigma, kid."

"Okay." Andy extended his finger to touch the blood, but reconsidered and withdrew his hand. "What's an enigma?"

"An enigma is something hard to figure out. A puzzle. You're a puzzle I can't figure out, but—as Pelt says—you were buried alive today, so I'll cut you some slack."

Andy finally looked up from the wound. "This is really gross."

"Thanks," Pelt said. "Not helpful."

"Do you think they'll cut your leg off to save you?" Andy asked. "I saw it in a movie once."

"No. It's just a deep cut," Pelt said defensively, but in the back of his mind he wondered. "How long till a wound becomes infected? Badly infected?"

"You're fine," Cole said. "It's not infected. They'll give you antibiotics when help comes. There's plenty of time. I think it takes days before shit like sepsis sets in. Help will be here before then. I'm sure."

At those words, they all glanced in the direction Zach had run. They kept their thoughts to themselves, but worried how long it would take him to find help, if at all. How many crazies lived around here?

They heard whistling again.

The gravedigger was back.

"Where's that coming from?" Cole whispered. It was impossible to tell. The tune carried so far on the wind; it could have been ten yards away or a thousand. Last they saw, he was headed up the road. Had he doubled back

ON GRAVEDIGGER ROAD

through the swamp?

Hezekiah can find us. He can sense where we are.

Andy's words stuck with the others. They shuddered at the thought they were being tracked by smell. By any means. Their eyes scanned the line of burning skulls and everything lit by them. No movement crossed the swamp or the road, except for the shadows of the skull pikes tugged back and forth by the wind. They created a horror show of silhouettes on the landscape. It would be hard to see a lone figure crawling among them.

"Hezekiah is big," Andy whispered. "But he moves like dust in the wind. That's what my mom said. She said he can be where he wants when he wants."

Cole displayed a thumbs-up. "Awesome."

The swamp surged back to life. More and more crickets rejoined their brothers' chirping, now that the rain had stopped and the moratorium on noise had been lifted. Frogs croaked. Life teemed all around them once more. It had always been there, but now it felt safe enough to speak out. Was it because morning loomed ahead? Or another reason?

Amid the loons and other water fowl came the caw of a strange bird. It didn't fit with the others.

This road is haunted.

"Hold on a minute. I know that sound." Cole stood on his toes and looked across the swamp. He yanked the camera from Pelt's hand, causing the lanyard to strain against his friend's neck.

"Hey, careful!" Pelt tried to get his camera back.

Cole held it to his eye for a second then handed it back. "Look, man. You see what I see?"

Pelt squinted through the lens. "Is that—?"

"Yeah. It is."

"What the fuck?"

CHAPTER 25

Jessica drank a mug of water before she departed. Her left hand clutched the salt as if it were her last two dollars. Hannah picked up the shotgun, removing any temptation the younger girl had for it, and ushered her into the kitchen. She didn't point it at her but held it against her shoulder.

"Go out the back way, dear."

Hannah leaned against the doorway between the kitchen and living room and watched her former captive walk out the back door. Jessica held the screen open and peered into the darkness. She was moments from freedom. But what was freedom on this dead-end road?

"He won't come after you," Hannah said, reading her fears. "Hezekiah won't hurt you."

"I know." She didn't know. Nothing was certain.

"Jessica. Remember, don't take too long. I won't be here forever."

Jessie looked back once more at the woman, then slipped outside and let the screen door slam. She hurried to the side of the house, then around to the front. Her steps grew faster, but she fought the urge to break into a run. She didn't want to appear scared. She passed the graves and their torches with scarcely a glance in their direction. When she reached the road opposite the tree and its swamp, she stopped.

Where the hell am I going?

This was obviously a trap. They were following her, letting her lead them to the boys. But what choice did she have? She needed to find them. Wandering the darkness alone held little appeal. She needed her friends back.

For the first time, she saw the laughing skulls. Her eyes went wide at the sight of their flame, their ghostly exhibition. Her fears shot up a notch. Curiously, she had felt safer in the house. Now, out here in the darkness, would the brother kill her? Did he know Hannah might not want that? Or were they both toying with her?

She wanted Cole to see her, see she was safe, but not come for her yet. How could she do that?

In the flickering shadows she thought she saw something farther up the road. Was that the brother? She turned back to the swamp, cupped her hands around her mouth and whispered.

"Cole. Cole! Zach?"

She waited and listened.

"Pelt?"

Her voice wasn't loud enough. If she shouted, both Hannah and Hezekiah would hear it. She would lead her friends into their trap, exactly as she was sure the two had planned.

She cupped her hands again and let out a *caw caw*

sound. It used to be Cole's signal to alert her he was outside her window at midnight. She made the sound twice more.

The oil lamp in the house went out. Hannah sat in the darkness and observed.

Smart. She can see me, but I can't see her.

Hezekiah also walked in the darkness, if that was him lit by the flaming skull lamps. She saw an outline of one side of a figure across from the church, but it had stopped walking. Was he facing her or facing the other way? She imagined him staring right at her, watching her every move.

She walked to the other side of the road to hide against the tree. Before she slid behind it, she saw him take a step away from the church and toward her. Still far up the road but moving in her direction.

The house seemed to follow her, the window a giant eye. She felt exposed. Hidden from Hezekiah, for now, but not from the house. If she hid behind the tree, Hezekiah would see her. There was no way to hide from both.

Shrinking into the tree, she scooched to the ground and touched the dirt with her hand. She wanted to duck into the grass and crawl away without being seen. If she zig-zagged, maybe she could throw them off her direction. She glanced at the house, then up the road. Hezekiah trudged toward her. Did he know she hadn't escaped, that she had been let go? Was Hannah watching?

This isn't going to work.

The figure walking toward her whistled, taunting her. Taunting them all.

She changed her mind. Now she planned to run back across the road and head for the bare trees behind the house. If she could get to the thicker green foliage behind the church, she could hide and surveil the car. That, she figured, was her best bet for finding the others. She crouched, ready to run at the right moment.

What are you waiting for? Go!

Ready, she leaned forward, her eyes glued to the house. Then she flashed one last look at Hezekiah closing his distance. His persistent whistle drilled into her like a needle to the brain.

Suddenly, a hand grabbed her shirt, yanked her back and covered her mouth as she started to scream. Only half a whimper escaped, but enough to be heard. Two arms dragged her back into the tall grass.

"It's me," Cole whispered in her ear. "It's me."

He let her go.

She whirled around, ready to fight, kick and yell, but didn't. She caught herself. Not the boogeyman. It was Cole. He pulled her to him and kissed her on the lips. She kissed and hugged him for half a minute, then pushed away and looked him up and down. He was a sticky mess.

"Are you okay?"

"I'm fine," Cole said. "What about you? What did they do to you?"

"I'm not hurt. But we need to go away from the road. He's coming."

"I know. Follow me. Pelt is hurt. Andy's with him." He took her hand and led her in a crouch through the grass. "Keep your head down. Try not to move the grass too much. I think he can see it move."

They wove their way back toward Andy and Pelt. Cole wasn't sure exactly where he had left them. He only knew the direction. The maze of weeds was confusing in the dark; the grass all looked the same. And walking in a crouch hurt his legs; he desperately wanted to stand up.

"Where are they?" Jessie asked.

"They should be here. This is it, I think. Or near. Where the hell are they?" He called out just above a whisper, "Pelt… Pelt."

Cole lingered a moment to get his bearings. This made no sense. Where were Pelt and Andy? This was the spot; he was sure of it. The grass was crushed, and shoe prints marked the mud. He sat on the ground to massage his right leg and immediately regretted it. Now his butt was muddy and wet.

"How did you get away, Jess?"

"She let me go. Hannah, that woman. She let me go, but I think it was to lead them to you. So… I think I did exactly what they wanted."

The whistling from the road petered out.

"I should run another direction, Cole. They'll find all of us here and kill us. If I run—"

"No way. I just got you back, babe."

"They won't kill me. Not if they don't find the rest of you guys. This is what they want. All of us together, so they can catch us at once."

"But we're not. We're not together. Where the hell are Andy and Pelt?"

He crawled forward and led her into a new area of broken grass. Fresh footprints in the mud proved someone had been here minutes ago. This was where Andy and Pelt had gone after he left them. He couldn't figure out why they would leave the first spot. The key to a rendezvous is to actually be at the designated location. Pelt knew that. So, why would he leave?

"There was a struggle here," Jessie said. "Look. There are hash marks in the ground, and the grass is destroyed there, and there."

"What the fuck! I only left them for ten minutes. Maybe fifteen, when I went to get you. Who could've found them? Jess, are there others out here? Do the creeps have help?"

Jessie nodded. "She said they have allies around the area. But I didn't think... I thought she meant in town. Not so close. Not here in the swamp."

Fifty feet away came the crunch of grass breaking under a heavy weight. Work boots? Hezekiah? It sounded like it was from the other direction, but Cole wasn't sure. A reed broke.

"Can you tell where that's coming from?"

"That way, I think."

A commotion stirred the wildlife into action. Water

fowl took to the air and smaller creatures scurried into the water. A scream came from the same direction and then a shout.

"Shit. That's Andy." Cole stood up, and this time he pegged the right direction. He grabbed Jessie's hand and ran toward the commotion, no longer caring to hide. They broke into a full run over mud and through the weeds.

"Hey, wait. Look!"

Jessie yanked Cole back and pointed to a green light moving through the weeds. It zagged left, right, then stayed in place a second before moving again, twisting through the weeds. It was Pelt's glow stick snaking through the grass.

"Hey, that's Pelt," Cole whispered. "Where the hell are they going?"

The green light traveled faster. Now they saw Hezekiah in the dim glow of the skulls, marching straight for the glow stick. He destroyed grass in a determined charge for Andy and Pelt, pausing only a second to load and shoot an arrow. It whisked through the air and landed in the grass near the green light. That sent the light running forward again.

"What the hell, Pelt." Cole couldn't figure out what had made them leave the spot where he left them, or why he would use a glow stick. It was like a beacon. "Where are they going? Don't they know they can be seen? They can be seen from space!"

They heard a splash and then the light vanished.

They had dived into the lake. It seemed unthinkable, especially given his leg wound. Unless they threw the glow stick in the water. But that splash was loud, too loud to be lighter than a body. And glow sticks float, unless they're being pulled underwater.

Cole drew Jessie close to him. "That lake leads to the shack, but it's murder to swim. He won't make it with his leg all cut up."

"His leg is cut?"

"Yeah. Pretty bad. And it'll leak blood into the water. Aside from getting infected…"

"What?"

"Can alligators smell blood? Like sharks do? Because there's a big one in there. At least one that we know of. We fed it a dog, but it still might be hungry."

"You fed it a dog?"

"Yeah. That's not important. I'll explain later. Right now, we need to get to Andy and Pelt. If a gator doesn't get them first," he motioned toward the shadow walking fast to the lake, "… he will."

"He's walking farther out, though."

"That's not good news. He's going for the footbridge. It takes you to the shack, but a lot faster. He'll meet Pelt on the shore, if not sooner."

"Damn. Why would they leave on their own?" Jessie picked a beetle off her arm and tossed it into the weeds with a scowl. "How long did you leave them?"

"I told you, only a few minutes." He stood up and tried to see; now even the gravedigger had disappeared into the darkness. "I heard a scream before. Maybe something happened to the kid. Stay close to me. We need to get to the lake."

A small dirt clod the size of a quarter bounced off his shoulder. Then another hit him in the arm.

"Ouch." Jessie stood, too. "Something hit me on the head. I have dirt in my hair now. What the fuck else can go wrong on this road from hell? Is it raining dirt?"

"Psst." Andy crawled through the weeds. He threw another dirt clump at Cole. When he finally got their attention, he swung his arm wildly, gesturing them to come his way. "Psst. Over here."

"Andy?"

Cole and Jessie fell back to the ground and crawled toward him. "Where's Pelt?"

"C'mon. Quick." Andy crawled in the opposite direction, leading them away from the lake; they did their best to keep up. The kid was amazingly agile, like a rabbit in the weeds.

Six yards up, Pelt was resting against a rotting log that didn't smell or look inviting. A six-inch centipede crawled over its trunk and ducked inside its hollow interior. Pelt was in so much pain, he was oblivious to the critters around him.

"Here you are," Cole said. "Why did you move? That was stupid. We almost lost you."

"Gator," Andy said. "We got attacked."

"What the—"

"It was small," Pelt said. "We got rid of it, but it bit

Andy."

"It bit him?" Jessie examined Andy from head to toe. "It bit you? Where?"

Andy showed them his right sneaker. It was torn and chewed, but he seemed unharmed. His foot wasn't even bleeding.

Pelt explained what had happened to them. "Small gator, two-footer, startled us and I think we scared it. I think that's why it bit Andy's shoe. I stabbed it a few times with the glow stick. When it got bent, it lit up."

"Glow sticks light when you bend them," Cole said to Jessie.

"Did you just explain to me a glow stick? I know what a glow stick is, Cole. I've been to concerts."

"Sorry. They're actually not meant for concerts, but never mind."

"Anyway," Pelt continued, "the stick got jammed in its mouth, caught in its teeth, I guess. It took off mad as hell. I don't know where it is now."

"It went for a swim," Cole said. "We saw it and thought it was you. And I think it did us a favor. That guy went after it."

"Really?" Andy asked. "Hezekiah left?"

"He's not gone, but he went toward the lake, out to the island. To the shack Zach and I found. It's pretty far."

"Where is Zach?" Jessie asked.

All three shared an uncomfortable look. Cole still felt guilty about letting him go. He took her hand.

"He went for help, Jessie."

"What do you mean?"

"He ran. He ran for the highway. He's gonna try to find help for us. That's the only way we're gonna get out of here alive. Otherwise…"

"I know," said Jessie. "There's no way off this road. Hannah, the way she talks, she knows we can't leave. That's why she let me go."

"Yeah, how did you escape, anyway?" Cole asked. "I couldn't believe it when I saw you outside on the road. We were working on a plan to get you out."

"She just let me go."

"Just like that?"

"Yeah. 'Cause I get the feeling she knew we couldn't go anywhere. Like letting a bird out of a cage into an aviary. It's just a bigger cage. They're arrogant. She is, anyway."

"What do you mean?"

"Like she knows we can't get away. She knows her brother will catch us eventually and there's no way to get off this road."

"She's wrong," said Pelt. "Zach will be back tomorrow with help. He's a good runner. And he's smart. He'll find someone to take him to the cops."

"Gotta be state or FBI," Andy said.

"Why?"

"Local cops are all *crupted*. They don't care. They won't come and help us none."

"You mean *corrupted?* Corrupt?"

Andy nodded.

"Zach's smart. He'll hit the highway," Pelt said. "He'll go to the State Police. I'm sure of it. I'm sure."

None of them were sure.

"What's the plan now?" Cole asked. "We need to hide for another day. The sun will be up in one or two more hours. It'll be easy as hell to find us when daylight breaks. We need to get someplace they can't see us or find us."

"We can go to the trees behind the church," Jessie said. "They're thick, not like the bare tree behind the house. We can watch the road from there and see if any help comes."

"I don't like the church," Andy argued. "They do bad things there. We gotta stay away from it."

"Yeah, he hates that place," Cole told her. "Been complaining since we were there and met up with that death clown, Hezekial, or whatever his name is."

Jessie's eyes narrowed.

"You're afraid of a church?"

"They do bad stuff there."

Jessie remembered Hannah's words.

He's a demon. And so is his mother. There are things even demons fear… some of those things are here, on Gravedigger Road.

"You know so much about Hannah and Hezekiah. And you're afraid of a simple church. What's up with that?"

You put this salt in the hand of young Andras. When you don't like what happens next, you come find me.

Jessie grabbed Andy's hand with the one still holding the salt. She clenched his in hers and ground the salt into his palm. His eyes widened in fear. He tried to back away, but she held him tight. She squeezed harder.

"Oww," he cried. "That hurts. You're crunching my hand." Andy looked to Cole for help.

"What the fuck, Jess?" Cole tried to separate their hands but couldn't. "What are you doing?"

"Ouch! Dammit! That stung." Andy wrested himself from Jessie and slapped the back of his neck, then his arms. He seemed to be having a fit.

"That salt hurt you, didn't it?" Jessie hissed. "Shit! Hannah was right about you. Salt burns you. Doesn't it? Doesn't it!"

Andy backed away from her.

She swore she heard him growl.

CHAPTER 26

Andy saw a bit of Hannah in Jessie, and it scared him. He knew what was happening here. Hannah had given her the salt. It was a test. But it wasn't the test Jessie thought it was. He had learned a lot from his mother; even more as Hannah's prisoner. This was part of her initiation.

Andy backed farther away from her and rubbed his neck. A three-inch grass spider crawled down his arm. He swatted it into the weeds where it crawled away and became one with the swamp again. Andy glared at Jessie and kept massaging his neck.

"Salt? No. Your hand was hurting me. You squeezed too tight. And then a spider bit my neck. Look. It burns."

Cole checked the red marks on the back of Andy's neck. Two tiny bumps. "Yep. He was bit alright. Looks painful. I don't know anything about grass spiders. Are they deadly?"

"No, but they hurt like hell." Andy slapped his arms to make sure no more spiders were on him. "What was that bullshit about salt? Are you one of *them* now?"

Andy looked ready to fight. He backed away with

the look of a cornered dog. His eyes shifted between her and Cole to see which way the older boy's support would roll. He clenched a fist in case she attacked him again. Small as he was, he could take down most adults—or at least make them earn it.

"Chill, she's not one of them," Cole said. "Shit, Jess! What's wrong with you?"

"Yeah, Jessie!" Pelt extended a protective arm around Andy and shepherded him further from her. "What the fuck? Have you lost your mind? The kid's been through enough today."

"I'm sorry. I'm… sorry." She looked at the last two grains of salt stuck to the sweat on her hand, a solid clump. "You don't know… She got into my head. It's confusing, you know?"

Andy rushed forward and slapped his hand on hers; he rubbed hard against her palm. "Satisfied now? I didn't turn into no werewolf!" He backed away again and shrank behind Pelt.

"I never said you would." Jessie clapped her hands to rid them of the last of the salt. "It's like brainwashing, you know? Hannah got into my head. That's all. You don't know what it was like in there. She kept talking to me. Asking me questions." She looked back and forth between them. "It was hard to think straight. And they gave me a drug, too. Yeah, they drugged me. I got confused. I'm still…"

I'm still confused.

Now Pelt looked at her with suspicion. "Drugged?

You mean you joined a cult while you were drugged? Can we even trust you now?"

"Yes! I didn't mean that—"

"Of course we can trust her," Cole said. He put his arm around Jessie and nudged her close. He kissed her forehead. "She's been through a lot today, too."

"I got mixed up. I'm not one of them."

"I know, babe."

"Stay away from me," Andy hissed under his breath. He walked to the other side of Cole, farthest from her.

Pelt reminded them they needed a plan. Arguing in the swamp wasn't the best way to hide. They needed to go to the church or find another place to hide. He asked about the shack again.

"It's a good place to hide," Cole said. "It's filled with bodies. And bugs. Disgusting, but we'd be hidden even in the day. Unless he looks for us there. But I still think he won't."

"You said he's there right now." Pelt shifted his weight and leaned on Cole.

"Yeah, he is, but he won't stay there forever. Not sure how to get past him, though. I'm not swimming in the lake again. Not after seeing the gator that ate the dog. No fucking way."

"We could do the obvious." Andy rubbed his neck again. The burning began to subside. "Hide in the graves. They'd never expect that."

"Put some mud on it," Pelt said. "That's what you do for a bee sting."

"Really?" Andy scooped up a finger of mud and rubbed it on the two bite marks. The burning subsided a bit and added a cool sensation; that made him feel a little better.

"That might infect it," Jessie said.

Andy shot her a dagger. "I don't need your help."

"Hold up. What do you mean hide in the graves?" Cole asked. "You mean bury ourselves?"

"Yeah. They'd never think we'd do that."

"Because it's crazy. And it's lit by torches, anyway. Even if I wanted to do it, they'd see us digging holes."

"Not go inside the graveyard part. We bury ourselves in the swamp across from it."

Cole reached for his cap again. *Dammit, still not there.* "Let's not even consider this. Guys, that's the worst idea ever."

"I hate to agree with him," Pelt said. "But I'm not gonna bury myself. Not even to hide."

The crickets sounded rowdier than ever now. Something had ratcheted them up. The mosquitoes had launched a new all-out assault, and it seemed grass spiders were on the prowl. This was the last place any of them wanted to spend the night. The thought of spending another day, possibly another night, sat like soot in the bottom of their stomachs. Nausea competed with hunger.

Jessie watched their bloated shadows wave across the grass—now barely moving as the breeze died off—and observed Andy from the corner of her eye. The kid still spooked her. Hannah may have lied, but there were many folds to this story and a deeper connection between the two, Andy and Hannah. And Hezekiah. This was more than an abduction.

There are things in this world even demons fear.

"We need to fight back," Cole said, all of a sudden resolute. "Fight them. I'm tired of being hunted down like a scared rabbit. I'm tired of everything here."

"Yeah," Andy cheered. "Yeah."

"Shh. Keep your voice down," Pelt scolded them both. "How the hell do we fight them? We slit his throat, Cole. We slit his damn throat, and he got up and walked away."

"Yeah. He did."

"That should've killed him, but he put a fuckin' Band-aid on it and got back out there. He's hunting us again. Like Jason fucking Voorhees. He walked away from death and got right back in the game."

"He's right," Jessie said. "Hannah told me he can't be hurt easily. He heals fast. Maybe it's like the reverse of an immune disorder. He can heal wounds faster than most people. I wouldn't believe it but... I saw it. There's something more to him."

"But the woman," Cole said. "She's not invincible. We can get to her. If we kill her, it weakens them by half. Right?"

"Or it just enrages the big guy." Pelt tried to reason with them. He didn't want to fight. "We shouldn't poke the hornet's nest any more than we have to. If we slink away, maybe they forget about us and we can move on. If we wait it out—"

"They won't forget about us," Andy said. Tired and weak, his voice cracked in a high-pitched squeak. "They came for me. They won't stop till they get me."

"Exactly," Cole said. "That's why we have to kill her. She won't ever stop coming after us. And then, we only have to take down the other one. Or maybe help gets here. The cops can take him. But first we go after the bitch. We kill her first."

Jessie shook her head.

"Kill her? Have you ever killed anyone, Cole? It's not so easy. It's… just not. And it changes you. I don't…" She lowered her voice. "I don't see you killing anyone." She looked at the others. "Any of you."

Killing changes you. I know.

"None of you can do it. You talk a big game, but we aren't… we can't kill her. We can't."

Well, maybe Andy. That kid isn't right.

I don't like him, but I'm not going to feed him to Hannah and Hezekiah.

"We're not going that way," she said. "We end this by being smart. Like you said, the sun will be up soon. We find a good place to hide."

"Daylight is the enemy," Andy said.

Because you're a vampire? You freak me out, kid.

Salt might not hurt you, but I bet a cross and holy water would tighten your skivvies.

"Right. We can be seen easier in day."

"We're going in circles." Cole ran his hand over his eyes and wiped sweat off his face and neck. "Fine. But I don't know where we're gonna hide. We're in the middle of nowhere at the end of the world. We're in the devil's backyard."

Jessie pulled her hair behind her head and begged the breeze to come back. "She said something weird. Hannah. She said Gravedigger Road doesn't stay here forever. What does that mean?" She looked straight at Andy. She wanted answers from him.

The kid shrugged. "Beats me."

"It was a metaphor," Pelt said. His leg grew angrier by the minute. He needed to sit down soon, but it was harder to stand back up each time. They needed a place to lie down for the day. "It means it changes. New graves. New people killed. I don't know for sure. But can we get out of here?"

Jessie still wanted to go for the trees. "We can hide on the far side."

But their time was up.

"It's better to—" Pelt stopped mid-sentence and gasped.

An arrow sank deep into his chest, just above the camera. It sailed through the air and pierced his heart with a powerful, sharp whisk. The *thump* on landing was louder than he'd have thought possible. His ears rang. He looked down at the arrow and clutched it with both hands. Blood gushed over his fingers and drenched his shirt. It oozed over his camera.

Then he felt himself slip down as he babbled, "That... too... the butter smell..."

Horrified, the others watched him spill backward onto the soft grass and mud, helpless to stop him. The ground fog seemed to part for him. The arrow remained in his chest, blood gurgled from his mouth, and—incredibly—he kept trying to talk. Nonsense words tumbled off his tongue. He described popcorn, how it was best when burnt a little.

Cole reeled back two steps, in shock.

"Do you... smell it?" Pelt asked. "It's popping... burning. I smell them. But... it's popping... too fast. It's nice... burnt."

Jessie knelt and put her hands on his face. She refused to look at the arrow, but the blood gushing from his mouth was worse. She made a pillow of grass under his head.

"Oh shit!" Cole snapped out of it and dove down next to him. "I can pull it out. I can take out the arrow and we'll bandage—"

"Don't!" Jessie said. She pushed his hand away. "It's in his heart, Cole. If you pull it out, it'll kill him."

"What the fuck do we do?"

But death was inevitable. Nothing would stop that now.

Pelt's babbling faded, and he stared up at the stars. And then at nothing. Life slipped away quietly. His eyes glassed over. Visually, it was an extraordinary show to behold, death reaching out and snatching life before their eyes. Extraordinary but chilling.

Cole's eyes grew moist. He blinked tears away and fought hard against the panic attack rising in his chest. His heart beat in his ears. Until now, death was something they could escape. It was a hard game, but a game it was. Now it landed like a hammer to the skull. It was real.

Pelt was dead.

His head lay at an angle on the grass with an odd quizzical expression on his face. There was a comical aspect to his look, which only added to the horror. Pelt was the first person Cole ever knew who died. For Jessie, he was the second.

Andy knelt down next to the body and closed Pelt's eyes. It was a peculiar gesture for a young teen. Reverently, he bowed his head and then let out a sigh. He had seen death his whole life. This was sad to him, but it was not new.

Cole needed to get them out of there. He swore not to let two more friends die.

"He knows where we are," Cole said. He wondered if an arrow was aimed at his back right now. Or at Andy's back! "We need to crawl away from here. Fast."

At the same moment, a distant pop exploded in the sky, miles off. They turned and saw an orange flare scream upward from the horizon. It arced and fizzled out. Cole knew the flare belonged to Zach. Only fifteen or twenty miles away, he hadn't gotten far. And he would only use it as a last resort.

Cole's heart broke. It was too much for him.

Zach, too, had been caught.

CHAPTER 27

The weeds became too thick to pass. Zach couldn't run through them, and walking was too slow. Lifting his legs to such a height with each step was taking a toll on his leg muscles. It felt like walking from the shallow end of the pool to the deep. He needed to get out of the swamp. It wasn't safe, but the only way he'd ever make it to the highway was to use the road.

Leaning north, he angled closer to the main road—such as it was. It was paved but hardly a center of traffic. After three miles, he met its edge but hadn't seen or heard a single car. The full moon shed enough light to show the end of the swamp grass. A few yards ahead lay the road they had turned off to enter Dead-End Road. Its paved surface was a lovely sight for his tortured feet.

A quick jog led him past the ever-thinning weeds to the side of the road. There he broke into a full run, breathing as he had been taught for marathons. He ran along the road's edge for two miles without seeing a person, a car or a house. It was desolate.

Eventually, he found a shack. Rundown and leaning hard to one side, its structural integrity inspired little confidence. He stayed on the opposite side of the road and ran past it as quietly as possible. Andy had said not to go to any of the local houses. Some were in league with the gravedigger's cult. No, he'd wait till he reached the highway and flag down a trucker.

Zach ran for two more miles. His legs were strong but began to feel the ache of the race. He had been running and hiding since that afternoon, from the moment they first saw the gravedigger. That was almost fourteen hours ago. Ignoring the pain, he pushed into the darkness.

Half a mile later, he squatted and enjoyed a ten-minute break, but remained alert for sounds on the road. That's when he spotted a beige object fifty yards ahead. It was hard to discern but gave off a small light, and he figured out it was an RV parked on the other side of the road. This sparked hope in him since tourists wouldn't be connected to anyone local. They might have a radio to call for help. Or they might drive him to the highway.

Or they might shoot me.

Waking someone up in the countryside at four a.m. was a risky proposition even if you didn't look like hell, and Zach looked worse. He rested his hands on his knees and panted. He poured a handful of water on his face to get some of the dirt off and thought about what he would say. Spitting out a rant about a lunatic cult capturing his friends, or a boy buried alive, might earn him a shotgun to the chest and a warning to move on.

Gotta play this cool.

Before approaching the RV, he took out Pelt's phone and turned it on. One bar. He dialed 9-1-1. The bar disappeared. It was worth a shot. He shut the phone off to save the battery.

His sneakers scuffed across the street to the RV, a giant house on wheels. Two windows to the left of the door were open, save for their tattered screens. A small light was on inside. It might have been a nightlight. Moths tried in vain to get at it. He gently rapped on the door. The cheap tin frame clattered. When no one came, he knocked again, harder. A shadow crossed the light and voices filtered through the windows. Someone moved a curtain and peeked outside.

The door flew open to a large man dressed in a white t-shirt and overalls. He didn't look like he'd just woken up. His hair was gray and disheveled, but Zach got the impression it was always that way. He looked like a farmer version of Einstein.

"Sorry to bother you, sir," Zach greeted him politely. "I need your help. My friends and I... we got stuck a few miles back. Do you have a radio? Or phone with reception? Can I call the police?"

The man stared down blankly at him, blocking the doorway. A woman appeared behind him, trying to get a look, and whispered to him.

"Who is it, Henry?"

"It's a young man. Says he's in trouble." The man continued to block the doorway and ogled Zach with dull curiosity. He blinked but didn't budge. He was examining the boy and considering his story. "He says his friends got stuck aways back."

"Well, let him in then." She pushed her husband aside and motioned for Zach to enter the RV. She wore a purple paisley dress and slippers with her hair tightly packed in rollers. Like her husband, she looked well over sixty. "Come on in before the mosquitoes get the scent and invade us like Alexander on Persia."

Henry stepped back and freed the doorway. He visibly favored his left leg, signaling an injury to his right knee. Zach followed the woman's lead and entered the RV. From outside it looked large, like a freighter on wheels, but inside it seemed tiny. He sat down in a small area of cushioned seats that likely served as their living room. He stared up at them and they down at him for a long minute, like wolves and dogs trying to decide if the other could be trusted.

He definitely hadn't gotten them out of bed and wondered what they were doing awake at this hour.

"Like I said, my friends are in trouble," Zach tried to explain. "Our car won't start and there are these people… who…"

He wondered how much he should share.

"My name is Henry, and this is Gretta," the man finally proclaimed. The boy's stammering was starting to annoy him. "Best you calm down and catch your breath. Now tell us, where are they? Your friends?"

"It's back on Gravedigger Road."

At those words, they exchanged a look with strange,

worried expressions, and he felt he had overplayed his hand. The name sounded bizarre and might scare them off.

"I mean, that's not what I mean. It's called Dead-End Road. A few miles back."

"Tell us what happened, son." The man's voice softened as if talking to a mental patient. "In your own words. What happened?"

When Zach started talking, words spilled out and wouldn't stop. Before he realized it, he was telling them nearly everything, even the ghoulish costumes of Hannah and Hezekiah. The kid they buried alive, how they rescued him, and the chase through the swamp. He left out the part about the drawers filled with bodies. That was an unnecessary detail that might make him sound insane. Not that the rest of the story didn't already paint him as a lunatic. Henry and Gretta regarded him without emotion or reaction. They listened intently until he finished his story.

Suddenly, Gretta jumped up. "Oh, where are my manners? You must be parched. I'll fix you some lemonade."

Thirsty, Zach nodded and smiled.

"I know this sounds crazy, but it's all true."

Gretta pulled a glass pitcher out of a mini fridge and stirred it with a wooden spoon on a small kitchenette countertop. "It all sounds so dreadful."

"How did you get here again?" Henry asked.

"I ran. I jogged through the swamp, then cut onto

ON GRAVEDIGGER ROAD

the road here. I planned to go to the highway but I found you first."

"Highway," Henry snorted. "No way you'd make it to the highway. That's not no cannon shot from here, son; it's far. What was your plan when you got there? Catch a bus?" He laughed. "Sounds like a half-baked plan to me."

"I guess I'd flag down a car? But maybe you have a phone or radio I can use?"

"Ain't got no phone. We ain't teenagers in the city, you know. We got a CB radio, but I want a little more info before we go callin' the cops in on this."

"I know it sounds nuts. I'm sorry—"

"Here, now you drink this and get your wits about you," Gretta said and handed him a glass of lemonade. "You're dehydrated, and that affects the mind. So, tell us, how do we find this place? Or how do we tell the cops to find it?"

Zach chugged the lemonade in one gulp. His hand shook a little from stress and fatigue. "About five or six miles back. Take a right onto Dead-End Road. That becomes Gravedigger Road and ends with the… you know, the graves I told you about."

"My goodness, you were parched. Here, have some more." She topped up his glass and put the pitcher on the small kitchenette counter. "Now tell us again about this boy. You say you rescued him. So, he's alive now?"

"Yes, of course he's alive; we saved him. Or he was when I left them. My two friends are with him now. And a third friend, a girl, is being held hostage. Those maniacs took her."

"Oh my," gasped Gretta. "Well, you catch your breath and finish your lemonade. We'll help you sort this out, right as rain."

"Anyone follow you here?" Henry looked Zach up and down, mentally frisking him. "You got no weapons on ya, do ya?"

Zach thought about the flare gun in his belt at his back. "No, sir. None."

"Well, the missus and I need to talk this over a bit." Henry gestured towards the door. "We'll be back in a spell. Don't, uh… don't touch anything."

"Oh, go on now, Henry." Gretta slapped her husband's arm and pushed him toward the door. "Leave the boy alone. He's had a hard enough night, seems. He ain't likely to break nothing in this dump."

"This *dump* got us all the way across two states, may I remind you."

The door closed; their voices became muffled and less discernible as they moved to the road at the rear of the RV. They were talking about the story he'd just told them. He could make out only a few words, but they mentioned the buried boy twice. They mentioned him by name. Had he told them Andy's name? He wasn't sure. Maybe he spooked them, and he'd be out on his ass in a minute.

Zach finished his lemonade—nectar from heaven to his thirsty body—and scanned the inside of the RV from where he sat. It wasn't fancy, but it wasn't half bad. They had all the comforts of a small apartment and could drive anywhere.

Then he saw it. The photo album leaning against the counter opposite where he sat. On the front was a photo of four people, all dressed in robes and made up like skeletons the way Hannah and her brother had been. The prickling up his spine ended with the hairs on the back of his neck. Trembling, he reached out and took the photo album. He flipped it open to the first page. Two more photos stared back at him with blackened eyes and ghost makeup. More photos of the cult—people in costume—filled page after page. Within it, he found Hannah and Hezekiah, their names written underneath the photo on the album itself. He felt his heart race. Blood rushed to his face.

They're with them.

They're part of it.

What if they take me back… or worse?

He ripped the photograph from the album and shoved it into his back pocket. The photo's absence left a square stain above the names penned on the page. He flipped through the rest of the album. His vision blurred as he searched for more recognizable faces. Then he started to feel dizzy; nausea churned his stomach. The album fell from his hands to the floor; he was incapable of supporting it any longer. His blurry eyes met the empty lemonade glass.

They drugged me.

It was after he told them the story of the road and the graveyard, the gravedigger in makeup and robe, that Gretta had offered him the lemonade. He had tipped his hand in the wrong direction. After freely entering the enemy's lair, he had told them exactly what they needed to know, and now they'd rush back to help Hannah and her brother finish off his friends.

I got help, guys.

But I got the wrong kind. Shit. Forgive me.

Struggling against the spinning room, he stood and staggered to the door. He slammed his body against it to force it open. Inhaling a gust of fresh air, he labored to hone his thoughts. The world beyond the door blurred into fuzzy lines. His mind strayed.

What am I doing?

Going... where am I going?

Get the hell out...

of here!

Outside, he propelled himself toward the front of the RV, away from Gretta and Henry. His shoulder slammed against the RV's mirror; he pushed himself off it and careened into the road. He wobbled and pinwheeled to stop from falling. It was the feeling of crossing slippery ice; he caught his balance, then teetered after two more steps. When he drove his body forward again, he toppled to the ground.

"I'll reel him in," Henry said with a heavy sigh.

"Oh, relax, Henry. He's not going nowhere. He drank two damn glasses full. Can barely stand up. Let him wind himself out."

Zach's mind went to a movie he once saw, *Invasion of the Body Snatchers.*

They're everywhere!

No way to escape them. They're all infected.

Am I a pod now?

Zach's mind slipped further, but he had enough control left to get his hand on the flare gun. He pulled it out, rolled onto his back and looked up at the stars, or the blurry lights he guessed were stars. He grasped the gun in both hands to steady its trembling. In his last act before losing feeling in his arms, he fired the flare into the sky. Its orange missile looked psychedelic to him and he smiled.

That was pretty.

"What in tarnation he do that for?" Gretta asked. "Ain't no one fixin' to see it 'round here."

The gun fell from his fingers and skidded on the pavement. Zach had no more feeling in his arms and legs. He was paralyzed. He couldn't see anymore, either, but he heard voices and the scuffle of feet around him. The last thing he heard before the world went dark and silent on him was Henry's voice.

"You take the legs. I've got his head."

CHAPTER 28

Cole crawled back to Pelt. He touched his forehead, felt his arms. He tried to pull the arrow out with one hand, but it caused more blood to gush. He fought the urge to vomit.

"We gotta go," Andy pleaded. "He's dead."

"No. No. He's not dead. He can't be."

With more strength than Cole had thought was possible in the young kid, Andy grabbed him by the arm and yanked him away from Pelt's body. He dragged him along the grass back to Jessie.

"Make him stop," Andy ordered. "Make him stop being this way. Crybabies get killed."

Crybabies get killed.

Her eyes dissected him. What had this kid been taught in his short young life? Who were his parents? Maybe his mother was a witch, after all, she thought. A child abuser is a kind of witch, a type of devil.

"Don't be so cruel," Jessie said. "He lost his two best friends." She couldn't hide her distaste for the urchin. Hannah's words hadn't left her.

ON GRAVEDIGGER ROAD

Cole pushed Andy away and stood up. He formed two fists. His body quivered, brimming with rage. Tilting his head back, he screamed into the air. He unleashed a horrible sound that frightened even Jessie. His screams sent a loon into flight.

"Get down, Cole. He'll see you."

"I don't care," Cole yelled through a flood of tears. "I don't fucking care anymore. I'm tired of this shit."

Suddenly, he broke free and sprinted toward the road, shooting through the grass. Without looking back, he crossed the road and entered the graveyard, where he wrenched one of the torches out of the soil and brandished it like a weapon. Its flame changed shape and waved like a multicolored banner of reds and yellows as he swung it through the air. He made a stand in the center of the road.

"Come on!" he screamed. "Come and get me, you motherfucker! I'll rip your heart out and feed it to you." The tears formed phlegm at the back of his throat and cracked his voice. "Come on, you freak!"

Hezekiah answered the challenge.

Having abandoned the bow, the gravedigger took up his machete and charged across the swamp like a rhino. His eyes were slits of yellow within the black that surrounded his sockets, his head bent with a steely look of determination. He had a purpose. There was no anger in his march; it was a cooler, more controlled form of excitement. An obsession. Controlled but violent.

The look said: *I'll kill you because it's what I must.*

Hezekiah didn't hate him. He'd kill Cole because it was his job.

But for Cole, it was pure hatred. Blind fury. A bitterness welled inside him and percolated into incredible strength of spirit and body. He gripped the torch in both hands as a warrior might hold a spear. In his mind, he would kill the gravedigger and end this now. And then he would put an end to the woman. In his mind, it was that simple.

But it wasn't.

Jessie yelled at him to come back, to run and hide with her. Andy cheered him on and begged him to kill Hezekiah. And Hezekiah simply marched forward with his eyes fixed firmly on his target, a straight path to Cole. He never looked away from the boy, never flinched. His right hand held the machete in a confident grip. No doubt lingered in his mind that he would kill this boy today before the sun rose. But also, no malice, no hatred, despite what they had done to his dog. Same as the four students, the dog was a casualty of war. He hated Andras, but not Cole. The killing would be merciful.

It simply had to be done.

He plowed through the long grass to Cole, only twice hacking the stalks aside. The fog swirled and parted for him. It appeared to recede from his feet, giving him a wide berth. The painted gravedigger inspired fear even in the elements.

When the two met in the middle of the road, Hezekiah swung his machete first. He was stronger, but

ON GRAVEDIGGER ROAD

Cole was faster. Or luckier. He dodged the blade and smacked his torch against the side of the man's head. Hezekiah grunted and wiped blood from his ear without taking his eyes off Cole.

Hezekiah swung again and Cole met the blade with the torch handle in a furious stroke that deflected it away from him. Cole threw his body forward; the torch slammed into Hezekiah's head once more and sent him to the ground. Instantly, Cole was on top of him. Using the pointed end of the torch, he drove down with both hands and shoved it into Hezekiah's chest. He tried to spear him through, but the point barely pierced the skin before the stronger man caught it with his free hand and shoved upward, throwing Cole off with ease. Hezekiah's strength was almost supernatural.

The two rose to their feet and squared off again. For the moment, Hezekiah's cold poise was no match for Cole's anger, but it wouldn't last long. Hezekiah was better at this. And he was biding his time.

Angry, Cole drove forward, swinging the torch. The flame spun through the air and singed the gravedigger's skin, as Cole hammered it into his neck, head and shoulder. He struck again and again. Hezekiah scarcely flinched. When he'd had enough, he raised his machete to meet the torch, first blocking it, then hacking it in two. It only took two swings. The torch's pole splintered in half.

Cole backed away to catch his breath. His heart pounded. He held both pieces of the broken torch, the flame in his right hand and the spear in his left. He waved the flame end at his opponent and screamed.

"Come on, fucker! Come get it!"

Hezekiah did not respond. He stared at Cole and tracked his movements, but his machete stayed at his side, and he remained in place. Cole hopped from foot to foot like a boxer, taunting him, but still the man did not move.

"Come on! Come get me, you asshole!"

Cole was a tightly wound mass of nerves, tattered and unraveled. He had released all his pent-up anger and frustration at once, and now he resembled a coke addict bouncing around the road. Half from fear, half from frustration, he didn't want this fight to continue. Even if it meant his death, he wanted it over. He wanted this nightmare to be done—regardless of the outcome.

At that moment, Hannah came out of the shadows and stood ten feet from the graveyard torches, shotgun in her arms. She lifted its barrel and aimed. Not at Cole, her target was Andy. She aimed it at the boy who was still cheering for Cole and getting dangerously close to the road.

"Fuck!" Cole saw then that he had been the bait. Andy and Jessie were both right. These people had never wanted him or his friends. They wanted to kill Andy. That's what they'd needed all along, and he had fallen for their trick. But Hannah was too far away to stop her.

"Andy, come here!" Jessie shouted.

"Run!" Cole screamed. "Jess, take Andy and run. Get out of here."

ON GRAVEDIGGER ROAD

Hezekiah made his move. He put one foot forward and swung his machete into Cole's left shoulder. Blood spurted into Cole's face, and he dropped the sharp end of the torch. He swung the flame end to block the next strike of the machete. Both instruments clashed. Then they clashed again.

The collision sent pain up Cole's shoulder. He backed away and looked down at his arm, slick and red with blood. Jessie screamed, but it didn't register. Andy shouted something, but that didn't come through, either. His ears rang. He looked up to see Hezekiah hammer the machete again; Cole blocked it but fell back. He stumbled to the ground, skinning his elbows, then scrambled backward, crab-crawling away until he got back to his feet.

Hannah cocked the shotgun and put Andy in her sights. Hezekiah inhaled deeply for a final charge. For Andy and Cole, at least, the world rested on a thin rope, frayed to a single strand. Death is sometimes as close as the next breath.

Until the next breath is interrupted.

The roar of a dragon bore down on them with two fiery eyes, blindingly bright. It was the headlights of an RV racing down the road at well over 90 mph, its engine revving. Both Cole and Hezekiah turned to face it and jumped to opposite sides of the road to avoid being crushed by its front grill. The beast screeched to a halt, sending its frame shifting forward on its wheels.

A woman hopped out of the passenger side. She had rollers in her hair and a map in her hand.

"I'm sorry to bother you. We are just as lost as June bugs in March. Can you look at my map?"

She reached behind her, but not for another map. It was a pistol. She aimed it at Hezekiah and fired twice. His shoulder jerked to the left. One bullet to the arm and one to the heart; the force of a third threw him onto his back in the middle of the road.

Hannah fired the shotgun at Andy and nicked his shoulder, spinning him to the ground. Then she swiveled toward the woman, but it was too late. A man was halfway out of the cab with both hands on a revolver; he had her in his sights and pulled the trigger. He missed her heart but hit the gun, sending it out of her hands and to the ground. He fired again, and so did the woman in rollers, but Hannah had already slunk back into the shadows. The woman moved like a ghost. If she had been hit, they didn't know it.

Andy picked himself off the ground—his resilience a privilege reserved only for the youth—and ran into the road to the woman at the RV. Jessie warned him to come back, but he ran on and looked like he might attack her. Instead, he hugged her.

"Aunt Gretta! You came."

"Of course we came, darlin'. Now where's your mama at?"

Andy broke the hug and pointed toward the graves with the tree branch crosses. "They buried her yesterday. Or day before. What day is it?"

The man had been squinting into the darkness and

fired one more bullet toward the house. "She's run off," he muttered and rounded the RV. "Gone but not a goner. Keep your peepers peeled."

"Let me look at that gash on ya." Gretta fussed over the light wound on Andy's shoulder. His brand-new Bud's Gator Museum shirt was torn but his skin was lightly scraped with only a small smudge of blood. "You'll be fine, but I want to douse it good with alcohol. Give you a once-over."

"Cole's hurt worse."

Cole still held the flaming torch. Both Henry and Gretta looked at Cole as if seeing him for the first time, unsure what to do with him. Henry reached a conclusion and aimed his gun at the boy.

"Don't shoot them," Andy pleaded. "They're my friends. They saved me."

"That's not our way, Andras," Henry said. He kept a steady aim on Cole. "You know it well as anyone. No outsiders."

"Please, Aunt Gretta," Andy tugged on her sleeve. "Don't kill my friends."

Gretta looked down at Andy's small face and brushed the hair from his big doll-like eyes. She held his cheeks in her hands and kissed his forehead. "I'm too soft on ya."

Henry exchanged looks with Gretta, who nodded. He lowered his gun but eyed Cole warily. Jessie ran through the grass and entered the road with her hands up. When there was no visible objection from Henry, she cautiously went to Cole and hugged him.

"Are you okay?" Jessie asked Cole. Blood from his arm stained her shirt. "You got cut really bad."

"I'm alive. My arm's fine."

"You're lucky he didn't skin you alive," Henry said. He ambled toward them with a slight limp. "You two have landed in the middle of a blood feud older than the hills. And you best be on your way out of it, if Andy will vouch for ya."

"They're my friends," Andy said. "They saved me. Please let them go."

"Well, then you better make tracks like lightning. A world of hurt is about to come raining down on this road. You don't want to be a part of it. Trust me."

Cole agreed. "I'd like nothing better. But our car is missing some parts. We're stuck. Can you get us out of here?"

Henry shook his head. "You can't go with us, son."

Andy ran to Hezekiah's body and shoved his skinny arm deep inside one of the man's pants pockets, despite his aunt's objections. He pulled out a few coins, then plunged into the man's other front pocket.

"Get away from there, Andras! He could rise up any minute now!"

Andy produced a set of keys on a plain gold ring and smiled, triumphant in his discovery. He trotted them over to Cole and placed them in his hand. His small fingers held onto Cole's.

"Take his truck. It's a piece of garbage, but it'll get

you away from here."

Cole squeezed the boy's hand, then held up the keys, a set of three that jangled. He wondered what the other two keys fit. Boxes with dead bodies? Potions containing eye of newt? He didn't want to know.

"Go on then," Henry prodded. "Get out of here quick. No need for you all to dawdle no more. We got work to do here, and you're plain in the way."

Gretta's voice was less harsh. "You kids have had a rough night. You best get on home now."

What about Pelt?

Cole gazed out at the swamp. Pelt's body lay there. Should he mention it? Should they take it with them? Or leave it for the cops to collect? Probably best for the police or FBI.

Andy read his thoughts.

"No time to get Pelt. He's gone now. I liked him, but he ain't with us no more. Please leave before Hannah comes back with her friends. Or before my aunt and uncle change their mind."

He pushed them toward the truck. Cole nodded to Jessie and walked to the driver's side. The door opened with a haunting groan. He slid behind the wheel and put the key into the ignition. It rattled to a start as soon as Jessie took the passenger seat. She was moving on autopilot, vaguely aware of her actions. She and Cole had absorbed a lifetime of trauma in one night.

The engine knocked badly as Cole put the manual gear shift into reverse. He'd never driven a manual before, but his dad had taught him how to drive a riding lawnmower when he was ten. This was close enough. With a tap on the gas, the truck reversed out of the driveway. He maneuvered carefully around the RV and Hezekiah's body.

Henry sidled up to the driver's side window, and Cole rolled it down.

"Piece of advice," said Henry. "You'll want to go straight to the cops. Don't. This fight ain't got nothing to do with you. My advice is to go home and forget you ever saw this place."

"We lost two friends," Cole said. "Their parents will want answers."

"Well, be that as it may, at the very least do not go to the local police. They'll be more trouble than help. Wait till you get to the next state up. Go north. If you feel you need to report this, do it far from here."

"Yes, sir."

Andy raised himself on his toes to make himself taller and extended his small hand. Cole slapped it in a goodbye high-five.

"Take care, Cole," Andy said. "I'm real sorry about Pelt and Zach. I liked them both."

"I know. Take care, little man."

Andy did not acknowledge Jessie, and likewise she remained quiet. The two were never destined to be good friends. She waved to Gretta as they drove away, and Gretta returned a tenuous wave of her own. The truck jounced over the road, sputtering wildly. It shook as if it might fall apart, but it didn't. It held together and carted them off the dead-end road. The two adults and their small nephew Andy grew smaller and smaller in the rearview mirror.

As Cole looked forward, the sun began to rise with a tiny spark of light. A cruel irony.

CHAPTER 29

With Cole and Jessie out of the way, Henry weighed the mess around them and contemplated the quickest fix. He picked up the broken torch and tossed it away from the RV; it was too close for comfort. Then he ambled to the RV and fetched a shovel.

"Where's your mother buried?" he asked Andy. "Time to dig her up."

"Over here." Andy scampered over the graves and pointed to where his mom had been planted. "Here, here. She's under here."

Gretta gestured toward Hezekiah. "What about him?"

Henry shot two more rounds into Hezekiah's body —one in the leg and one in the chest. "That'll hold him for a few hours. Maybe more."

He stepped respectfully around the graves to where his nephew was still hopping up and down, pointing to his mother's plot. Henry stabbed the shovel into the dirt —now turned to mud from the rain—and sloshed it to the side. He formed mounds to the left and right, digging deeper while Andy looked on impatiently. Eventually,

Andy dove in with his own two hands to help ferry the mud aside. Gretta held her gun ready and patrolled the four corners of the graveyard in case Hannah returned.

By the time Henry's shovel scraped the burlap cloth surrounding Andy's mother, the sun was on the eastern horizon and swelling by the minute. Something stirred inside the grave, and Andy jumped in to help his mother out. She fought to remove the burlap and screamed as the salt burned her skin. Andy's hands worked fast to brush it off her.

"Help me," she croaked. Her voice grated like sandpaper.

Henry dropped the shovel and grabbed her under the arms. He dragged her free of the grave while Andy continued to brush the salt and dirt off her. Gretta tossed her a bottle of water, which she downed in one gulp. Her dress soiled and her hair a dirty rat's nest, she rested on the edge of the grave and hugged her son close to her.

"Careful, ma." He pulled away and slapped his hands together to make sure he was free of salt. Then he hugged her again. "I missed you, ma."

"How are you doing that?" Henry asked. He squinted down at Andy's hands. "How are you touching the salt?"

Andy formed a crooked smile, pleased with his clever ruse. He tore one end of the tape off his left hand. It peeled off like a Band-aid. He winced from the pain of removing it, and some of his skin looked chafed and irritated beneath, but it lifted smoothly.

"It's *surgial* tape."

"What? Surgical tape?" Henry closely inspected the boy's hand. "Well, I'll be damned. What gave you that idea?"

"It was in the basement where they kept me afore they buried me down in the dirt."

"They buried you, too, honey?" Gretta asked. "You poor dear." She glanced at the house. "Animals!"

Andy's mother stood on shaky legs and brushed dirt off her purple dress. "They're vicious dogs, those people. All of 'em."

"You're a smart kid." Henry glowed with pride for his nephew. "Smart as a whip."

Gretta agreed. "He'll be stronger than any of us once he gets his powers. Two more years. And by the time he's twenty, he'll be eating the likes of Hannah for breakfast. Look! Your arm's already healed."

Andy's mother pointed to the body in the road. "Cousin Hezekiah won't stop coming after us. He's in with that bunch of cockroaches, tight as thieves."

Gretta spat on the ground. "Traitor to the clan."

Henry grunted. "Nothing we can do about him now. None of us can kill him. You know that. But for the moment, he's down for the count. Let's be happy we found you two, that's all I'm saying. Take what we got and go."

Andy's mother turned to the house and uttered an incantation in the dead language of her people. The door shook but it didn't come off or explode into flames. "Dammit. I was never good at destruction spells. No damn good at this crap."

"I'll take care of them, ma," Andy promised. "When I'm older."

"Sure you will, baby. Sure you will." She kissed the top of her son's head.

They believed he would be the strongest of them all, once he matured. They predicted him as the next king of their people, bound to lead them in the war against the angels and humans, like Hezekiah and Hannah. Andras would be hell on earth.

For now, Andy was only a kid. Like any kid, he picked up a rock and threw it at the front window. It cracked and left a spiderweb pattern in the glass. He started to look for another, but Henry told him to stop fooling around and help him gather their things.

Gretta went to her sister and rubbed dirt off her face, gave her a gentle kiss, and faced the house. She tossed fire from her right hand in a stream that ate the door frame and cast an orange hue across the porch. She recited a spell that sent fire up to the roof where flames devoured it. The house would burn from the top down.

"You're just tired, Griselda," Gretta consoled her sister. "We'll get a rose in those cheeks by week's end." She tapped Griselda's nose with a finger.

"I hate to rush you two, but we gotta go," Henry said. "Hannah will be warning the others in her clan. So… reinforcements might be here any minute." He paused and looked over the graves. "Anyone here we know? Anyone else we oughta dig up?"

Andy's mother shook her head. "They're all done. Bodies 'ave been down there too long. They rotted and their souls went on below. Nothing left of 'em up here. I could feel it while I was down in the soil. Nothing much left at all. A damn shame."

They spared the three remaining torches, left them burning and toted the shovel back to the RV. Gretta, Andy and his mom climbed inside. As Henry opened the driver's side door, shots rang from the woods at the end of the road. A bullet ricocheted off the RV's front bumper.

"Hannah."

She was lying in the grass with a new rifle—snagged from one of her secret stashes—firing at the escapees. A bullet struck Henry's leg an inch above the kneecap.

"Dammit! That's already my bum leg!" He shimmied into the cab and started the RV.

More bullets peppered the vehicle as he spun it into a wild U-turn. The frame rolled violently, throwing its passengers from their seats. When the turn was complete, Gretta hung out the window with a semi-automatic rifle. She fired a barrage of bullets into the woods and over the flaming house, smashing windows. To keep Hannah down, she continued raining bullets on the dead trees as the RV sped away. It rocketed up the road, bouncing over bumps much faster than safety dictated. Gretta stopped firing when they rounded the bend.

They left Gravedigger Road.

At the top of Dead-End Road, where Cole and Jessie had turned left, they turned right. They would thread the back roads into a safer zone and spirit their way across state lines. Their home was no longer secure; they had been found. Now they needed to find a new town.

"We'll take what we got here in the RV," Henry explained. "Can't go back to Sackville or even Janus, for that matter. We'll head northwest. Wyoming has some safe spots, nicely hidden. You need anything, we'll get it on the way."

He ignored the blood running down his leg. Later he'd extract the bullet and start to heal. Right now, time was essential, and they had none to spare.

A long road lay ahead of them.

* * *

Hannah slung the rifle over her shoulder and dragged herself up from the ditch. She assessed the damage with cold eyes: the burning house, the open grave, her brother bleeding in the road. Work needed to be done and with some urgency. It was time to gather the others. Those kids would draw attention to this place, and very soon it would be best it no longer existed here. Best to be gone by nightfall, at the latest.

A bullet had nicked her hand, and the wound would

need attention. Being human, she wouldn't heal as fast as Hezekiah; she'd need real medical care. She ambled to the back door and entered the house to fetch the first aid kit. Fire didn't bother her. She'd have ten or twelve minutes, at least, before the flames reached the kitchen.

Out on the road, as the RV was turning off Dead-End Road and Hannah was wrapping her hand, Hezekiah's right leg twitched. His fingers moved and clawed at the dirt beneath him, and his knee bent.

Sluggishly, he rose.

CHAPTER 30

Cole put the truck into first gear and pressed down hard on the gas pedal. The truck bounced forward at 30 mph. He turned left at the end of Dead-End Road and breathed a sigh of relief. It felt good to be off that cursed dirt lane.

"Can't you go any faster?" Jessie asked.

Cole floored the pedal. The truck jolted and sputtered. Its frame shook, and Cole could feel the vibrations in his teeth. They hit 42 mph. This road, though poorly maintained, was at least paved and not as narrow as Dead-End Road. Potholes marred the aging asphalt surface, but it was a straight shot after a light curve to the right, a straightforward path to the main highway.

"This is as fast as it goes, babe."

Jessie tried her phone, but still had no reception. "I think we're still forty or fifty miles from the interstate."

"It's fine. We'll get there in half an hour. I'm going to slow down. This bitch might blow up." He eased off the gas and rubbed the dashboard with one hand. "Hang in there, baby. Don't quit on me."

"Don't touch anything in here! Those freaks rode in here."

"She just needs some care. I'd put her in second gear, but I'm afraid to. Barely got it into first. The gears stick like hell."

"*She* belongs to the freak show."

"And she'll get us where we need to go. Relax, baby. We made it." He pulled her hand to his lips and kissed it, but his eyes never left the road. They were the only two traveling this morning and had the world to themselves.

But Pelt hadn't made it out.

Nor had Zach.

Remembering them, he suddenly felt like throwing up. For Jessie's sake, he kept a smile and hoped she didn't smell a fake. He didn't want her breaking down into tears or a rant until they got to a police station. And he didn't want to collapse into hysteria himself, either. Pretending they were okay was the best way forward for both of them.

Blood had soaked his left arm; it throbbed badly. He didn't want to draw attention to it, but it was soon going to be a problem. "Babe. I need you to tear a piece off my shirt and wrap it around my arm."

She ripped one of her own sleeves off instead and reached over him as he drove. He eased off the gas as she tied it tightly around his left arm.

"That looks bad, Cole."

"I'm fine. See if there's a map in there."

Jessie opened the glove compartment and rooted

through a stack of papers. She pulled out a dilapidated map and unfolded it with great care. Torn in two, she had to hold the pieces together to locate the nearest State Police barracks. It was sixty miles due north on the highway.

They followed the road's winding path in silence, save for the hiccups of the truck and the extraordinary vibrations; it was a hellish ride. Cole wondered if he might lose a filling. He also felt uncomfortable sitting so high off the road, but he understood why the other man had liked it. A high perch made it easy to spot his victims.

"Is this a truck or a damn helicopter? Sounds like we might lose a fuckin' propeller any minute now."

"I don't care," said Jessie. "Fly us out of here."

She rubbed her bloodshot eyes and didn't want to open them again. Sleep called to her, but she fought it off. Cole might need help. Most of the drug was out of her system, but not the wine. A new headache formed at the back of her head and mushroomed.

"I'm just glad to be leaving. I'd ride a donkey to get out of here. Anything to get back home."

The truck was too damn slow. Cole tried to put it into second gear. He fought with the stick and lost; it slipped back into first. A rock in the road sent him flying off his seat, and his head hit the cab ceiling. After a few expletives, he decided speed wasn't the only problem. He slowed the truck down to 28 mph, worried the engine might overheat and crap out, leaving them stranded.

A glint of light caught his eye. A police car emerged in the dirty rearview mirror with its red and blue lights flashing. He gave them room to pass, but they stuck to his tail. A second later, its siren blared.

"Thank Moses and Mary," said Jessie. "Finally! We're saved."

"Are you sure? Andy said locals can be… unhelpful. Isn't that what he said?"

"Doesn't matter. They'll connect us to someone who can help. They're the police, Cole. They have to help. Right?"

"Right. Sure."

He wasn't sure of anything, but Andy had seemed sure the locals were bad news, and Cole found him convincing. *Crupted*, the boy had said.

Cole considered plowing forward to the highway, but this junk-bucket wouldn't outrun a mule. Reluctantly, he banked the truck to the side of the road, certain they'd be wasting their time with these hicks. He wrestled the gearshift into park and turned the key. The truck knocked for a few seconds before it shut down.

Through the side mirror, he watched the cop car pull up behind them and park a dozen yards back. The siren and lights shut down.

Instinctively, Jessie fixed her hair and tucked it behind her ears. She wondered what she might look like to them; how frightening and haggard her face must appear. And she wondered if the cops would believe their story. They were in a stolen vehicle, after all. She worried she and Cole looked more like criminals than victims.

One patrolman stayed in the car, writing notes on a clipboard while talking on the radio. He wore a wide-brimmed trooper's hat that hid his face as he bent to his work. The other officer exited the car and sauntered up to the truck with all the confidence of a shark in a swimming pool where new swimmers had jumped in for a dip. His hat and sunglasses were only outdone by the revolver strapped to his belt. This was his world. Small though it may be, it was his. Any guests were here under his authority.

On his way, he paused and examined the truck bed. It contained a shovel, a box and a scattering of loose soil. And a small streak of blood in one corner. Suspicious even for a gardener. Cole hoped the box didn't contain a human head. They hadn't checked before stealing the ride.

The officer finally made his way to the driver's side. The window was already rolled down; Cole drummed his fingers anxiously on the knob. Up close, they could see his uniform had a patch that read **Brayerville Parish Police**. The officer bent down and examined the inside of the truck through the window, gave Jessie a good up and down, then looked hard at Cole.

"Good morning, officer," Cole said. His voice cracked. He craved some water.

"Morning," the cop replied through a thick wad of gum. He flipped open a notebook and started writing. "Where you kids off to this morning?"

"It's hard to explain," Cole began. "It's a long story. Our car broke down… or I mean… the parts were stolen. Back there on a side road. We saw a crime, and we got chased…" He realized he was rambling and sounded ridiculous. After two deep breaths, he started again. "Sir, we need your help. We've been chased by a couple of crazy people back there. We witnessed a crime. A murder."

"Yeah," Jessie piped in. "There's two dead bodies. We need to report…" She stopped when it didn't seem the policeman was listening to her.

The officer finished writing in his book and looked up, constantly chewing his gum. His jaws never stopped, like a cow chewing cud. "You kids take any drugs in the last twenty-four hours?"

"No, sir," Cole said.

"Any alcohol? Weed?"

"No, sir."

"Do you have any alcohol or drugs in the vehicle or on you at this time?" He stressed the words *at this time* very officiously.

"No, sir."

"Do either of you have any weapons on you or in the vehicle?"

In the vehicle? Cole had no idea. He had to think hard whether anything on him constituted a weapon. Was there anything stashed under the seats? What did the gravedigger keep in his truck?

"No, sir. No weapons."

ON GRAVEDIGGER ROAD

The cop tilted his head to look at Cole's blood-encrusted arm. "You cut yourself shaving, boy?"

"No, sir. I was attacked. Like I told you... the crazy people. On that road."

"Uh uh. Crazy people," the cop repeated with a generous portion of ridicule in his tone. "On that road back there, you said."

"Yes, sir."

"Okay then." The cop took off his sunglasses. "Driver's license and registration, please."

Cole felt for his wallet, but it wasn't in his back pocket. He must have lost it in the lake or the swamp. "Sir, I lost my wallet. And this isn't our truck. We took it to get away from... I told you, there was a murder."

The cop settled his hands on his hips. "A murder? Where was this?"

"Back on Gravedigger Road. It's at the end of Dead-End Road. Back a few miles, you take a right—"

"I know where it is, son. I'm no tourist. I know every inch of this county."

"Yes, sir. Anyway, that's where this cult is. I mean, these two people from a cult, they killed my friend."

The cop chewed on gum and sighed. "Maybe you need to tell me everything from the beginning, son. Nice and slow. Don't leave anything out."

Cole gathered himself and his thoughts and told their story. The boy buried alive, the painted faces of Hezekiah and Hannah, the chase through the swamp, and the horrific death of Pelt. He ended with the RV rescue and Henry shooting Hezekiah with a handgun. That last part seemed to be the only detail the cop latched onto with great interest.

"Describe the RV, son."

"It was an RV. Like any RV. Beige. I don't know. It had a big back end. It was beige. And big." Cole tried to remember. It was the most nondescript vehicle on Earth. "How many RVs can there be out here? Just look for any RV."

"You get its license number?"

"License number? What? No! Why would I? I just wanted to get out of there."

"Well, son," the cop leaned in against the window frame, "if I witnessed a man shoot another man as many times as you said he did, I'd sure as hell want the license plate of that vehicle."

You weren't there, you asshole! We were fighting to stay alive.

"No, sir. I didn't get the number. I'm sorry." He squeezed his hands on the steering wheel in frustration. "You're missing the point. The other two are the killers. They tried to bury a boy alive. He said they killed his mother. You're... I think..." Jessie calmed him with a gentle hand on his arm. "I'm sorry, sir. I didn't get any license plate number."

The officer stood a moment and looked at Cole, sizing him up. It was clear he wasn't impressed by him and still thought they were both on drugs. Finally, he sighed and said, "You two stay put. Please place your hands on the dashboard where I can see them at all times and keep them there."

They complied, and the cop walked back to his patrol car. He leaned in and exchanged words with his partner. They heard the word "RV" said a few times. His partner got on the radio and talked again at length to someone on the other end. Then the first officer got back in his car, and his partner stepped out and circled to Cole's side of the truck. As he did, he also examined the contents of the truck bed.

"Sounds like you kids had a real interesting night," he called up to them as he checked the truck closely. He kicked a tire. "A rough one. A real fright."

"Yeah," Cole called out through the window.

"Well, don't you worry. It's about over."

When he got to Cole, he tipped his hat back and they could see his face.

It sent chills up the backs of their necks.

He had face paint on his upper left cheekbone. Black around his eyes, but white only on part of his skin, as if he'd been called to duty halfway through his prep routine. He smiled at them, a crocodile grin.

"Yeah, you can relax now. It's just about all over." He winked. "Morning, kids."

Fuck! He's one of them!

He's one of Hezekiah's people.

Cole swallowed. He tried to say something, but only a wheeze came out.

"Shit," Jessie hissed.

"Yeah," the officer said. "It's gonna be one of those days. But like I said, it's all over now."

The officer drew his revolver from its holster.

And he fired.

PART III

"The bones of a ghost are easily broken…"

ROD LITTLE

CHAPTER 31

The State Police Barracks of District 57 was arguably the least interesting in the state. Few daily arrests were made, if any, but they got some action once or twice a week. It existed primarily to process traffic fines and take complaints. This stemmed from their off-road location north of the interstate, far from any metropolis or border. On a good day, they caught someone smuggling in fireworks. On a really good day, drugs or guns. They patrolled the least interesting highway in the union.

Lieutenant Frank Millstone arrived on Tuesday after a long three-day holiday with his wife and kids at Holly Beach, a cheap resort in the south. It was boring, even by beach standards. He never saw the point. But it made his kids and the wife happy, and it wasn't Disney World. Anything that wasn't Disney World was aces in Frank's book. So, win-win. But today he wasn't unhappy to be back at work. It was good to be back.

"Afternoon, Frank." Trooper Lynn Broderick looked up from her paperwork. "You back today?" She glanced at her watch.

"Yeah. I'm on deck for the afternoon and evening."

A few other troopers interrupted their work and threw him a wave. Dave Winshaw was still pissed over being reprimanded about late paperwork; he merely nodded.

"How was the beach?" Lynn asked.

Frank shrugged. He poured a cup of coffee from the pot. It looked like sludge. "It's the beach. A bucketload of sand and water. And you know what else? Sand and water. Not much more you can say about it."

"Well, if you swim into a school of jellyfish, there's something to say about it." She tucked a pencil behind her ear and leaned back to have some fun. "Is that why you're afraid of the water, Lieutenant?"

"I ain't afraid of no—" Frank spat the coffee back into the cup. "Damn, that's toxic." He poured it down the sink next to the coffee station. "Make me a fresh pot, will ya, Lynn?"

"Sure, Frank. But you know women can do more than cook and clean! One day, a man's gonna learn how to make a pot of coffee and the world will shake in its boots."

"Only in New York or Boston," Frank said as he disappeared into his office. He came back a minute later with a stack of reports in his hand. "What's all this? You have a busy weekend?"

"You know, we *do work* even when you're not here, sir. The cat's away at the beach but the mice still protect and serve."

"Seriously, what is all this?"

"Sunday we arrested a drunk driver who hit a Honda and caused a three-car pileup. Almost—by a hair—almost caused an eighteen-wheeler to roll. Thankfully, he got lucky. But the first driver was drunk, so we booked him. He's still back there, waiting on his wife to bail him out."

"But it's Tuesday."

"Yeah. I guess she ain't in no hurry."

"This second one? Kid with no ID. I don't see a booking slip."

"Yeah. That one's a puzzler." She had filled the filter with coffee grounds and poured water in the coffee maker. Now she hit the brew button. "See, Frank. It's a button. Even you can hit a button."

"I think it's more than that. The filter gizmo and all that crap. I never seem to get it right. Back to this second file…"

"Yeah. Some kid we found by the side of the highway. Drunk as a skunk. I'm telling you, he reeked of whiskey as if he'd bathed in it. Out like a light. Could've been hit by a car."

"He was in the road?"

"Well, no. But not too far off the side. If someone had taken a notion to steer outside the lines, they'd have smashed him up into a pancake. Anyway, lucky for him no one tossed him. Still in holding back there."

"No booking?"

"Nah. Nothing to book him on. Technically he hasn't broken any laws. No law in *this* state against getting drunk, is there?"

"Maybe up in New York," Frank chuckled as he read over the report. The *or Boston* was implied. He hated northern cities. His thumb flipped the page. He could read but always preferred to be filled in verbally. He loved a good story.

"We're only holding him until he wakes up," Lynn said. "He mumbled a few words in his sleep, but no interview yet."

"You picked him up yesterday?"

"Yep. Late afternoon someone finally spotted him and called it in."

"Long time to be passed out." Frank whistled. "That'll be one helluva hangover. And no ID?"

"None. Only a few things left beside him, listed there on the report. Weird, huh?"

"Six shades of weird, but I'm not too worried about a drunk kid. High as a kite, I bet. Wonder how he got there, young kid like that. Fight with a girlfriend and she tossed him out of the car?"

"Could be. Good-looking kid, though. Must have been one heck fire of a fight to toss him out." She watched the coffee drip down into the cup. "If he doesn't wake up soon, I may have a go at him."

"Nice. Don't even joke like that. We need another lawsuit like we need another hole in the wall." He accepted the cup she handed him and took a sip. "Wonderful. You're a peach, Trooper Broderick. I thank you."

"Sure thing, Frank."

Frank shuffled off to his office with the reports. "I'm gonna sift through the rest of these. Knock if the prisoner wakes up. I want to question him. Or if the other one's wife ever gets here. I wanna meet *her*."

Lynn laughed. "Sure thing, Frank. I want to meet her, too."

Frank listened to the chatter outside the glass walls of his office. The inane conversation was normal. He wondered how many years it might take him to get command of a real barracks with real crime.

"They want me to appear in court tomorrow." Bill Johnson's muffled voice could be heard through the glass. He was always complaining. A pain in the ass, but good with computers.

"On what case?" the trooper at the desk across from him asked.

"That domestic disturbance last month. It's finally going to court tomorrow. The prosecutor is charging the wife. Can you believe it?" He sounded surprised.

"Well, she did shoot her husband."

Johnson held out his hands. "He's not dead."

"Oh, yeah. You're gonna be a great witness for the prosecution. Remind me not to call you up when my wife finally shoots me."

"Duly noted."

At four in the afternoon, Sergeant Rangsit popped his head through the doorway. "Hey, Frank, that foreign kid is awake. You said you wanted to talk to him?"

Frank looked up from his paperwork and took off his glasses. "No, I'm swamped with reports. You interview him. Find out his name and look him up in the IC database. If there are no warrants, let him go." Then he added quickly, "*With* a warning to cool off the drinking."

"Sure thing, boss."

As Frank handed the folder to Rangsit, a photograph slipped out, wrapped in plastic. He caught it in his left hand and straightened the plastic to get a clear look at the picture. It was a man and woman dressed liked skeletons. "What's this?"

"Ah, sorry, that shouldn't be in there," Rangsit apologized. "That pic was in the kid's back pocket. It should go with his personal belongings. I bagged it in case we found warrants and wanted a fingerprint."

"It's a Polaroid," Frank marveled. He hadn't seen a Polaroid in years. Decades.

"Yeah. Go figure. Some of his friends at Halloween, my guess."

"No. It isn't." Frank rubbed his thumb across the plastic and stretched into his memory. "I know this one. This man on the right. We had a BOLO out on him… what was it, maybe three years ago?"

Rangsit furrowed his brow. "Are you asking me?"

"No, dammit, I'm telling you! And if this kid's got something to do with that character… let me try to remember… what was the case?" He closed his eyes but couldn't bring the name into view. When he opened them, he almost had it. "Change of plan, Rangsit. You put the kid in Room 2. Have Johnson find me the case with this guy in the photo. Back then he was all made up like a ghoul, same as here. I'll interview the kid myself."

"IR 2. You got it, boss." He left with the Polaroid for Johnson.

Frank Millstone had been assigned the case three years ago, a year before becoming Lieutenant. He grappled to remember the reason they were searching for this guy. The character had a weird name, but that detail escaped him, too. He hoped Johnson could find the file.

CHAPTER 32

The room had stopped spinning, at least—and that was a plus—but he couldn't shake the nausea pestering his stomach. The smell of whiskey didn't help. And it was coming from his own clothes. He stood up and leaned against the bars; they felt cool against his skin. It eventually sank in that he was in a jail of some sort, but little else fit together. A puzzle with all the pieces cut wrong.

Shouldn't I be dead?

"Hello? Hello!" he called out through the bars.

Maybe this is what death is like: in a prison cell, left alone for all eternity.

He clawed his way to the conclusion that he wasn't dead, but he wondered how he'd landed here. He was sure death had been his next stop. But the RV people hadn't killed him. Instead, they somehow got him arrested?

This makes no sense.

A state trooper plodded down the hall to his cell, keys jangling on his belt. The man had a thick mustache and was heavy but not quite fat. That was still a few years

ON GRAVEDIGGER ROAD

away; but he was headed that direction for sure.

"Sleeping beauty. You're awake, finally."

"Hey, where am I? Why am I here?"

"Hold up. I'll tell the LT you're back in the land of the living. Sit tight."

"As opposed to what? Leaving?"

The man ignored him and meandered back up the hall, keys jangling on his belt. Fifteen minutes later, the officer came back and escorted him to a small interrogation room with a mirror on one wall and told him again to sit tight.

"Don't I get a phone call?"

"Nope. Ain't under arrest."

"Then can I leave?"

"Nope. Sit tight."

And with those words of wisdom, he exited and shut the door.

Zach drummed his fingers nervously on the table. He looked at himself in the mirror, a grisly sight. Bags under his eyes, hair uncombed, and his clothes wrinkled. He was probably the healthiest, nicest looking person, perp or victim they'd had in these cells in months; but to himself he looked bad. He combed his hair with a nervous hand.

Half an hour later, another man came through the door with two white coffee mugs. He looked fit and more like an officer of the law. There was no sluggish boredom in his eyes, unlike the previous man. A keen aroma of coffee followed him in. It was glorious and yet a bit sickening. Zach couldn't decide if the nausea was leaving him or coming back.

"Lieutenant Millstone," the man said and extended one of the mugs. It was filled with water. "You're at the ass end of one helluva party, I'd say. You drank too much, son. That's not good."

Zach drank the water in a single gulp and put the mug on the table. "I didn't drink at all. Well… except the lemonade."

"Yeah, well, someone spiked your punch, maybe, but you still drank too much. Here. Drink this now."

The second mug contained black coffee, the source of the wonderful smell. He sipped it, too hot to gulp, and inhaled the steam through his nostrils. It revived him. His senses began to return. His stomach even felt a little better.

"I had one or two glasses. That's all."

"You smelled like a whiskey bottle, son." The cop sniffed and wrinkled his nose. "Still do."

"I don't know why. Unless they poured it on me. Makes no sense."

"Who are *they*, son?"

"The people in the RV. I was trying to find help for my friends, and I found this RV. But the people inside were part of the cult."

"Ah. Now there's a cult. Interesting." Millstone sat back and folded his arms. "I'm listening. Tell me about this cult. Tell me what happened to you that landed you on the side of my highway drunk as a skunk."

"How did I end up here?"

"Like I said, we found you by the side of the highway. Drunk and out like a rock. My troopers brought you in so you wouldn't get run over or robbed. Or killed. Can we start with your name?"

"Zach. Zach Saetang."

"Where are you from?"

"Chicago."

"I mean, originally."

Zach frowned. He knew what the man meant but refused to make it easy. "I was born in Pittsburgh. Originally, I'm from Pittsburgh."

"That right?"

"Yes. Except now I live in Chicago. Well, except that I go to school in Pittsburgh. Again."

"You don't look American to me."

"My passport says I am. My grandparents are from Thailand. That what you want to hear? You gonna throw me over the wall now?"

"Relax, son. I'm merely trying to drill to the bottom of this fiasco. Tell me everything that happened to you, everything you remember before you blacked out."

Zach explained how he and his friends found the road, how they saw a man bury a kid alive, the chase through the swamp, the search that led him to the RV... every detail. The last time he told this story it ended with him being poisoned. He hoped today was headed in a better direction. At the end of his story, he finished the coffee and shook the last drop into his mouth.

"And my three friends are still out there. They need your help. And the kid, Andy!"

"I understand, son. We'll get to them."

Another trooper entered the room with two files in his hand. He whispered in the lieutenant's ear and handed over the files, then left. Millstone laid the files on the table side by side and flipped both open. The Polaroid was on top of the left one. He lifted it.

"These people. They're the ones who chased after you?"

It was the photo he had stolen from the RV!

"Yes. Hezekiah and Hannah. That's what Andy called them."

"Where did you get the photo, son?"

"From the RV. I think they were connected, working together. I'm worried they went to help chase down my friends."

"And you swear you never met this man before?"

"No. Never. Not before two days ago."

"This man was wanted a few years back for kidnapping. We never found him or the victim. You had nothing to do with that?"

"What? Are you crazy? Three years ago I was a freshman in college. I never left campus, not that whole year. That entire year I didn't leave Pittsburgh. You can check."

That made sense to the lieutenant. He didn't think there was a connection, but he needed to dot the i's. He didn't see how this kid was going to be of any use in the search for Hezekiah, either.

"Okay, son. I'm gonna let you go. You'll get your phone back so you can call your folks. I want you out of my state by tomorrow."

"What the fuck? My friends are still out there."

"Mind your language, son."

"Sorry. But you need to send a SWAT team to that damn road back there. They're still out there!"

"There's nothing there, son."

"Just send a squad car. Please."

Millstone leaned back and sighed. "We did. You've been moaning about that road in your sleep all day. There's nothing out there. We also got the Brayerville County police to help out. They're keeping an eye out for your people in the Halloween get-ups and for your friends."

"You didn't find them? That doesn't mean they're not lost in the swamp."

Millstone shook his head. "I'm not launching a swamp drain over the story of a drunk kid. You call your folks and go home. I'll bet your friends are already on their way back to Chicago right now."

"Pittsburgh."

"You said—"

"We go to school together in Pittsburgh. Listen, you gotta believe me—"

"I don't gotta do nothing but pay taxes and die, kid. Now, do you want to leave, or do you want to sleep another night as a guest of my station?"

Zach backed off. "I want to leave, sir."

On his release, he collected his possessions at the front desk, along with Pelt's phone, a water bottle, a granola bar and a handwritten note on a crumpled piece of paper.

"What's all this?"

"Those were on the ground next to you when we found you," the trooper at the desk said. "And the note was in your front pocket, sticking out."

Zach unfolded the note and read it.

Thank you for saving Andras. Don't look for your friends. Go home. Good luck.

That's why they didn't kill him. Because he'd saved Andy. And that meant something to the RV people. They knew Andy. But that hardly seemed possible.

Were they in the cult or not?

Answers were not in the cards today.

He used Pelt's phone to call his parents. He explained that they had car trouble, and that the others were missing. His dad paid for a rental car at a place nearby so he could drive home.

The lieutenant ambled out to the front desk to see

him off. "I'm keeping the photograph, just in case I need it. Seeing as how you stole it, anyway."

"Yeah. That's fine. I don't care." Zach gathered his things and looked out the front door. "How far is Budreau Car Rental from here?"

"Twenty miles. Give or take."

"Any chance of getting an Uber way out here?"

"I'll have someone drive you," Millstone said. "Lynn. Can you…"

"Sure thing, boss. I'm finished in an hour anyway. I'll drop him off and run by checkpoint two."

"Thanks," Zach said. He felt lost and followed her outside on autopilot. Nothing seemed less than a dream today. He wasn't sure what day it was.

Outside, Zach and the female officer were about to get in the state police car when Lieutenant Millstone burst through the front doors.

"You know what, Lynn," he said, scratching his head and looking up the stretch of highway they were perched on. "Never mind. I'll drive him."

"You sure, Frank?"

"Yeah. Yeah, I want to get out and get some fresh air. Too much paperwork today."

"Okay. Fine with me."

"Do that highway check and call it a day. I'll see you tomorrow, Lynn."

Lynn Broderick winked and got into her car.

"This way," Millstone said. "My car's over there. Sit

in the front, not the back."

Zach and Lieutenant Millstone drove onto the highway and Zach eyed him suspiciously. "You're not gonna kill me, are you? Beat me up and say I jumped you?"

"Holy Moses! You watch too many movies, kid. No. I'm not going to beat you up, lunatic college boy. I'm taking you to Dead-End Road. I want to check it out for myself."

"Really? Thank you, sir."

"You can get your rental car later tonight."

"Thanks. Really. Thanks."

Millstone said nothing. He tapped the Polaroid in his shirt pocket.

At the road leading to Dead-End, they both looked for signs of the RV. Zach pointed out where he had found it parked, and Millstone slowed down to look over the area but didn't stop. They continued forward and turned right on Dead-End Road. The car bumped over rocks and came to a halt five hundred yards down the road. Weeds and brush grew where the road had existed a few days ago. Millstone parked and they got out.

"What the hell!" Zach yelled. "This wasn't here before. It was a road. It became Gravedigger Road. There was a sign and everything. It went down a mile or two and there was a church and a small house. There's an island with a shack full of bodies. It… it was here. Down there. I swear it."

"There's nothing here, son," Millstone said. He examined the ground and kicked a rock aside. "You sure this is the right place?"

Zach looked at him as if he were suggesting they eat grasshoppers. "Yes. I'm sure. Are you nuts? I wouldn't forget the worst night of my life. It was here. I swear it."

Millstone kicked around more dirt, marched into the swamp a few yards and looked out over the expanse. He scrutinized the weeds for tracks or any clues, but there were none. It looked as he expected it would: empty. "Son, no one's lived around here in decades, maybe longer. I don't think a house or church was *ever* built here. Nothing ever lived on Dead-End except for mean alligators and loons."

"They were here. I swear it!"

"And you're sure it wasn't the drugs? Some kind of mind trip you imagined?"

"I wasn't drugged when I was here! That came later. I told you! I told you all of this at the station."

"Calm down, son. We've got a riddle here, and riddles don't get solved by themselves. We need to look at the facts." He took a few steps into the swamp, careful not to get his shoes stuck in mud. "Problem is… some riddles can't be solved at all. Least not in the way we think."

Zach kicked at the grass, only two feet high. It grew taller a dozen yards deeper in the swamp but no place above three feet. It wasn't as tall now as he remembered seeing it before, when he and his friends were running from the gravedigger. None of this was the same.

"This isn't right," he told the cop. "It was different before. I swear it."

"It sure doesn't look like you described it, son. And this puzzle is six ways from being solved. Your friends aren't here. No church, either."

"So, what do we do now?"

"Help me understand this, because those facts I mentioned are only on your say-so. Makes them shaky at best. And there's no proof here. So, make me understand how that is."

"I don't know how. But I swear everything I told you is true."

Zach paced back and forth along the grass. There had been a dirt road extending from this line, where now he walked on weeds and grass. Shrubs sprouted every few yards and looked to have lived there for years. All of it had taken a long time to grow, but he was sure this was a road two days ago. It wasn't a great road, but it did exist.

"This is where Gravedigger Road starts," Zach insisted as he drew a line with his shoe. "I swear it. There was even a sign on that tree. It led us to the church and the set of graves."

"Where kids are buried alive."

"No. Yes. I mean, I don't know who else was buried there, but there were a lot of graves. We only saw the one kid, and we dug him up." He walked into the grass along the path where the road once existed. He followed an imaginary line where, in his mind, it still lay. "There was a bend here. It led to the church. The graves. I told you… it's where my friends… where I left them."

"There's nothing here, son. I wish I could help you, but… there just isn't any road here."

"But there *was*." Zach fought back tears of frustration. Something boiled in him, emotions he couldn't understand or contain. Fear crossed with disappointment; a dam ready to burst. "And my friends are out there still. How can I make you believe me?"

The sound of tires on gravel got their attention. A Brayerville County police car pulled onto the short road and parked behind Millstone's car. A tall, slim officer angled himself out of the car and swaggered their way with his hands on his hips, resting against a revolver on each side. If Zach hadn't been with Lieutenant Millstone, he would have been afraid.

"Can I help you guys?" He was chewing gum. "This is a private road you're on, ya' know?"

Millstone saluted with two fingers. "Lieutenant Millstone, State Police Barracks fifty-seven. We're checking on a possible missing persons case."

"I understand. But we already got the call and we're handling the case from this end. It's in our jurisdiction. We been keepin' our eyes open but ain't found nothin' yet. You know, this swamp is dangerous. Best let us handle it."

In our jurisdiction were the words Millstone hated most of all. He took an instant dislike to the local cop.

Feathers officially ruffled, he raised a brow and grunted. "It's fine. I'd like to have a look myself, if you don't mind. All things being equal."

The Brayerville cop ambled closer to them.

"Well, truth be told, I kinda do mind. See, this is our jurisdiction and... well, you know, too many cooks and all." He laughed and revealed a missing tooth. It was the scariest grin Zach had seen since Hannah's. The local cop stepped closer. "We've got our county under control, Lieutenant." He said *Lieutenant* in the way Millstone might say *Commie*. The instant dislike was mutual.

Millstone returned a steely gaze, unwavering. He was not a man easily intimidated. This was still his state, regardless of what local Keystone cop said otherwise. "We'll have a look, just the same."

"Suit yourself. Nothing in there but gators, and it's gonna be dark soon. If you get eaten, I'm gonna have to fill out paperwork for days. So, I'm gonna call this in, if you don't mind. And make my objection known."

Millstone decided he didn't care. In his younger days, he'd have caused a stir. But he was more mature now. "Your warning is noted. I know my way around an alligator. We'll only be a few more minutes."

"Hmm. Your boy. You wanna catch him?"

The cop pointed to Zach who had now made it several hundred yards into the swamp, down what used to be Gravedigger Road. Shielding his eyes from the glare of the failing sun, he tried to find any sign of the church or house, the graveyard or the lake island. He hoped he'd see his friends waving their shirts as flags to get his attention. He hoped a lot of things, but none of them came true.

Briefly, he doubted himself. Had he been drugged two or three days ago? He couldn't even be sure how long it had been. Had it all been a hallucination? He wished, he really wished that could be true.

Millstone caught up to him and grabbed him by the arm. "That's far enough, my young friend. He's not wrong about the alligators, not to mention snakes, and some of them are poisonous. There's also pits you can fall into and be neck-deep in water. Then the leeches will get ya. So… let's head back."

"No. It can't be all gone."

"Son, I don't see anything for miles. For sure, no church ever stood here; the ground's too wet. It's not building-quality ground. It's swampland." He tugged on Zach's arm. "Now we've got less than an hour of sunlight left. I'm going back and you're coming with me." He tugged again. "That's not a request."

Zach scanned the horizon one more time, then gave up. He followed Millstone back to the car and had more than a bad feeling about the Brayerville cop. Zach ducked into Millstone's car and put his hand up to hide his face. For some reason, he didn't want that cop to see him close up. Maybe it was Andy's warning about locals that subconsciously clicked into place, but he didn't want to be seen by or hang around the local law. Suddenly, more than anything, he wanted to go home. Even if it was alone.

The Brayerville cop waited until they had left, then pulled out and followed them until he was sure they were back on the highway. At the intersection, the local cop turned around, and Millstone gave him the finger in his mirror. It went unseen. Zach didn't speak again until the rental car agency.

"He's in on it," Zach said.

"What? Who?" Millstone wasn't happy about any of this, but he had other things on his mind—real cases. He was ready to move on.

"That cop is in on it."

"In on what? Hiding a road and a church and a graveyard? You realize how ridiculous that sounds, right?" But Millstone had to agree this case stank. He wouldn't admit it out loud, but something wasn't right with the Brayerville police force. He never liked them. Today, however, it was a problem he couldn't tackle. "You drive home, and I bet your friends show up tomorrow."

Millstone stuck around to make sure Zach got his rental car, that the kids' dad's credit card worked with no fuss or problems. Before leaving in his rented Saab, Zach thanked him for taking him back to Dead-End Road. Millstone shook his hand.

"I don't have any words of wisdom for you, son. I'm going to admit I only believe part of your story. I could lie to you, but I won't. I think the drugs sent you on a wild ride and let your imagination do the rest. But I'll keep my eyes on the roads down here for anything out of the ordinary. That's all I can promise, at least for now. At this point…"

"I understand. Thanks again."

"Have a safe trip home."

Millstone escorted him twenty miles up the highway toward the border, then returned to the station. Zach drove home, nothing registering in his head except the yellow lane lines. He stared through the windshield and watched the rental car eat one mile of highway after another. Without a break, he kept going till he reached the suburbs of Chicago.

CHAPTER 33

Over the next two months, the gears of law enforcement ground slow but true. Cole's parents filed a missing persons report, followed by Jessie's parents and then Pelt's single mother. That got the FBI involved. The FBI task force combed the swamp that used to be Gravedigger Road, but found nothing. The Brayerville cops assisted in the search, or hindered it. Zach's belief leaned toward the latter.

The group's cell phone records were of no help. The last pings from Cole, Jessie and Zach's phones were from the morning of Bud's Gator Farm, at the breakfast diner miles before the farm. Zach still had Pelt's phone.

None of the missing students were found. It wouldn't be the first time students went missing in the Deep South. And no kid matching Andy's description had been reported missing from Texas. In fact, no proof of his existence could be ascertained at all.

For a few days, Zach was a suspect. The FBI called him in and questioned him for hours. But there was no evidence he had anything to do with his friends' disappearance. When people in their twenties disappear it's not the same as with a minor. The assumption was that no crime had been committed; that Cole and Jessie ran away to elope. Pelt joined them for some reason, and the three of them left Zach out in the cold. They drugged him at a party—maybe—but that was the only crime committed here.

Soon, the missing persons cases faded; they drifted from the top of the stack to the bottom. The cases became cold. Bigger, hotter cases took their place. Aside from the parents, no one cared.

In September, Zach returned to Pittsburgh and tried to focus his energy on classes. It was difficult concentrating. It was even harder sleeping, often waking up in cold sweats. He began seeing faces in the dark. His world wasn't coming back together, it was disintegrating. He started seeing a psychologist. She even hypnotized him. But when he told the same tale under hypnosis, she concluded the procedure had failed. It's hard to believe what you know can't be true.

In the evenings, he searched online for any new information, not only on the missing persons cases but on Hannah and Hezekiah. And anyone else who may have seen them or their cult. He bent over his computer, often deep into the night, chasing leads on anyone that matched their description. The leads always turned out to be Halloween costumes or pranks. His searches came up dry.

Until October.

Two October events, a year apart, would change Zach's world forever.

The first came that year on the fifth night in October. He woke up to find Hezekiah standing at the foot of his bed, whistling in the dark. He was dressed in his brown robe and skull makeup. The full horror. There he stood in the shadows, taunting him with his song for a minute and a half, as Zach lay paralyzed; none of his limbs would respond to his brain's commands.

Where are Cole and Jessie? Where's Pelt?

"Where? You bastard!" He found his voice, and that one came out loud.

Hezekiah's answer was blunt and to the point. He grabbed Zach by the ankles, yanked him out of bed and threw him across the room with uncanny strength. Zach landed in the corner with a dislocated shoulder and bruises all over. He screamed. True to form, the man did not speak. Not one word. But his eyes glowed.

Still unable to move, Zach watched him drip blood onto the bed from a cut on his wrist. Then Hezekiah dipped his finger in the blood and wrote the words "Seek No More" on the wall. The S was written backwards. He faced Zach and uttered a sound between a grunt and a growl. Finally, he descended on Zach and knocked him out with his fists.

Zach woke up in the corner, but his shoulder was uninjured. There were no bruises on his body or head and no blood stains on the bed. There was no writing on the wall. It was only a nightmare.

But it wasn't.

He believed Hezekiah had been there in some form. Maybe he stole his way into Zach's dreams to give him a message, or maybe it was a vision. If the man couldn't be there in person, he could cut into Zach's mind.

Seek no more.

Seek no more what?

Stop searching for you? Stop looking for my friends?

After that, he rarely slept. When he did, it was fitful and filled with sweat. He kept a large knife under his bed and another in his sock drawer. He was convinced the dream was a hybrid of reality. Maybe next time he could stab at the vision. Was anything impossible?

Nightmares continued to haunt him despite every drug he tried, downing everything from Xanax to Valerian root. Bad dreams persisted, but Hezekiah did not return in them. That, at least, was a gift. A better sleep eventually came—not every night, but sometimes. That was also a gift.

Stranger gifts were yet to come.

"Life is like riding a bicycle. To keep your balance, you must keep moving. —A. E."

Zach etched his favorite quote from Albert Einstein on the front of his school binder and read it often. He thought it meant one should not dwell on the past but look forward. Or maybe it meant to keep pushing on, keep trying. Either way, it spoke to him.

Though he didn't want to give up the search, his will was evaporating. Every month, there was less starch in his mission to find Hezekiah's cult. Doubts multiplied, even doubts in himself. Depression began to weigh heavy on him, along with the grim possibility that he'd never see his friends again. Depletion of the spirit happens so gradually, it's scarcely noticed. And then, one day, you wake up with no clue where to go or what to do. Or what the purpose is.

He was tenacious, but even the bravest, most steadfast man can break over time. Failure and loss can cripple the mettle of any soldier. And yet, he still had one small drop of will that needed answers. So, with a broken spirit, he plowed on.

Each day wore down the edges of his heart a little more, steadily dulling them. Until something amazing happened, something he never would have imagined. The impossible came to be true.

A year from Hezekiah's night visit, fifteen months from their ordeal on that phantom dead-end road, it happened. In the most unlikely place, he saw something that changed the direction of his search and revived his will to continue, instilling in him equal parts hope and despair. But most of all, it proved he wasn't insane.

The second October event revealed a clue.

And this one was big.

CHAPTER 34

Zach dropped out of the University of Pittsburgh in January before the new semester started. He couldn't concentrate, so it was pointless to go to class. Instead he returned to Chicago and, in February, started a job at a trendy café. By day he served caramel macchiato lattes, and by night he surfed the internet for evidence of Gravedigger Road or traces of anyone connected. Hannah, Hezekiah, even Andy. Any hint to what had happened in the Louisiana swamps that night. He searched for photos of any of the players or anyone dressed the same as Hezekiah. He even emailed Lieutenant Millstone, but it went unanswered. Maybe not the lieutenant's fault, he couldn't be sure it hadn't wound up in the police station's junk folder.

Life went on, dismal and bleak but moving forward. Progressively, he opened back up to the world, went to more events and socialized. He dated for two weeks, then went back to flying solo—best to keep the crazy to a party of one. It was hard to enjoy concerts or parties knowing Pelt, Cole and Jessie were missing and possibly being held captive in a dungeon somewhere.

I wonder what tortures Hezekiah might perform on them. Or that woman, Hannah. What might she do?

What are they doing now?

Had Pelt, Cole and Jessie been buried alive?

Buried dead?

He shuddered at the thought.

Still in possession of Pelt's phone, he scanned its photos, but there was nothing from their trip, nothing from that road. Pelt used his camera for everything; he rarely took photos with his phone. There were a few images of the group: a selfie of the four of them the day the trip began. Another of Zach and Cole together. Several of Jessie by herself. Did Pelt have a crush on her?

In a special folder was a photo of the water tower they'd marked with their initials and a fine Charlie Brown. The time|date metadata showed it was taken five years ago. Zach remembered that trip. The three of them went out to the tower after their first year at college. They were amazed the graffiti was still there. Weathered and faded, but still there.

Zach smiled wanly and put the phone away.

Weeks passed. He nudged himself into each day—there was no thrust left—and kept his metaphorical bicycle going. Often it teetered, but he stayed on. Spring turned into summer, and summer turned into fall. Within a blink of an eye, time had evaporated—it didn't stop to chat; it simply passed on. Each day dies and the next one is born to take its place. It lingers not a second longer

ON GRAVEDIGGER ROAD

than it needs.

In September, he enrolled in one class at the University of Illinois to keep his parents happy. Already he had skipped it twice.

And it was that fall, in October, that he saw the unthinkable come to life. But that's how the unthinkable happens, when and where you least expect it.

Two of his friends invited him into the heart of Illinois to the Moretown Pumpkin Festival. He agreed to go only to get away from the grind of his routine and the nagging of his parents to re-enroll full-time in school. Both would still be there when he got back.

The festival was bigger than he had expected, lively and filled with everything orange, autumn and pre-Halloween. And, of course, anything to do with pumpkins and pumpkin-related fodder. A Ferris wheel towered nearby. Styx played Crystal Ball on the radio, WROCK Peoria, loud and clear through five colossal speakers.

Of course it's Styx, it's Illinois.

The Halloween playlist blared as Folks waited for the band scheduled to take the stage. Zach wondered if it was an original band or a cover band. Or an 80s band with one original member. He didn't care, either way.

His friends gravitated to a row of games—darts with beanbags, and then bingo—and got lost in the competition. He appreciated their *joie de vivre* but declined and wandered off by himself. He examined a row of jack-o'-lanterns to be judged and browsed a few of the craft displays—some more creative than others, and a few downright weird. A cup of pumpkin cider warmed him from the crisp air. In October, each day was chillier than the last. Tonight, as the wind kicked up, it seemed downright cold to him. He zipped up his jacket. A million miles from the hot sweaty swamp he'd endured more than a year ago.

A million miles.

But it was right here, always. In front of his head. It occupied prime real estate in his mind 24/7.

Zach sipped his cider and smiled at the kids who played around him. He enjoyed the spectacles, the smiles and laughter of the attendees, old and young. And as his eyes grazed the crowd, he saw her.

It was her.

Fuck.

Oh fuck!

It was the woman, Hannah, her face painted with a skull pattern that ran down her neck—same as he remembered. Here amid the Halloween decorations, she was not out of place. To Zach, she was the devil incarnate, but the spectators were charmed by her act. He stared at her in disbelief, sure she was a vision or a ghost, a waking nightmare like Hezekiah at the foot of his bed. But this was no dream. She was real, as real as the crowd around him. Unless this whole scene was a dream.

No, man. It's real.

Go to her!

Hannah was seated at a table with tarot cards spread out in front of her. A woman sat across from her and held a hand over her mouth, suckered into a reading of her future. Her five-year-old daughter fidgeted impatiently as the reading proceeded. Hannah smiled her awful smile and turned the cards over. Spectators gawked and were pleased by each turn, every aspect of the reading. They oohed and clapped.

Zach's fingers tightened on the cup. A swell of excitement and fear washed over him. This is what he had been looking for night after night, and there she was! But… what now? What could he do? Confront her? Kill her?

Kill her with what? My bare hands?
Holy fuck!
Shit! She's right fucking there.

He had questions that she held the answers to. He needed to ask her what happened to the others. That much he could do. She wouldn't attack him in front of all these people. She couldn't.

Or could she?

Then he wondered if Hezekiah might be near. Perhaps in the tent behind her or lurking in the shadows. Behind him? Zach whipped around, sure he'd see that awful face in the crowd. All he saw were adults and children playing the arcade games. A child screamed. He scanned the crowd and expected to see Hezekiah sinking his machete into a woman. But it was a scream of joy. A child had won a prize.

Zach turned back to Hannah. He forced his legs to walk forward. He needed to go to her.

What is your plan, man?

Fuck do I know?

He kept walking toward the table.

And then his legs froze.

Someone had come out of the tent behind Hannah. A girl that looked like...

It can't be her.

It was Jessie. She smiled and handed a piece of candy to the child fidgeting next to the woman whose fortune was being ceremoniously read. Jessie laughed and touched the child's cheek. She looked... she looked happy.

How is this possible?

She doesn't look like a prisoner to me.

He stood there for an eternal minute, watching both Jessie and Hannah. The wind blew his hair into his eyes, but he didn't brush it away. If this were not real, he'd be better off. If he blinked and they were a mirage, that suited him fine. He willed them to vanish, but they remained. This was no illusion. They were as real as the pain in his heart.

It was only a matter of time until the woman would see him. He wondered how she'd react, what she'd do. Throw daggers at him?

But Jessie saw him first when she looked up from the child, and her smile fell. Her face became sad and frightened at once. Their eyes locked and there they remained for a year of seconds. It seemed like the world was spinning, and a lifetime passed for them.

Two kids, running and playing, collided into him and broke his trance. Hot cider spilled over his shirt and pants. He scrambled to brush it off, holding his cup away from his body.

"Oh sorry," one of the kids said, then both scampered away laughing.

"Are you okay?" a woman asked him. "Let me get you some napkins."

"No, I'm fine," he insisted. "It's no problem."

When he looked back at Jessie, she was gone. Crowds of people thronged in front of him. He fought his way into them; it was like parting a flock of geese.

"Excuse me, excuse me. Sorry…"

He forced his way through the crowd, but when he reached Hannah's table, the woman—like Jessie—had vanished. He rounded the table and tore the tent flap aside, then burst into the tent uninvited. No one. It was empty except for a few pieces of a costume on the floor. He rushed back outside and searched the tent grounds for either of them.

He called out into the crowd.

"Jessie! Jessie, please. Where are you?"

A few people looked at him, wondered what was wrong. Jessie didn't answer his plea. The woman with the napkins found him first and started dabbing motherly at his shirt.

"Did you see the woman at this table?" he asked her.

"She was reading cards."

"No, dear. Did you lose someone?"

"I... I can't find them."

He called out to Jessie, louder this time. After a few times, he even called out Hannah's name and was starting to attract attention. It didn't matter. He pushed the napkin woman away and frantically searched the grounds, running from stall to stall. That expression on Jessie's face haunted him. She hadn't been relieved to see him; she had looked upset, even scared.

She didn't want me to find her.

Why the hell not?

And where is Cole? Where is Pelt?

Jessie didn't look like a victim of torture. She looked happy helping Hannah. That seemed almost surreal, but it had been there, right before his eyes. You can't fake that kind of enthusiasm. She wasn't being forced into this; she wanted it. Two dogs can perform tricks, but you always know the beaten dog from the happy puppy. Jessie was happy.

Why? Why would she want to help Hannah?

What the hell ever happened to Andy?

Questions piled up like garbage on a collection strike. None were getting answered, and his head was overflowing. Any more and he might go insane. As he searched the fair grounds for the two women, he listened to the sounds, the laughing and screaming, the music. He swore—for only a second—he heard Hezekiah's whistling. It was that song he whistled while he and Cole were on the roof of the shack.

That shack full of bodies.

... had a little lamb... little lamb...

Later he would chalk it up to imagination, but at that moment it terrified him. If he saw Hezekiah, how would he react? How would Hezekiah react? Was the gravedigger here, delighting children with a demonic magic show?

Jessie or Hannah he would confront. Hezekiah, he wasn't so sure. He might just pee himself and faint. The air felt damn cold suddenly, and the fairgrounds seemed endless. What looked like a small venue on arrival now appeared to stretch for miles. He searched every booth and tent.

Zach stayed until midnight, when the last of the displays had been disassembled, the last tent rolled up. He found the lady in charge of the festival and asked about the woman they had hired to read tarot cards.

"Oh, none of the stalls on the right were hired," the tired lady said. She was helpful, perky in the day—he was sure—but exhausted tonight. "We hired the band; weren't they so good? And the arcade games and rides we paid for. But all the others are volunteers. The money is for charity and anyone can come and set up a booth."

"You don't have their names? Addresses?"

"Why no, dear."

"I wanted to hire some of them for a charity event in my town. Next month."

"Oh, I see. That's lovely. Well, you can advertise the

way we did online, but I don't have any contact information for most of the stalls on the right. Well, I do know a few of them. I have Betty Kenner's phone number. She bakes the pies. And I know Jim Benson. He sells the wooden clocks. Weren't they amazing? So much detail."

"But you don't know the card reader?"

Her face fell into pity. "I'm sorry, young man. Do you want the other numbers?"

"No. Never mind. Thanks anyway."

He started to leave, but she stopped him. "You're not really having an event, are you?"

"No. I'm not."

"You're chasing after a girl. I saw her. She's very lovely. Beautiful brown hair. I'd kill to be that age again."

"You saw Jessie?" So, he hadn't imagined it.

"I don't know her name. She was with the tarot card woman, the one in costume. I'm sorry, I don't know anything about them. I have no way to help you find her, but I hope you do. Young love is so rare and so wonderful."

"Thanks. Thank you. Have a good night." Head down, he walked away more depressed than if he'd never seen Jessie tonight.

He returned to Chicago and began a new search. This time he scanned social media sites for other festivals around the country. He tried to find photos of a tarot card reader and her assistant. Picture after picture flew past his eyes until they blurred—by one or two in the morning most nights—and then he'd fall asleep and dream nightmares of a swamp filled with ghosts and demons.

One night in November, he was searching the net when a beep signaled a new email. That was uncommon these days; he had so few friends left. His obsession had isolated him. The email came as a surprise and its contents a shock. It was from: jessitsme at yourmail dot com. It read:

> **Stop looking for me. The others are dead. If you keep looking, they'll kill you too. I am okay. Stop. I love you. J.**

He read the email twice, then replied as fast as he could type:

> **Jessie where r you? What happened to Cole n Pelt? And Andy? Why are u with that woman, Hannah? Tell me. Please. Tell me.**

The reply came back as a mailer-daemon. The email address had been closed, the account deactivated. He tried again and again, but the email failed each time. He read her email over and over. She wanted him to stop; she didn't want to be found.

Stop looking.

This made no sense. It was ludicrous.

Hannah must have written the email. It's a conspiracy, and they're holding her prisoner. Maybe they tortured Cole and promised to do more if she didn't cooperate.

But he knew that wasn't true. The look on Jessie's face spoke volumes. She was no prisoner. Happy in her work beside Hannah, she was not doing anything under duress. And that look: she was scared of him, of Zach. She didn't want him to find her.

Rejected and excluded.

Sometimes we're on the wrong path to reach what's needed. These are the toughest truths to accept. Zach spent the next four weeks unraveling Jessie. He imagined a dozen scenarios, but the only one that fit was the one where Hannah had broken open something in the younger woman. A layer had been peeled away, and now the two women worked in tandem.

Why would she work with a killer?

She wouldn't. Which meant some of what Hannah said must be true. Andy… that's who he had to find. He was the key to all this. The centerpiece. Zach had been looking in the wrong direction. He should have been searching for Andy!

He started a new internet search, this time focusing solely on finding the kid. That strange little kid who stabbed Hezekiah in the rain. With only his memories to go by, he faced a hard task. Pelt's phone had no photos of Andy, but Zach searched it again anyway and came up dry.

He heard Hezekiah's whistling a few more times. It came to him in crowds, sometimes at the mall or on the campus where he worked. Twice it came to him while lying in bed. He opened the door to his apartment, looked out on the fire escape; but no one was there. It didn't make the whistling less real. He knew he wasn't imagining it.

One night I'll open my closet and Hezekiah will be there. He'll stab me and end all this.

And that might not be so bad.

The thought didn't frighten him anymore. In fact, he might simply say, "Hello, old bean," and greet the costumed man before accepting his fate. As long as he'd answer a few questions first.

Fair trade, old bean. Tell me the truth first.

But no one was in his closet. Not yet.

CHAPTER 35

Zach's parents insisted he move back into the dorms, enroll in more classes and participate in school life. He didn't mind. In fact, he felt safer surrounded by people on a busy campus, even if his roommate was rarely home. His roommate's busy party life left Zach free of distractions to surf the web for Andy. And in January, Zach found the first clue to Andy's whereabouts.

An online news story broke about a twelve-year-old boy in Oregon who beat a man to death to save his mother. The photo was grainy, but it was Andy. No doubt. Zach followed the breadcrumbs to his mother who lived with the aunt and uncle in a suburb of Portland. In the background of the interview with the aunt was an RV. *The* RV.

"Can't run from social media," he squealed at the screen. "I've gotcha."

Twice more he replayed the video. The aunt tried to downplay the event, but none of that mattered. He took a screen capture. Now he had a photo of the RV.

He packed a single backpack and ran out the door. Thanks to his credit card, fast approaching its limit, he caught the next morning's flight to Portland, landed in the afternoon and rented a car. There was no need to rush. He knew they'd be gone by the time he got there—probably fled two hours after the interview—but the starting point would still be there, and some clues would remain. South to California was too crowded. They would want to be away from cell phones and cameras for awhile. That RV would be on the road north, further from the world.

People always leave tracks.

At the mall outside Portland, he spoke to anyone involved in the incident, anyone who might have known or seen Andy. Most people shook their heads and waved him on.

"I really didn't see much," was the answer most gave him, usually with a shrug and a look of pity.

His bag felt heavy, but less so than his heart. A cocktail of hope, fear and dread drove him forward. There seemed little chance of success, but he had to try. No thoughts of work missed or school unattended. None of that mattered.

At the shopping center where Andy attacked another man, Zach interviewed every shop owner and as many shoppers as would give him a minute of their time. Most didn't want to be bothered, but one man kept a close eye on him and never strayed far, always within earshot. Old and haggard, a cowboy hat keeping strings of gray hair from blowing away, he looked like a homeless wretch. And yet he wore a gold pocket watch he checked regularly. The man eavesdropped on Zach's questions until, finally, Zach confronted him.

"Can I help you, sir?"

"Yes, you can," the man said.

"You're very interested in my investigative work."

"Is that what you call it?" The man took out a pipe and lit it. This wasn't likely legal in the parking lot of a shopping center, but the man didn't care. "I thought you were looking for a lost brother."

That was his cover story. He needed to find Andy, but few people talked to police, reporters or P.I.'s. Maybe they'd talk to a relative. The big bro to an adopted little brother who ran away.

"Yes. I am."

The man chuckled. "He's your brother. You're Chinese. How's he your brother?"

"Adopted."

"Right." The man puffed on his pipe. "Can I offer you some words of advice?"

"Yes. Please do."

"Go home. Stop this nonsense. Forget you ever knew him and get on with your life."

Zach's eyes widened. He stepped closer. "You know him. You know Andy, don't you?"

The man shook his head. "Just go home, friend."

"Please help me find him. He might be able to lead me to my friends. We lost them last year. He was there." Zach started to grab the man's hand, then thought better of it. "He was there. He knows. He has the answers, or some of them anyway. Please, sir."

"He can't help you."

"Maybe he can."

"Go home, friend."

This man was a blocked road. Nothing would convince him to take Zach to Andy. Obvious as the wrinkles on the old man's face, he wouldn't help anyone find the kid. His mind was set.

But maybe he'd carry a message.

"Tell Andy I need to see him. Can you do that? Let him decide. I'm sure you people know how to find me."

"What people?"

"Just give him the message. Please."

The man puffed twice on his pipe. It was almost imperceptible, but he nodded his head.

Zach packed and went home.

* * *

The next day, after his morning shower in the shared dorm bathroom, he saw a message written on one of the seven steamed mirrors. It said "Seek No More." The S was backwards. More words materialized underneath. "And go not into the path of evil men."

Three other boys were showering, and another was combing his hair two mirrors down. Zach asked if he had seen anyone writing on the mirror.

"I didn't pay attention, man. What does it say?"

When the other boy looked, the words were not there. They had been replaced by a smiley face drawn in the steam. It drooped as the steam dissipated.

"Smile. Right on," the other boy said and went back to his own mirror. "Nah. Didn't see who did it."

Zach recognized Hezekiah's message, the same from the dream. Hezekiah knew. Somehow the man knew he had gone to find Andy.

Zach wiped the smile off with his hand. The message never returned.

* * *

Two weeks later, he came home to his small dorm room and found his desk lamp lit. He hadn't left it on. As his eyes adjusted, he made out an old woman sitting in the armchair next to the desk. Wearing a rumpled dress, she looked even worse than the old man, her hair a spider web of strings. Her voice was thin and reedy.

"Don't be frightened, Zach."

He wasn't. He put his book bag and jacket on the floor and watched her twist in the chair. Something was wrong with her right side. Maybe she had been the victim of a stroke; he didn't ask. Her face didn't look right, and her right arm didn't move when she shifted her frail body.

"Do you know me?" Zach swallowed. Though he wasn't afraid of her, he wasn't entirely at ease, either. He guessed who might have sent her.

"I'm Griselda. Andras is my son."

"Andy? Is he okay? Did he get out alright?" Stupid question. If he beat a man last month, of course he got out alright. At least he escaped Hezekiah.

"So sweet," she said. "You care for him even now. Mighty brave of you to go an' save him. Ain't many would do that for a stranger."

"He's a kid… they buried him."

"I know." She coughed. It went on for a few seconds and sounded like death rattling in her rib cage. "I know, child."

"Are you alright? Can I get you some water?"

"Don't worry on me none. They tried to poison me. This body, anyway. Not entirely successful, but I'm partly paralyzed on my right side." She wiggled the fingers of her left hand. "Slow me, sure. Ain't stopped me, though. Not yet."

"Sorry."

"You're the boy who saved my son. He said you pulled him out of the grave."

"Yes. That was me."

"So, because of that, I owe you. I owe you everything." Her right arm trembled, but she ignored the tremor. "And I'll grant you a favor. More important, for what you done, we won't kill you. We'll leave you be. But I must insist you stop looking for Andras."

"I only wanted his help to find Jessie."

"She's not with us, child. She's departed. I know it's hard, but it's best you forget about her."

"I saw her! At a fair, I saw her. She's not dead."

"Nevah' said she was dead. Physically, she's alive. No argument there. But her mind's done gone to their side. You can't help her no more."

"You said you'd grant me a favor."

"Yes, I did."

"I want you to help me hunt them down and kill them. Hezekiah and Hannah and anyone else in their damned cult."

"No. That ain't the favor. To repay you, I intend to give you the answers you been searchin' fo' like a dog with a bone."

"What answers?"

"About your friends."

"You know where they are?"

"I do." She coughed again. It took her a second to get her voice back. "They're not prisoners, dear child. None of them are. Not now, not ever."

"What do you mean? How do you know?"

"Well, at least I can fill in some blanks for you, and that might put your mind a bit at ease."

"What blanks? What do you know?"

"Andras says Hannah and Hezekiah killed your friend. He called him Pelt, I believe. They put him down in the swamp. An' I found out through the withered grapevine that aftah-wards they killed the one named Cole, right as the two lovebirds were fleeing town. As for the girl, she up an' joined their clan of her own free will.

ON GRAVEDIGGER ROAD

I can't say she condoned the killing—probably not—but she did sit there and witness it, an' then she joined that bitch Hannah, anyways."

"You're lying. You can't know that."

"I do a lot of bad things, child, but I never lie. Ain't no liars in my clan, I can promise you that!"

"They're dead?" It shocked him, but he didn't know why. Deep down, he already suspected they'd be dead. He'd known for a while. But the actual news hit him harder than expected. Suspecting the worst and knowing it are two different animals. They live in the same zoo, like a cobra and a zebra, but one is so much worse than the other.

"So, you don't need to go that way," she wheezed. "Chasin' ghosts is a fool's errand. Forget them."

"Never gonna happen, lady. I want to do something. I want to find those two freaks." Zach felt blood rising to his face. "I hate them. They took my friends, all of them."

"You're just feelin' sorry for yourself. Pity is a lovely pool to wallow in, ain't it? You lost someone, and you're feelin' abandoned. You're lonely. Get over it!"

His face flushed a deeper red. "Fuck you. It's a lot more than that. I want to make those ghost-painted freaks pay for what they did!"

"Oh. I see. You want revenge. Well, that there's a dangerous game, child. They say if you go out lookin' for revenge, best be sure to dig two graves."

"I don't care. Someone has to pay."

"Pay? You don't know from payment, child. Payment for a killing, that's not something gets settled with knives or guns or even iron bars. You don't know nothin' about payin' revenge."

"You said you'd give me anything I want. You owe me. Revenge is what I want."

"And Jessie?"

"I just want to talk to her."

"Oh, but talkin' will be off the table, if y'uns go after her clan. It's not a cult; it's a clan. And she's a part of it now. You may hafta kill her, too. You sure you can do that? I don't think you can."

"I don't care. I want to go after the others."

"Aha. You do, do you? You know, you're asking for somethin' that carries a powerful price."

"I know."

"*Sheet*. You don't know nothin'." She shifted in the chair again and winced from the pain in her bones. "I believe I will take that water you offered."

Zach fetched a bottle of water from his mini fridge, twisted the cap off—he was fairly sure she couldn't manage it herself—and handed it to her. She drank two sips and held the bottle trembling in her left hand.

"Somethin' wrong with your tap?"

"I don't have one. It's a dorm room. Bathrooms are down the hall."

"Fair enough. It's cold, anyways. Thank you."

"By the way, how did you get in here?"

She looked back as if it were a stupid question. Maybe she and her kind could go among the shadows unseen. It made him wonder.

"Little chance this will end the way you want," she said. "They say the bones of a ghost are easily broken, but that don't slow it none. Not one bit. So, I'm askin' you again: you sure you want to wander down that road once mo'? With me? Because I don't go to play bridge with 'em or to siphon gas from their car. I go to kill. And I do it so they can feel it. I do it so's they hurt."

Zach didn't need to think. He'd spent months doing that already. He had decided thinking was overrated. He nodded.

"I need to hear the words," she said.

"Yes. I want this. I want revenge. Help me find them all. Yes."

She leaned back and regarded him for a second. "I see there's no changing your mind. But first, let's get one thing straight an' clear, child. I'm not helping you. You're helping me. You do as I say. I'm steerin' the boat, as it were."

"I understand."

"This will end badly for you," she said again.

"I don't care." He knew it wouldn't be a walk in the park.

"You said you'll help me kill Hannah and Hezekiah, but what about the girl? What about Jessie? You ain't committed to that one yet. You'll be alright if I end her, too?"

She watched them kill Cole. And still she went with them. Who could do that?

"Yes. Even her," he said firmly.

Griselda didn't smile. The look on her face, always grim, never wavered. If she was happy Zach had joined her side, she didn't show it. If anything, she looked disappointed. He could see the pity she had for him. It made him uncomfortable. Her voice sounded stronger when she spoke again, but there was an echo of despair in her tone.

"So be it, child."

He nodded. Nothing else to say.

"You do know you're on the wrong side of right, don't you?" she asked. "My family isn't the holders of the holy grail. We're no angels."

"And Hannah's clan?"

"She's not so holy herself. But her intentions are a might better. She's a bit more on the good graces of heaven, you might say. And your friend, Jessie, picked the right fight. At least, that's what you're going to think. So, don't go into this with no wrong impressions. No misconceptions, you got that?"

"Why are you telling me this? Don't you want my help?"

"No, I do not. I want you to forget all this bullshit and live a long and happy life. Pardon my swearin'. And I'm sure Andras wants that for you, too. He likes you. But I can see you're set on comin' and you need to know the truth 'bout what you're fixin' to get mixed up in. No cards up my sleeve. I won't lie to you."

"So, what's the truth?"

"That this isn't going to end well for you."

"I know that. I don't care," Zach repeated.

"Don't you, now? And you don't care that you might be on the wrong side?" Her breathing was increasingly labored.

"They took my friends from me," hissed Zach. "They took Jessie and killed Cole and Pelt... if you're telling the truth, and I think you are. So, I want them dead for that. That's not unfair."

"No, that's not unfair. And like I said before, I always tell the truth," Griselda promised. "I'm a very bad person, but I don't lie. Hell has a special dark corner for liars."

"Fine. Where do we start?"

Griselda struggled out of the chair. "Help me up. I move like a drunk one-eyed peg-legged pirate these days. And I'm ornery as one, to boot!" Her laugh came out as a cackle that immediately morphed into a cough.

Zach hurried to her left and steadied her arm with his. He was afraid to touch her right arm. Slow quivering steps took her to the door in plain scuffed shoes, simple, like something worn a century ago. Old lady shoes. She continued to lean on him. Another cough forced its way out of her, violently jarring her body. Zach leaned away but kept one hand under her left arm for support.

"You're not... contagious, are you?"

"Poison ain't catchy. No. But my wicked temper is

catchy, so don't spend too much time with me. See? You've already made a bad decision."

"Where do we start? Tell me," he insisted.

Small and brittle, hunched over, her right side trembling again, she was a horror show tableau. He wondered what his classmates would think if they saw her in the hallway. She looked up at him through milky eyes.

"You start by going to bed."

"No, I'm going with—"

"It'll take time to find it again. They can't reappear often, only after a number of full moons, and they disappeared last year. When we see it again, that's where it'll be for some time. I'll contact you when the time is right. Not sooner."

"Contact me how?"

"You'll know. And won't be soon, neither. It'll be a few months, at least. So, meantime, you rest a spell and get your strength back."

"But I want—"

"Patience. That'll be the greatest skill y'an can harvest. If you ain't got that, you've lost already and you're not no use to me. You ever hunt elk?"

"No, ma'am."

"It takes a load of patience. Most of the time, you're sittin' quiet and waiting, watching. When ya spot one, gotta have a hand steady as a rock. You be patient and get strong. If it takes a month or it takes a year, that's what it takes. Same as huntin' anything else."

"I get it."

She grabbed his arm tight with her withered left hand. "Like I says, a powerful price for what you're askin' to do. Mighty powerful."

"I understand."

"No. You don't! But you will."

She released her grip on him, turned away and took hold of the doorknob. "You can still say no. When it's ready, when I send a message to you, I want you to ignore it. Get some sense and go a different way. No hard feelings on my end. None at all." She kept her head bent toward the door, away from him. "But if you're a fool, if you still want to be a part of this, you need to tie a red bandanna around that light pole in front. Someone…" She set into a coughing fit and took nearly a minute to recover. "Someone'll come for ya soon after that."

"I understand."

"I hope I don't see no bandanna, child. And I hope I never see you ever again. Good luck, either way."

"I understand."

"Now, go to the window. Tell me if you see anyone out there, down by that gorgeous maple tree I saw on ma' way in."

Zach went to the window and peered out. From his seventh-floor room he could see most of the walkway to the science building. The campus was dotted with light poles carrying lit orbs, and one shone on the maple near his window. He looked closely but didn't see anyone standing under the tree. A few students walked past, but no one stuck around.

"It's late," he said. "Not too many people outside."

She didn't reply.

"No, I don't think there's anyone out there. Are you being followed?"

When he turned around, he was alone in the room. He went to the door and opened it. No one was in the hallway. How had she slipped out? He wondered if she had become a wisp of smoke and evaporated. It wouldn't have surprised him, even if she had done it before his own eyes.

One of his classmates came out of the bathroom with a towel wrapped around his waist and a toothbrush sticking out of his mouth. "What's up?" the boy said as he passed by.

"Hey," Zach replied absently, scanning the hall. He walked to the end, turned the corner and looked down the next corridor. The old woman wasn't there. The elevator doors opened, and a student emerged and jerked his chin up in a hello as he passed. Zach nodded and walked back to his room.

When he tried his doorknob it didn't turn, even though he hadn't locked it when he left. He fished for his key and opened the door. Inside, the room was dark; his desk lamp was off. He flipped the wall switch and noticed then that he was still wearing his jacket and book bag.

I didn't dream that old lady... from the elevator to

the door. Did I?

If he started questioning his own sanity, it would unravel pretty fast. That wasn't the best way to find Jessie or get revenge on Hannah.

If Andy's mother hadn't been there, why would he dream about her? He'd never met her.

When he turned on the fan, something flew out from under the chair. He chased it down and swiped it off the floor. A dozen strands of gray hair twisted together. They might have been from the old lady.

If she really was here.

Were they left on purpose or had they fallen off her?

A million ways a clump of hair could find its way into a dirty student dorm. But these hairs were gray. That was unusual. He opened the window and let the wind take them.

CHAPTER 36

The next day, Zach bought a red bandanna and kept it in his pocket, always ready. Every day he watched eagerly for a signal that he knew was likely months away. No matter when it came, he would be ready. His leg bopped up and down while he sat in class, or anywhere for that matter, anxious and on edge. One of his classmates joked that he must have walked a hundred miles a day sitting down. He laughed the humorless laugh of a man in a cancer ward not wishing to upset his family with the harsh reality of his pain.

He signed up for classes the next semester, with only a vague intention of attending them. He pretended to have put the past behind him and let the world roll on as usual. The old lady said a few months or a year might pass, so he carried on as if his life were normal.

That weekend he went to a party thrown by two students in his economics class. They lived in a house with five roommates, and this night it bubbled over with students on both floors and in the backyard. He mingled and drank. His mind felt more at ease now that he had a partner, of sorts, and a plan. Drinking and chatting, meeting new people, it all seemed surreal.

Life continued.

* * *

After nine months, Griselda had yet to send him a message of any kind. He came to realize that she never intended to contact him again. Never wanting him to be a part of her war, she had put him off, hoping he would forget about revenge. She got her wish. He had no choice but to wait… or give up. She was the only connection he had left to Hannah or Gravedigger Road. Zach was cast out of the game with no hope of getting back in. At first, this translated into anger. Soon it morphed into depression.

Then it hit him.

Two ideas came together at the same time, and he suddenly understood what he had gotten wrong.

In the fall, he attended classes regularly, and he figured out a piece of the puzzle during his biology class. The teacher was lecturing on hibernation, and to make his case he pointed to the cicada. Periodical cicadas come out every seven to twelve years, while annual cicadas come out once a year. In the meantime, they hibernate. They hide underground and cannot be found.

That's what hadn't occurred to him before. That road that disappeared, Griselda said it was on a cycle. It goes away and comes back. But that doesn't mean it moves.

Gravedigger Road doesn't *move*.

It *hides*.

And some things, like the chameleon, can hide in plain side. If you don't see it, is it there?

The teacher also handed out photo cards of cicada eggs, photos he had been using for decades. They resembled Polaroids and reminded him of his visit to the State Police barracks. Lieutenant Millstone had given him the biggest clue of all: three years earlier, Hezekiah was seen in the area and was wanted for kidnapping.

The same area. Three years ago.

Hezekiah's road was there three years before. And then again that year he and his friends found it.

He played Griselda's words over in his head. She had said it shows itself after a number of moons. It *shows* itself. She didn't say it moved; that was the assumption he got wrong. And the Brayerville police were in on its concealment. They obviously couldn't move. They would stay where their charge will be again in the future. They'll stay to guard it.

I'll contact you when the time is right.

But the time would never be right. Griselda hadn't lied. She'd never thought the time was right for him. If she ever thought he should be a part of this, if the time ever were right, she'd contact him. That time was not today and not tomorrow. And it would never be. He surrendered to the truth; no message would ever come.

So, it was time to stop waiting.

ON GRAVEDIGGER ROAD

That day, he emptied out his savings account and bought a used '92 Ford Tempo for $880 and filled it with gas. At the pawn shop on Adams Street, he sold his guitar, class ring and watch. He kept his phone, even though he didn't think it would be useful where he was going. It had pics of Cole and Pelt on it. And the water tower. If nothing else, those might comfort him.

He wrote a note to his parents and attached it to a stack of pages, a handwritten manuscript of what had happened on that road that night. He had been working on it for months, piecing together what he knew. He titled it: "On Gravedigger Road" and signed it K.D., their nickname for him as a baby. It stood for *kaidee* which is something a shop owner in Thailand says when he's had a good day. It had been their inside joke since he was two.

As for the story, he'd told it a dozen times already—sometimes to blank stares, more often to sympathetic looks of tired disbelief, full of pity—but now it was in writing. That was important to him, if to no one else. Stuffed into a manila envelope, he stuck two rows of stamps on it and dropped it in the mailbox on Fifth Avenue, minutes before the last pickup. By the time his parents got it, he'd be on the road.

That night, he cleaned and tidied his side of the room. Old habit. Don't leave a mess behind.

The next morning, the second of October, he left his dorm at five-thirty while his roommate still slept. The air was cool and crisp, the pre-dawn fog a fitting send-off. A few morning birds sent tweets to him, and he stood a second to acknowledge them. The street lamps were still lit; the sun slept in later each day.

He passed the lamp in front of his dorm, then paused and went back to it. He plucked the red bandanna from his pocket and tied it around the pole, where it fought against the breeze to stay in place. There it would last a few days before a janitor took it down. For now, its bold wave signaled his departure.

"In case someone is watching," he murmured. "They'll know where I'm going."

No one saw him plant his flag. He was the only human soul astir this hour. Even the morning joggers were yet to make their annoying tracksuit-lined appearance. He got in his car, pulled out of the student parking lot and waved goodbye to the sleepy guard for the last time.

On his way south, he popped into a sporting goods store and bought a tent, a sleeping bag and boxes of supplies. Flashlights, mosquito repellent, binoculars. He paused at the sight of a flare gun.

Sure. That, too. Why not?

Did he need a first aid kit? This trip wasn't likely to have survivors. He bought it, anyway.

After purchasing hunting weapons, he bought three guns. It was surprisingly easy. He bought a hunting rifle at the sporting goods store that very day. A twenty-dollar bill and a nod to the salesman got him the address of a man on a farm in Missouri who sold him an automatic pistol and a revolver. He threw the revolver in the trunk with the rifle, neatly stashed under a blanket, and packed the automatic in his backpack resting on the passenger side floor. An array of knives already slept in a box on the back seat along with a crossbow. On the passenger seat lay two thick books on the subjects of demons and witchcraft. It was likely all rubbish, but they might prove to be useful. He didn't have much in his arsenal.

Not for what he was hunting.

After three coffees and an hour spent picking at a stack of pancakes—so high no one could ever finish—at the Pancake Hut off I-55, he ordered a coffee for the road. The same road they had taken on their first drive this way, two years ago, for Jessie's big project.

He was returning to where it all started. First back to Bud's Gator Farm. Then to the dead end that led to Pelt's and Cole's deaths, and maybe would lead to his. He wasn't asking permission anymore. He would hide the car in the woods and walk the rest of the way in. He'd camp out under cover, somewhere hidden in the swamp, and wait for the road to come back. After that, it was anyone's guess what would happen. How long it would take was another unknown. But he intended to ride it out, no matter how many nights passed in the tent in the swamp. That was the plan.

Griselda's words hung over him.

This will end badly for you.

Maybe. Probably. Still, he drove on.

With each mile, his resolve hardened. He missed

Cole and would do anything for him. Pelt deserved better, too. And Jessie… She had questions to answer. Hard questions. Those answers more than anything were the whales he chased. Nothing would topple his bicycle now. Momentum was with him.

He hoped one day he would stop hating, but he would never stop hunting. Looking for answers. For revenge. Always searching for what he lost that night on Gravedigger Road.

For more information about this and other books by **Rod Little**, visit the author's website:

www.rodlittleauthor.com

From the bestselling author of EARTHWEEDS
ROD LITTLE
THE
WHISPER KILLER
He's their worst nightmare. And their only hope.

THE WHISPER KILLER

**Wolf Hollow is not like other towns.
It gets what it needs.**

Ben is a baby-faced serial killer who can charm his victims with a smile. But when he stumbles into Wolf Hollow to hide from the FBI, it's the town that charms him and convinces him to stay.
Because Wolf Hollow gets what it needs,
and it needs Ben.
It knows his secret.

Under cover of a blinding snowstorm, a bitter enemy returns to Wolf Hollow, hell-bent on revenge, resolved to wipe out the entire town and leave no survivors.

Only Ben has what it takes to stand in its way.
He is their only hope.
Because some evils can only be met by a greater evil.

THE WHISPER KILLER
is now on sale at your favorite bookstore.

Excerpt from The Whisper Killer

Ben climbed into the truck and slammed the door. "Thanks for picking me up. Most people are afraid of hitchhikers."

The driver was a husky man with a ponytail poking out from under a cowboy hat. He wore sunglasses and sported a thick mustache. "No worry. I ain't afraid of no one." He chewed a toothpick and drove forward.

"Well, I do appreciate it. My name is Ben."

"Hooper," the driver said. "I ain't going all the way to Sioux City, but I can take you as far as Bakersville."

"That's fine. Hooper, eh? You play basketball? Hoops?"

"Nope."

"How did you get a name like Hooper?"

The man ignored the question.

"You know," the man said, gnawing the toothpick, "a young boy like you outta be careful. You got those innocent little boy looks about you, says maybe anyone can take advantage of you. Sure as hell don't look like any hitcher I never saw. For sure."

"Really? What do hitchhikers look like?"

"They don't look like a scrawny kid, or like a doe-eyed cross between Zack Morris and one of the Hardy

Boys. For sure."

"I don't know who those are."

"Google 'em. You're a dead ringer for one of 'em. Though I bet the ladies would stop for ya. You got the looks to charm the scales off a snake."

"Women don't pick up hitchhikers," Ben snorted.

"No?"

"Not in my experience."

"Your experience?" The man laughed. "You ain't old enough to got no experience. What are you, sixteen? How long you been hitching?"

"I'm twenty-two, but I've been hitching off and on since I was about sixteen."

"Kid, you don't look twenty-two. And that's a long time to be on the road. So, you're a runaway."

"I'm not sure an adult can be a runaway."

"As a kid you were. Am I right?"

"I guess so."

"Hitchin' the road since sixteen." Hooper whistled. "Long damn time. You always been out on the road? Roamin'? No family?"

"None to speak of."

"So, no one knows where you are," Hooper said. It wasn't a question. He glanced in his rear-view mirror. "You're alone. Something happened, no one would miss you."

"Not a damn soul," Ben said.

Hooper drove faster. "Ain't something you outta go

advertising, son. People might think about doing something to ya. If no one gonna come to find ya, and they know it. If you know what I mean."

"Do what?"

"Kidnap ya, rob ya, kill ya? Or worse." He switched the toothpick to the other side of his mouth. "Hard to say, hard to say. For sure."

"Are you trying to scare me?"

Hooper stared ahead at the road. "Maybe. Is it working?"

"A little bit. Yeah."

"Good. Fear will make you stronger. Toughen you up. Make your balls drop."

"Never heard that before." Ben shifted in his seat. He checked to make sure his door was unlocked. It was. Ben never wore a seat belt while hitching. One never knows when it's about time to bail. People can be weird. The ones who pick up hitchhikers can be downright freaks. Not always. But it happens.

And for Ben, that's not always a bad thing.

But today he didn't want trouble.

When the truck slowed down and pulled to the side of the road, he sensed his wish would not be granted. When the man unbuckled his seat belt and got out of the truck, he was dead certain.

"Gotta take a leak," Hooper said. "You should take one, too. It's a long drive."

"I'm okay. I don't need to."

Hooper walked around to the other side of the truck. He opened the passenger door, pulled out a revolver and waved it at Ben. "Afraid I must insist, son."

Ben sighed, jumped out of the truck and let the man take his backpack. "You don't want to do this, man. I've only got sixty bucks to my name. It's not worth it. Let me go, I won't say a word."

Hooper pointed the gun at Ben and pushed him toward the cornfield. "I know you won't. And best you don't tell me what to do, hitcher boy."

Ben worried this was about more than money. Freaks on the road, they were into everything.

Hooper rifled through Ben's backpack, found nothing of interest, then dropped it to the ground. They marched into the cornfield with Hooper only a foot behind Ben, the revolver nearly touching his back. Rows of corn quickly swallowed them.

* * *

Noah slowed the car and squinted through the windshield. "What's that up there?"

A shiny new GM Sierra was parked askew on the side of the road with no driver or passenger. Nothing disturbed this stretch of highway save the breeze raking the cornfields on both sides. A mile ahead, three trees surrounded a lonely farm house, but there were no other cars this late in the afternoon. None except the station wagon carrying Beth and Noah Murphy halfway through a six-hour drive to their twenty-year high school reunion.

Noah pulled over and parked the station wagon behind the truck. A continuous warning beep sounded from the truck's passenger door, left ajar.

"You think someone's in trouble?" he asked.

"Maybe they've got a flat," Beth said. "Or out of gas. Maybe they walked to get some?"

"Where? Last gas station was thirty miles back, at least. And why leave the door open?"

They got out of their car and circled the truck. The two were an unlikely pit crew, with Noah in his pressed pants and Oxfords and Beth in her dress and high heels. But they established that the tires looked fine.

"Expensive truck." Noah clicked his tongue. "Looks new. Nice one. But the hood's not up."

"I'm gonna guess the driver went into the corn to do some business, if you know what I mean."

"I do, I do," said Noah. He, himself, suddenly felt the need to take a piss. "But why leave the door open? Maybe we shouldn't bother him ... or them. It could be two kids, you know. Having fun."

"In a cornfield? Really, Noah, don't be vulgar."

Noah opened the passenger door wider and poked his head inside. It smelled of mint, freshly detailed. The gas gauge read half full. He reached for the glove compartment, but his wife stopped him.

"Noah! You can't go looking through people's private stuff without their permission," she whispered.

"No need to whisper; I don't think anyone's around

to hear you, dear."

But he withdrew from the truck's cab without touching the glove box. "I guess they went for a walk. And as far as I know, that isn't against the law. Nothing much we can do if we can't find them." He closed the door to stop the infernal beep.

"Well, we can't just assume they walked away," Beth insisted. "He or she or they might be hurt."

Noah glanced at his watch. "We're running late, dear. I'll call the police when we get back on the road. Have them check on it."

"Look, there's a backpack."

A large gray backpack lay against a corn stalk at the start of a corn row. Unzipped, some of its contents had spilled out, including a blue flannel shirt sleeve.

"See, dear. I told you, kids having fun. There's their clothes. Probably down to their undies by now … somewhere in the corn rows."

Beth didn't buy it. She peeped a "Hello?" that barely carried.

Noah cupped his hands and was about to shout a heartier "Hello," when a man emerged from the maze of husks. He was wiping blood off a hunting knife onto a torn rag. He halted and looked up from the knife, surprised to see the Murphys. They stared at him, and he stared back. He stopped cleaning the knife and looked to be calculating how best to diffuse the situation. He opened his mouth as if to say something, hesitated, then said, "Oh, crap."

Unlike the truck driver, Noah recognized the man from the news. It's not every day you meet a serial killer wanted by the FBI; it's a rare and horrifying treat. He knew this was the end for him and his wife but knew no way to stop it, like the moment after you fall off a cliff before you hit the ground. They were seconds from hitting the ground with a splat. He grabbed his wife's hand and ran for their car.

"Son of a bitch," Ben said and dropped the rag. "Why do they always have to run?"

He easily closed the distance and hit the man hard on the back of the head with the knife handle; the man collapsed to the ground. Restroom paper towels might have put up more of a fight.

Ben faced the woman.

"Money and cell phones, lady. Hand them over," he said. "I don't have much time, so I'll give you twelve seconds. Unless you'd rather I kill you both and take the phones myself?"

Beth's hands shook. She emptied her purse on the roof of the car and found two twenties. She handed them to Ben. She started to pull out credit cards, but he waved them off.

"Keep 'em, lady. No use to me. Where are your phones?"

"The phone is in the car. We only have one."

"Get it, lady. Seconds count."

Noah got up, rubbing the back of his neck. "Look, guy, we don't want any trouble."

"It's your lucky day, then," Ben said. "Neither do I. As a matter of fact, I woke up this morning thinking just that: I don't want any trouble."

Ben retrieved the phone from the woman's trembling hands and the wallet from the cowering man, and left them with a tale to tell their friends for years to come. The truck spun gravel and ate up the road at 60 mph. The Murphys froze in place and watched the truck get smaller until it vanished from sight.

"He didn't kill us," Beth said.

"That was him, it was him," Noah babbled. He had pissed his pants. The urine stain grew down his leg. "That was him. Right there in front of us."

"He didn't kill us," Beth repeated. She was in shock.

They hugged each other and checked the bruise on Noah's neck, then watched the road for another minute before driving to a gas station and calling the police. For a long time, no one thought to search for Hooper's body in the cornfield.

* * *

THE WHISPER KILLER
ISBN-13: 9798643428978
408 pages
on sale now

ROD LITTLE

EARTHWEEDS

"In a post-apocalyptic world, beware the creatures you awaken."

Sam and his brother return from a camping trip to find their city empty. The world is gone with no explanation why. When they are attacked, Sam's spark takes on a vital role. Mutated creatures roam the earth, giant lizards and spiders.

The few remaining human survivors form separate camps, struggling against each other and the new horrors brought by this strange apocalypse. When probes are found across the land, the mystery begins to unravel. Sam and his brother must find the truth to survive the terrifying end of the world.

"A sci-fi/horror tale with a twisted ending."
Sons of Neptune: Book 1
EARTHWEEDS
ISBN-13: 978-1547268566
358 pages
on sale now

About the Author

Rod Little has written for countless horror and science fiction magazines over the past twenty-five years. He has also written for the Wayward Pines series and has released nine novels, including his own series, ***Sons of Neptune,*** and the celebrated horror novel, ***The Whisper Killer.***

Born in northern Illinois, Rod later moved to Pittsburgh, Pennsylvania and worked as a translator. In 1994 he opened a sci-fi & horror-related gaming store called Starbase One on Pittsburgh's famed Forbes Avenue, which he kept open for eleven years of fantastic fun. In 2006 he moved to the tropics to begin writing again and maintains residences in the US and Asia.

"Reading should open your eyes and make you think, but it should also be entertaining."

Follow Rod on Twitter: @rodlittleauthor

Books by Rod Little

○ ○ ○

THE WHISPER KILLER
ON GRAVEDIGGER ROAD

○ ○ ○

Wayward Pines: Dark Pines

○ ○ ○

Sons of Neptune:

Earthweeds

Revenge of the Spiders

The Last Starbase

The Boneyards of Nebula

○ ○ ○

Angry Galaxy:

Hidden Planet

Emperor of Two Moons

○ ○ ○

Official Website:
www.rodlittleauthor.com

Printed in Great Britain
by Amazon